UNDER COVER OF CLOSENESS

LEANNE WOOD

Copyright © 2025 Leanne Wood All rights reserved. No part of this publication may be reproduced, distributed, or transmitted in any form or by any means, including photocopying, recording, or other electronic or mechanical methods, without the prior written permission of the publisher, except in the case of brief quotations embodied in critical reviews and certain other non-commercial uses permitted by copyright law. For permission requests, send email to the author at author.kylie.price@bigpond.com with the phrase "Permission Inquiry" in the subject line.

Printed in the Australia
Printed 2025
Paperback
ISBN: 978-0-9953804-8-6
Ebook
ASIN: B0DP1WMFKY

This is a work of fiction. Names, characters, businesses, organizations, places, events, and incidents either are the product of the author's imagination or are used fictitiously. Any resemblance to actual persons, living or dead, events, or locales is entirely coincidental. The author accepts no responsibility for any thoughts you may form after reading her works.

This novel is set in Australia, so I've chosen to use Australian spelling and style to enhance its authenticity. Australian English typically aligns more closely with British grammar and spelling conventions rather than American ones. For my American readers, please note the extra u's and instances of s in place of z are intentional and reflect the regional language differences.

BOOKS BY LEANNE WOOD

The Belonging
Torment
Under the Cover of Closeness

Secrets Series

#1 Pages of Your Life: The Secret Life of Shirley Rumming
#2 Travels Through My Mind
#3 Where Secrets Lie

Dedicated to...

For those bound by birth, and those bound by choice.

Table of Contents

Copyright	4
Books by Leanne Wood	5
Dedicated to…	7
Prologue	13
Chapter One	15
Chapter Two	20
Chapter Three	23
Chapter Four	25
Chapter Five	30
Chapter Six	34
Chapter Seven	38
Chapter Eight	41
Chapter Nine	48
Chapter Ten	51
Chapter Eleven	55
Chapter Twelve	58
Chapter Thirteen	61
Chapter Fourteen	63
Chapter Fifteen	68
Chapter Sixteen	71
Chapter Seventeen	78
Chapter Eighteen	80
Chapter Nineteen	85

Table of Contents

Chapter Twenty	91
Chapter Twenty-One	94
Chapter Twenty-Two	97
Chapter Twenty-Three	103
Chapter Twenty-Four	106
Chapter Twenty-Five	109
Chapter Twenty-Six	113
Chapter Twenty-Seven	119
Chapter Twenty-Eight	128
Chapter Twenty-Nine	132
Chapter Thirty	138
Chapter Thirty-One	142
Chapter Thirty-Two	150
Chapter Thirty-Three	164
Chapter Thirty-Four	168
Chapter Thirty-Five	173
Chapter Thirty-Six	179
Chapter Thirty-Seven	186
Chapter Thirty-Eight	192
Chapter Thirty-Nine	198
Chapter Forty	205
Chapter Forty-One	212
Chapter Forty-Two	223

Table of Contents

Chapter Forty-Three	229
Chapter Forty-Four	234
Chapter Forty-Five	239
Chapter Forty-Six	246
Chapter Forty-Seven	256
Chapter Forty-Eight	262
Chapter Forty-Nine	278
Chapter Fifty	283
Chapter Fifty-One	290
Chapter Fifty-Two	297
Chapter Fifty-Three	304
Chapter Fifty-Four	312
Chapter Fifty-Five	318

UNDER THE COVER OF CLOSENESS

Prologue

Lorna Martin's Diary
Saturday, 2nd March, 2024

As an identical twin, the notion of our shared existence had always held a mesmerising allure for me. The idea that Cara and I were once one entity, seamlessly halved into two distinct individuals, felt like a wondrous feat of nature. The unspoken understanding and unimaginable bond we shared was enviable. Our closeness was exclusive, sealed by our ability to communicate thoughts and feelings without outside input. Cara, my mirror image stood by my side, we were loyal equals, our shared features echoed in every gesture, yet as time passed things began to change. Fractures. Beneath the surface, lay the subtle distinctions that set us apart. Despite our identical physical appearance contrasting personalities were beginning to emerge. Being identified as one and being likened to an individual who held conflicting views was no longer attractive; in fact, it was something I found deeply repulsive.

Little things at first. Cara and I became locked in a perpetual battle. What began as typical squabbles between sisters escalated into full-blown warfare. Lies. Accusations. Distance. And finally, silence.

Over a decade had drifted by since the rupture in our bond, since Cara, my mirror image, vanished taking her two young sons and departing from the family fold. Losing them was profoundly distressing. Their sudden disappearance left a void filled with shock, confusion, anxiety and sorrow. I was lost without closure or understanding. Anger surfaced. Why had Cara made such a drastic decision? How would she explain my absence to the nephews I adored? My sister knew how to twist words, how to manipulate people and situations. For years I clung to the possibility of their return, then finally I grappled with the painful acceptance they might be gone forever. I found solace in the tranquillity of my own existence, never forgetting the echoes of Cara's lies and manipulations, her venomous words. I preserved evidence of her deceit, tangible proof of the truth concealed behind her facade of innocence. It would serve as a reminder to be cautious moving forward. I would never be so gullible to be fooled by Cara ever again.

Yet why after all this time was Cara in the forefront of my thoughts? Why did I sense her distress from afar? A nagging worry. A primal instinct whispered something was amiss.

One

Saturday, 9th March, 2024
The Unforeseen

Lorna sat snuggled on her lounge by the fireplace, the warmth making her weary as she read. Wiping her eyes she looked towards the clock on the mantel, the hand ticked away the seconds, each one amplifying the silence. It was nearing nine o'clock. One more chapter and then it's bedtime.

Suddenly, a startling knock at the door shattered her stillness. It was sharp and urgent, Lorna jumped, her eyes darting to the door as the knocking continued. Who could that be at this hour?

The knocking stopped. Lorna took a deep breath, trying to steady her racing heart. The knocking started again, louder this time, a desperate insistence she couldn't ignore.

She rose slowly and steadied herself placing her book on the coffee table, then made her way to the front door. Each step filled with trepidation, her hand trembling as she grasped the cold brass knob. Pausing for a moment, she questioned, "Who… who is it?"

"It's Jakob, Aunt Lorna," he said, his voice low and strained. "I need your help."

Lorna's eyes widened; she flung the door open and stood frozen in the doorway, her heart pounding as she stared at the young man before her. It had been just over a decade since she last laid eyes on Jakob, her sister Cara's eldest son. The last memory she had of him was at their father's funeral, a solemn occasion clouded by grief and family tension. "Jakob," Lorna said, her voice barely a whisper. "What... What are you doing here?"

Jakob shifted uncomfortably, his gaze flickering between Lorna's face and the ground. "I... I came to see you, Aunt Lorna," he said, his voice tinged with nervousness. "It's been so long, and... Well, there's something I need to talk to you about."

Lorna's caution deepened. She couldn't shake the feeling there was more to Jakob's sudden appearance than a simple desire to reconnect with family. Beside the fact it was late and he would have travelled hours to her house, Cara had made it abundantly clear over the years she wanted nothing to do with Lorna. Why after all this time was her nephew here? "What is it, Jakob?" Lorna asked, her tone guarded.

Jakob took a deep breath. "It's my mum," he began. "She's... She's sick, Aunt Lorna. Really sick."

Lorna felt a pang of sympathy for her sister, despite their strained relationship, she and Cara had been inseparable as children. "What's wrong with her?" Lorna asked, her concern genuine.

"She needs a kidney transplant," Jakob replied. "Her kidneys are failing, and the doctors say she doesn't have much time left unless she gets a transplant."

Lorna's heart sank. She couldn't imagine what Cara must be going through, facing such a grim prognosis. And yet, a part of her couldn't help but wonder if there was more to the story than Jakob was letting on. "And you want me to donate a kidney?" Lorna asked, her voice tinged with suspicion.

Jakob nodded. "Yes, Aunt Lorna. Please, you're her best hope. I know things have been... difficult between you and Mum, but this is her life we're talking about. You being her twin and all, you'd be a perfect match. You could save her."

Lorna hesitated, torn between her desire to help her sister and her lingering resentment. "What does your mum say? What does she think about you being here?"

"She doesn't know."

"She doesn't know?" Lorna repeated, shocked by his reply. "Jakob, your mum will kill you if she finds out you've gone behind her back."

Jakob shrugged. "I don't care. What she doesn't know won't hurt her. I have to try. Surely, she'll understand."

Lorna shook her head. "I guess that's between you two. As for what you asked me…Nope, I don't think so, nope… nope, I don't think so. Your mum wiped me. Packed up and left. Left with you boys. Left with no forwarding address. No word. No explanation. No Goodbyes. Just gone. Do you know how I felt? Do you know what that did to me? …I'm sorry, Jakob." Lorna paused and looked towards her nephew. "This is too much. After all this time, it's just too much… I mean, if the roles were reversed…" Lorna chuckled bitterly. "Your mum said she wouldn't spit on me even if I was on fire. Time. Too much time has passed."

Jakob looked at her with pleading eyes. "Please, don't commit now, Aunt Lorna. Think about it. You're in shock. It's been a long time. Please don't shut me out."

Lorna looked beyond the young man and saw the boy with the sad, begging eyes. She saw the boy who had lost his dog, who had said goodbye to childhood friends, farewelled his grandparents, and who had been separated from the aunt he had adored. Tears welled in her eyes. "I'm so sorry, Jakob. I can't give you the answer you want, but I'll… I'll think about it," she finally said.

Jakob gave a half smile. "Thank you, Aunt Lorna. I'm

sure you'll do what's right, and I know you have to think about it. That's all I can ask. Well, I'd better let you go; I've found a place to stay in town." Jakob smiled, then nodded. "Good night, Aunt Lorna, and thank you." Jakob turned and walked towards the front gate.

"Oh, Jakob, hang on a minute," Lorna called. "Before you go, I should give you my phone number just in case you want to call me. You were too young to have had it before."

Jakob paused, turning back towards Lorna with a curious expression. "Sure, thanks," he replied, waiting as Lorna disappeared briefly into her house.

Returning, Lorna handed Jakob a slip of paper and smiled. "I didn't think you would have remembered it."

Jakob examined the number written on the paper. "It's the same," his eyebrows furrowed, "you never cut it off?" he asked, with curiosity in his voice.

"Yep, it's the same," Lorna replied, shaking her head. "No cutting here. Why would I cut off my phone? Always had it, will always need it."

"Oh okay," Jakob nodded, "I thought mum said you'd cut it off. Never mind. I've got it now. Thanks."

Lorna smiled as Jakob put the paper in his pocket and waved goodbye. "Mum said you cut it off," Lorna mumbled quietly beneath her breath. Nothing surprised her when it came to Cara, absolutely nothing. As he walked away, Lorna's heart ached with the weight of the decision she faced. She watched him disappear into the night. Alone with her thoughts, she knew the decision she had to make would shape their lives forever.

Closing the door, she leaned against it, feeling the cool wood against her back. Tears welled in her eyes. Everything was fine, everything was wonderful. Why did he have to show up now? Memories of her childhood with Cara flooded her mind: the games they played, the secrets they shared, the arguments that felt monumental but were trivial in hindsight. They'd once been inseparable, two halves of a whole. But time had eroded their bond, they were no more.

With a deep sigh, Lorna pushed herself away from the door and wandered into the living room. She sank into the comfort of her lounge by the fireplace, and stared into the darkness, her reflection faintly visible in the glass cabinet on the opposite side of the room. How had they come to this point? The rift between them seemed insurmountable, yet Jakob's visit had stirred something deep within. The memories of shared laughter and sisterly bonds tugged at her heart, competing with the resentment that had built up over time. Had Cara ever looked at her reflection and wondered how Lorna was?

Lorna got up and walked over to the mantle where a collection of family photos stood. She picked up a picture of her and Cara as children, they were hugging each other, their faces bright with happiness. She traced a finger over the glass, as if trying to bridge the gap between past and present.

Could she really turn her back on her sister? Could she deny Jakob's heartfelt plea?

Two

1975
Cracks Surface

Lorna retreated to the comfort of her lounge, still shaken by Jakob's sudden visit. Seeing him had stirred up memories she'd long buried. Her thoughts taken back to her earliest childhood, days spent side by side with her twin sister, Cara. She closed her eyes, and sank deeper into the soft cushions, the memories flooded in, taking her back to when it all began. Back to the days when they were inseparable, back to 1975.

Signs of tension had been there from early childhood, hidden under the cover of closeness, their twinship. If Lorna had something, Cara wanted it too. A doll, a toy, whatever caught Cara's eye became something she had to have. As the eldest, although only by a matter of minutes, Lorna had felt responsible to give in to her sister's desires. She hated seeing Cara upset; if Cara was upset, Lorna felt upset. It was as if their emotions were entwined. Handing over her latest find was a small price to pay for peace.

To the outside world, they were an adorable pair, indistinguishable in their matching outfits and shared mannerisms. "Oh, aren't you two so cute? I can't tell you apart," people would say, their smiles bright and voices bubbly. "What's it like to be a twin? Can you read each other's minds?" they would ask. Lorna had always thought these questions reasonable, but hearing them day after day became a burden. She didn't know what it felt like to be anything other than a twin, no more than a singleton could comprehend the absence of a twinship bond. It was simply their reality.

Not everything about being a twin was frustrating. Being the mirror image of another had its advantages, you could pretend to be your sibling in order to avoid or gain. They could divide and conquer when asking permission from their parents, listening to the most suitable response. Then there were the secret smiles across the dinner table, the shared giggles without a single word spoken, and the unspoken understanding that came from a lifetime spent side by side. Cara was her permanent companion, her partner in crime, and the one who offered unwavering support against the outside world.

It wasn't until the summer of their eighth birthday that Lorna finally started to feel and see a shift. She could still picture it... Cara, perched precariously on a stool in their parents' bedroom, a forbidden room in their home. Lorna had stood quietly in the doorway, watching with curiosity. Cara, meticulously moving stacks of clothes to the side. What was her sister up to? What was Cara looking for? Lorna stepped forward trying to see.

"What are you doing?" she had asked, her voice trembling with apprehension.

Cara had turned, her eyes wide and wild, like a predator caught in the act. "I was just looking for something," she said, her hands moved quickly, but Lorna had seen the flash of an old yellow butter container and heard the clinking of its contents. Coins.

"You put something in your pocket," Lorna snapped, "I saw you."

"No, I didn't."

"Yes, you did, and I'm going to tell." Lorna was furious at her sister's lie.

Cara laughed and jumped off the stool. "You won't tell, because if you tell, then you'll be in trouble too. I'll say you were with me, so we'll both get punished. Go on, I dare you, dobber." Cara pushed Lorna and Lorna shoved Cara in return. The two scuffled to the floor. Coins fell from Cara's pocket. The sound of their parents' car pulling into the driveway had frozen them both, their allegiance diverging and then converging in a flash. Lorna promised not to tell, as long as Cara promised to keep her mouth shut about the bedroom and to never go there again. Their shared silence sealed their pact.

Lorna grasped the cushion. That incident had been one of the earliest fractures within their twinship. She'd learned then that being a twin meant sharing not just toys and clothes but also the consequences of each other's actions. They were forever seen as a single entity, especially when things went wrong.

And things had gone wrong many times. She remembered another summers day, a few years later, when Cara had pushed her off the swing as she hung upside down. Lorna had fallen, her shoulder snapped. Cara had wanted the swing and when Lorna failed to listen, she'd taken it by force. "It's your fault," Cara claimed, "because you wouldn't share."

Lorna sighed and rubbed her shoulder, opening her eyes to the soft glow of the fireplace. Jakob's visit had stirred emotions and her head was pounding. As she rose from her lounge, Lorna felt a sense of clarity as she reminded herself of an important point; worry would get her nowhere and she couldn't change the past.

Three

Sunday, 10th March, 2024
Reflection

Lorna sat in her cosy country home, the light of the rising sun filtering through the lace curtains. Sleep had been limited the night before, Jakob's unexpected visit replayed in her mind, leaving her with a swirl of unresolved emotions and questions.

In the years that had passed since she last saw him, Jakob had grown from a boy into a young man, almost unrecognisable. His presence had unearthed a flood of memories she had worked hard to suppress. Lorna found herself wondering if he had a mobile phone. It seemed odd he hadn't offered his number, was he distancing himself, or did he assume she wouldn't want it? And why hadn't she thought to ask about Henry, his younger brother? Little Henry, with his curious eyes and infectious laughter, had been such a light in her life. Lorna's heart ached at the thought. What had become of him? Why hadn't Jakob mentioned him? Was Henry, okay? And then there was Uncle Bernard, why no word of him? Uncle Bernard, was the quiet and reflective academic in the family, his aged existence revolved around reading news articles on the internet and watching the share markets. A self-proclaimed procrastinator whose greatest concern was being forced out of his home and into a nursing home. Lorna had enjoyed their regular telephone conversations. Uncle Bernard was the last surviving relative on her father's side of the family. Cara had openly resented their relationship telling Lorna he only talked to her out of politeness. And so, when opportunity knocked Cara took all necessary steps to ensure Uncle Bernard ceased contact. Was he still alive?

Jakob's visit had not just stirred her curiosity; it had awakened the pain of the past, reopening wounds she thought had long healed. She wondered now if she should have invited him in, given him a chance to bridge the years of silence. But the boy she remembered was not the young man who stood before her, a decade of separation had left them as strangers.

As she pondered, the weight of Cara's situation pressed down on her. Had she been picking up on her sister's illness? Over recent weeks Lorna had been experiencing severe, sharp pain on her left side and back. And now she'd been told Cara, her identical twin, required a kidney donation. This was the same Cara who had severed all ties, sold her home, moved away with her sons without leaving a forwarding address, and declared on social media that Lorna was dead to her. Lorna's life had been tranquil since Cara's departure, free from the chaos and manipulation that had once defined their relationship. She cherished the simplicity of her existence, the connection with friends and family who chose to be in her life. Yet, the news of Cara's need for help left her torn between her own peace and a lingering sense of duty to her twin. Lorna sighed, her gaze drifting to the fields beyond her window. Life had indeed moved on. People had focused on those who remained close, letting go of those who'd distanced themselves. The tranquillity she enjoyed had come at the cost of severed ties, but now, with Jakob's visit and Cara's illness, the past seemed to be demanding her attention once more.

Four

1979
A Package Deal

And the past had been demanding, exceedingly so, Lorna and Cara were perpetually viewed as a single entity. In school, where they were taught one plus one equals two, but the maths never seemed to apply to them. For twins, you got two for the price of one. Need a hand? Ask the twins. Here comes the package deal: ask for Lorna, expect both Lorna and Cara; ask for Cara, anticipate both Cara and Lorna. In their younger years, life had been a mix of smooth sailing and rough, turbulent waters, marked by mutiny and warring factions forced to share the same boat, each twin yearning for land and separation. Lorna's mind drifted to an incident from her later years in primary school. She and Cara had just finished their lunch when Lorna, wanting a break from her sister, decided to join her classmates who were playing on the far side of the sports oval. As she wandered across the grass, she spotted Mrs Hayden who clearly looked irritated as she marched towards her. Mrs Hayden pointed back towards Cara. "Go back to your sister," she barked.

Lorna slowed, glancing over her shoulder at Cara, who was still eating alone. Everything seemed fine. *Why am I in trouble?* she wondered. *I just need some space. I haven't done anything wrong.* But Mrs Hayden kept coming, her eyes narrowing as she approached. She stopped in front of Lorna, hands on her hips. "You don't need friends, you have a twin," she snapped.

Lorna's stomach sank as she struggled to blink back tears. *Why can't I have friends?* The comment made no sense. The unfairness hurt, but Lorna was too scared to argue with a teacher. Head bowed, she turned and walked back to Cara, swallowing the lump in her throat. *Surely, I deserve the chance to make friends too.*

Mrs Hayden's words echoed in her mind, along with the stories she'd heard from other twins. Some spoke of being labelled "the terrible two," as if their bond was inherently troublesome. Others recalled relentless comparisons, being measured against their "equal" in every way, academically or physically. Questioned about why they weren't identical in their achievements, with some made to feel inferior, as if their uniqueness was a flaw. Yet despite everything, they never doubted their twin connection; it was something that ran far deeper than words, an unspoken bond most would never fully understand.

For some, the pain came from forced separation at school. They described the experience as devastating, as if a vital part of them had been torn away, a limb suddenly missing. They remembered how teachers would reunite them briefly just to soothe their uncontrollable sobbing, only to separate them again, leaving them in tears for days, sometimes weeks.

For others, it wasn't about physical distance or the constant, suffocating comparisons. There was a different kind of pressure. Even when they felt moments of frustration or difference, like any siblings might, they were expected to stay together… because they were twins. It was unthinkable to acknowledge they could disagree or need space from one another. To do so was seen as ridiculous, even selfish. How could those who weren't twins possibly understand what it felt like? Being forced to remain by someone's side, even in disagreement, constantly compared, never given personal space, never allowed to breathe or exist as an individual?

No one wanted to acknowledge the twin who just needed some space.

By the time they reached high school, Lorna craved freedom, new faces, and the potential for individual friendships. The yearning for autonomy grew stronger as she dreamt of stepping out of the shared shadow that had defined their lives for so long. It wasn't that Lorna hated her sister Cara; on the contrary, she loved her fiercely and would defend her to her last breath. The issue lay in the feeling of being absorbed by their twinship, her identity gradually swallowed by the person to whom she was closest. Lorna yearned for recognition as an individual, distinct from Cara. Despite their identical appearances, they were not identical in thought and feeling. Lorna felt trapped, frustrated no one seemed to understand or even listen. It seemed easier for everyone to classify them as one, even reducing their names to the impersonal "Twinny," a nickname that denied them of their separate identities.

Yet in exams, their twinship ceased to be a marvel, replaced instead by suspicions and accusations of cheating whenever their results matched. To be accused of cheating was devastating for Lorna. How could their twinship be marvelled at in some circumstances yet so quickly disregarded in others? The same closeness that was celebrated in one moment became a source of suspicion and doubt in another, leaving Lorna to grapple with the bitter irony of their situation.

UNDER THE COVER OF CLOSENESS

Lorna broke down and started crying. Over the years, she and her sister, Cara, had disagreed about many events. A particular incident from their childhood had haunted their conversations: the push bike incident. Cara's recollection was vivid. She claimed, "I was on the front and Lorna was trying to climb on with me. Lorna slipped and fell off the seat onto the rear wheel. I remember Lorna yelling, 'Don't push me off,' but she didn't hang on. I know it was her fault because she let go of my waist. I remember feeling her one second and the next she was gone, screaming as the bike suddenly stopped." But Lorna's memory was different. She insisted she'd been on the bike seat, with Cara perched on the crossbar. Lorna believed that Cara, wanting the seat for herself, had pushed her off without warning, causing Lorna to be thrust onto the rear wheel, leading to a sudden stop.

These conflicting memories were symbolic of their strained relationship. Each memory, too minor for their parents to recall or too private for others to have witnessed, contributed to the friction between them. Both sisters clung fiercely to their versions of the past, their differing perspectives keeping them perpetually at odds. Lorna had long pleaded with Cara to move beyond their petty differences, to let go of the past. "Why can't we agree to disagree?" she would often ask. But Cara always responded the same way: "Why would I agree to disagree when I know I'm right?"

And so, their differences remained unresolved. Their struggles to be recognised as individuals continued, even as the unique bond of their twinship inevitably drew them back together whenever an external threat loomed. And defend they would; mess with one and you'd deal with two.

Lorna wiped the tears from her cheeks. The thought resonated in her mind: *mess with one and you'd deal with two*. Maybe she needed to speak with her doctor about donating a kidney. Was it a valid request? What would the procedure entail? Would she have to involve Cara, Jakob had come to her without his mother knowing? Would Cara even want her help? Most importantly, did Lorna want to jeopardise her life for someone who couldn't agree to disagree and from all accounts hated her. Questions swirled. Being a live donor had never crossed her mind until now.

Five

Monday, 11th March, 2024
The Logic

Lorna sat in the waiting room, her hands clasped tightly together, her mind filled with questions and nervous anticipation. When her name was called, she followed Dr Cornelius to a consultation room.

"Good afternoon, Lorna. How are you feeling today?" Dr Cornelius asked with a smile.

I'm good, thank you. Just a bit nervous," Lorna admitted as she took a seat.

"What seems to be the problem?"

"It's been over ten years since I last saw my identical twin, Cara. Now, Cara's eldest son, Jakob, has come to me with a desperate plea for help. He explained his mother's health issues and asked if I would consider donating a kidney.

"Oh, I see." Dr Cornelius listened intently as Lorna described her situation. His eyebrows lifted slightly, yet his eyes stayed focused on her.

"And Cara has no idea that Jakob has approached me, I have no idea what to do. I'm so overwhelmed and nervous, to be honest I'm torn between what to do," Lorna said, her voice beginning to tremble, her hands gently tapping her chest. "I feel the weight of the decision pressing down on me, I have so many questions and want to do what is right."

Dr Cornelius nodded. "I understand this is a complex

situation. Let's take this step by step and address any concerns you might have."

Lorna took a deep breath and relaxed a little. "I'm really unsure about what to do."

Dr Cornelius listened carefully before speaking. "It's important to acknowledge the emotional and psychological aspects of this situation. Reconnecting with a family member after such a long time, especially under these circumstances, can be challenging. But let's focus on the medical aspects first and see if we can provide some clarity." He began by explaining the detailed steps involved in the donation process. "Firstly, there is an initial medical evaluation, you will undergo a comprehensive medical evaluation to ensure you are a suitable candidate. This includes blood tests, urine tests, imaging studies, and a thorough review of your medical history. We need to ensure you are in good health and have no underlying conditions that could complicate the donation. There is compatibility testing, being identical twins means you have a high likelihood of being a perfect match, which significantly reduces the risk of rejection. However, we will still perform blood typing and tissue typing to confirm compatibility. All potential donors must complete a psychological assessment. Given the emotional complexity of this situation, a psychological evaluation is crucial. It will help ensure you are mentally and emotionally prepared for the process. This assessment will also explore the impact of reconnecting with Cara and the potential outcomes."

Lorna nodded slowly, absorbing the information. "What are the risks involved in the surgery?"

"As with any major surgery, there are risks such as bleeding, infection, and reactions to anaesthesia. However, because you and Cara are identical twins, the risk of rejection is significantly lower. Long-term, most donors live healthy lives with one kidney, but there is a small increase in the risk of developing kidney disease in the future."

Lorna looked down at her hands. "What if I need a kidney in the future?"

"Living donors are given priority on the transplant list if they ever need a kidney," Dr Cornelius reassured her. "But it's important to remember living with one kidney is typically very manageable, and most donors do not experience significant issues."

"And what support is available during and after the process?"

"There's a robust support system in place," Dr Cornelius explained. "You'll have access to a dedicated transplant coordinator who'll guide you through every step. Additionally, there are support groups and counselling services available both before and after the donation."

Lorna looked up; her eyes filled with uncertainty. "I haven't seen Cara in so long, and she doesn't even know Jakob asked me. How do I approach this?"

Dr Cornelius leaned forward slightly. "This is indeed a delicate situation. It might be helpful to have a mediator or counsellor facilitate the initial conversation between you and Cara. This can help manage the emotional complexities and ensure both of you have the support you need."

After discussing a few more details and talking about organ donation in general, Dr Cornelius concluded, "Let me print a fact sheet from Kidney Health Australia, it's about deciding be to a living kidney donor, you can even speak to someone who has been a live donor. The decision is yours and it's not something I would suggest you rush into without all the information. Take your time to think this over, Lorna. Talk to Jakob, consider discussing it with a counsellor, and ask any more questions you might have. This is a big decision, and it's important you feel fully prepared and supported."

Dr Cornelius's calm and steady presence conveyed a thoughtful consideration of her words. Lorna left the appointment feeling heard and understood, she was now more informed, but the decision ahead was still huge. She knew there were many steps to take and emotions to navigate, with the support of her medical team, friends, family and the possibility of reconnecting with Cara, she felt a glimmer of hope amidst the uncertainty.

Six

1982
Enough Is Enough

Lorna returned home after her appointment with Dr Cornelius, clutching an envelope filled with information about being a living kidney donor. She dropped her keys on the kitchen counter and made her way to the lounge, sinking into its familiar comfort. The house was quiet. Nausea swirled; the weight of the day's emotions pressed heavily on her. Opening the envelope, she began to read through the pamphlets and booklets, absorbing the details about tests for compatibility, the surgery, risks, and the recovery process. The words began to blur as her eyes grew heavy, and before long, she drifted into a deep sleep.

In her dreams, she was back in high school, the year was 1982 and she was walking the hallways with Cara. The constant strain of being treated as one entity made Lorna more determined to carve out her own identity. She studied harder, pushing herself to excel, hoping academic success would grant her a semblance of individuality. Every night, she would study in secret, hiding under the covers with a torch. Her hard work paid off when she was finally moved to a higher-grade class, where she found new classmates who recognised her as Lorna, not just one half of a twin. During breaks, however, she was thrust back into the world of twinship. Despite her efforts, the distinction faded, and she yearned for freedom. Finishing year ten was enough for Lorna; she couldn't wait to escape the confines of school and live her life on her own terms. Getting a job and earning her own money felt like a breath of fresh air. *I can breathe*, she thought, relishing her newfound independence.

Working in Sydney was exhilarating. Her coworkers knew nothing of her twin sister, and for the first time, Lorna experienced life as an individual. She had the best of both worlds: the freedom of being a singleton and the comfort of returning to twinship whenever she and Cara reunited. As soon as they turned sixteen, they both got their learner's permits, pooling their savings to buy an old, second-hand car. They dreamed of adventures once they obtained their provisional licences. The world was their oyster, and the freedom of travelling together reassured their parents of their safety. They drove to beaches, over the mountains, and spent weekends away, revelling in their shared adventures. But things took a turn for the worse. After a heated argument with their parents, Cara took off in the car while still on her learner's permit. Lorna, unaware of Cara's plans, was accused of knowing her whereabouts and was punished for not telling the truth. Their parents called the police who informed them nothing could be done unless she was caught in the act. Lorna was distraught, fearing Cara's arrest. When Cara finally returned, both sisters were in trouble: Cara for driving unlicenced, and Lorna for supposedly allowing it. Their punishment was equal. They were grounded for a week and banned from driving the car, which only deepened Lorna's resentment. She couldn't stop her sister from taking the car, and she genuinely didn't know where she'd gone.

Later that night, Lorna confronted Cara. "You need to tell them I had no part in this, Cara. I didn't even know where you were!"

Cara laughed. "I'm not telling them anything. And I'm getting out of here." She opened their bedroom window and started to climb out.

"Don't, Cara. Please," Lorna begged, grabbing her arm. They argued, pushed, and shoved, but Cara was determined, pushing Lorna to the floor as she climbed out the window and disappeared into the night.

Their parents discovered her absence. "Why didn't you stop her? Why didn't you tell us what she was doing? Where is she?" they demanded.

Lorna insisted she didn't know, feeling trapped and powerless. Her mother grabbed her by the arm and slapped her on the leg. "Liar! Go to bed." Lorna burst into tears and rushed to her bed from where she listened to her parents. Anger changed to desperation and then worry.

"What happens if someone kidnaps her and we never see her again," her mother cried.

The next day, Cara strolled in the back door as if nothing had happened. "Oh, my goodness, you're home, thank goodness you're home safely. No one hurt you, did they?" their mother cried.

Cara put on the waterworks. "I needed to get away from Lorna, she wouldn't stop nagging at me about the car, sorry mum," Cara said. Her only punishment was a promise not to drive unlicenced again.

Lorna was furious as Cara giggled, recounting how she'd hidden in the boot of their car, the broken lock providing her a hiding spot. She'd listened to their parents' frantic search and Lorna's denials when they'd been standing outside within meters of the car, then when everyone went inside, she snuck under the house, cosy in the comfort of their old cubby house. "I told you I was going and you can't stop me from anything. You're not as perfect as you think you are," Cara said, laughing. "I heard you crying when Mum slapped you."

Lorna's legs ached for days from the slap, the bruises fading slowly. As everyone else moved forward, the memories and resentment lingered in her heart. She shifted on the lounge, the dream fading as she awoke. The ache in her heart was as fresh as ever, the memories of betrayal and pain intertwined with her current dilemma. She sat up, feeling the weight of her past and the uncertainty of her future pressing down on her. The journey ahead was daunting, but she knew she had to face it, just as she had faced everything else.

Seven

Monday, 11th March, 2024
Shocking Stats

Lorna was shocked, realising her sister, Cara, had become part of a grim statistic. The numbers were staggering: about one thousand people in Australia were waiting for a kidney transplant. One thousand lives in limbo, anxiously awaiting a life-changing phone call. Some had been waiting for years. The median wait time for a kidney transplant was just over two years, but it wasn't uncommon for people to wait up to seven years. Tears welled in her eyes as she grasped the severity of organ failure. People were extremely ill. People were dying. People died on the waiting list. Why?

She remembered something Dr Cornelius had said about being on the Australian Organ Donor Register during their appointment, a reassurance that echoed in her mind: "The decision to use your organs is based on medical criteria, not age. Don't disqualify yourself prematurely. Let the doctors decide at your time of death whether your organs and tissues are suitable for transplantation."

It was a simple statement, but it carried a profound message. Anyone over sixteen could register as an organ donor in Australia, including elderly people and those with chronic conditions. The process took one minute. One minute to potentially save a life. One minute to potentially save multiple lives. Registering as an organ and tissue donor took less time than drinking a cup of coffee and this could result in being a life-saving hero. A gift of giving once you were gone. Lorna reached for her phone and googled, 'how to register to be an organ donor in Australia.'

She read how most common fears about donation were usually more myth than fact. She wasn't jeopardising her life by going on the register. Doctors and emergency staff's first priority was to save a life; organ and tissue donation was only considered when a person had died or death was inevitable. At that time, the Australian Organ Donor Register was checked, and the family was asked to confirm their loved one's donation decision. She would feel no pain; her body would be treated with the same degree of respect as given to a living patient. Being on the register was the first step for action at a later date, which could be years away. It was as Dr Cornelius had stated. Yes, it was your choice, but one your family needed to know.

Lorna was disgusted with herself. For years, she thought she'd been registered on her state's driver's licence, that system no longer existed, and she still needed to join the Australian Organ Donor Register.

Name, email address (optional), date of birth, postcode, Medicare details, and a dropdown box for what prompted you to register today. Registration Complete. Lorna smiled and relaxed into her chair as she read the lovely message that acknowledged her registration: 'Thank you for taking one minute to register to be a donor. You could one day save and improve the lives of many Australians through the gift of organ and tissue donation. Now that you are registered, make sure you talk to your family about your wishes.'

Tears welled in her eyes. Her first real steps in organ donation. The thought of Cara passing away hit home, she hoped her sacrifice, should she proceed with the live kidney donation, would be seen for what it truly was… a gift of life, free from the complications of their past. It was time for some more reading. She had her sister to think about and the process of being a living kidney donor. The journey ahead was uncertain, filled with risks and challenges, but it was a path she was willing to explore, not just for Cara, but for herself, and for the possibility of healing the wounds time had failed to mend.

Eight

1983
Sticky Fingers

Lorna had been eagerly looking forward to the weekend, when she arrived home, she found an envelope addressed to her on the kitchen table. Opening it, she couldn't believe her luck. After months of hard work and persistence, she'd finally secured a transfer at her job, bringing her closer to home. Squealing with excitement she jumped around the kitchen flapping the letter as she imagined the ease of walking to work instead of enduring the long train rides. Without transport costs she could save a substantial amount of money, which would go towards her dream trip to meet her pen pal, Wendy. They'd been writing to each other for over five years, and with both of them turning eighteen next year, Lorna had planned to surprise Wendy by visiting her and celebrating their birthdays together.

"I got a transfer. I got a transfer," she squealed.

Cara looked up from the TV she was watching in the living room. "So, what. Why don't you get lost, I can't hear the TV."

With Cara not interested, Lorna retreated to her bedroom. Their parents had gone away for the weekend, leaving the sisters alone in the house. Turning on her stereo she danced around the bedroom revelling in her good news as she put away her work clothes. Opening her sock drawer, she decided to check on her savings she'd carefully hidden away. Shock. The envelope was noticeably lighter. Her heart sank as she counted the money. Panic. A significant amount was missing. A quick recount. A good chunk of her hard-earned saving gone; her mind instantly raced to one person. Lorna stormed into the living room. "Cara, did you take my money?"

Cara looked up from the TV. "What are you talking about?"

"The money I've been saving! It's gone. Did you take it?"

Cara stood. "Why would I take your stupid money? Stop accusing me."

Lorna's frustration boiled over. "I wasn't accusing you, I asked you. I can't believe you'd be so nasty. I'm going to tell Mum and Dad when they get home."

"Tell them whatever you want, Lorna," Cara spat. "They'll believe what they want to believe and besides how can you prove anything, it's your word against mine. You have to prove I knew you kept your money hidden in your sock drawer."

"See, see!" Lorna pointed towards Cara. "You did take it. I didn't tell you where it was. It had to be you, you're the only one who's been here."

"So, what. Prove it. Prove all of it. Who cares about your stupid money."

"I do, I care, its mine, I worked hard to save it. You know I'm saving to surprise Wendy."

"Oh, poor Wendy and Lorna's little dream. I don't care about any of it."

"I can't believe you would do this to me!" Lorna shouted. Unable to contain her anger, she stormed out of the house, she paced in the backyard, her thoughts a whirlwind of hurt and betrayal. She couldn't understand why Cara thought she had the right to take what wasn't hers.

After a few minutes, she turned back towards the house, hoping Cara would own up to what she'd done and hand over the cash, but when she tried the door, it was locked. Lorna pounded on it. "Cara, let me in!"

No answer.

Infuriated, she rushed to the window next to the back door and banged on it. "Cara! Let me in!"

"No way!" Cara's voice echoed back.

"Cara! Let me in!"

But Cara ignored her sister.

In her frustration, Lorna pounded harder. The force too much. Glass shattered. A large shard sliced deep into her palm. Blood poured from the wound. The pain instant and intense. "Cara!"

Cara rushed to her feet and quickly unlocked the door, her face going pale at the sight of her sister's blood. The argument forgotten. "Oh my God, Lorna! What happened?" Cara pulled Lorna inside and grabbed a towel, wrapping it tightly around Lorna's hand to slow the bleeding.

"It's... it's bad, Cara. We need to get to the hospital, you'll have to drive, the glass is stuck in my hand," Lorna managed to say through clenched teeth.

Without another word, Cara helped Lorna to the car. The drive to the hospital was tense and silent. Both sisters were too focused on the severity of the injury to think about their recent argument.

"Listen, Lorna," Cara said, as they pulled into the hospital carpark. "When we get inside, tell them you walked out the back door and thought you'd jump down the back steps. Say you accidentally swung your arm and hit the window. I'll say I was lucky to be there to help you. It was all a horrible accident."

Lorna nodded.

UNDER THE COVER OF CLOSENESS

In the emergency room, Cara was the first to speak, Lorna nodded as her sister told the concocted story, agreeing with the version of events just as she'd been instructed. Cara stayed close, repeating the story to every staff member who asked. The medical team worked efficiently, cleaning and stitching the deep cut. As Lorna lay on the hospital bed, the painkillers finally taking effect, she watched Cara from the corner of her eye amazed at how quickly she could come up with a lie and how convincing she'd been with her story telling.

It was late by the time they returned home. Cara helped Lorna to her room, ensuring she was comfortable before heading to bed herself. Not a word was spoken about the broken window. As Lorna drifted off to sleep, she couldn't help but think about the day's events. The argument, the accident, and the way Cara had stepped up when it mattered.

The next day, Lorna checked her money again and was surprised most of what had been missing had been returned. Cara had put it back. Maybe it was a gesture of guilt or perhaps Cara's way of making amends. Either way, Lorna decided not to say anything about the money and stuck with Cara's story, feeling trapped by the official account they had given at the hospital. It was best to let it go.

Their parents returned that evening, and when they heard about the incident and saw the broken window, they were annoyed and disappointed. "Lorna, you'll have to pay for the replacement glass," her father said. "Consider it a lesson in being more responsible."

Meanwhile, they showered Cara with praise. "Thank you, Cara, for helping your sister," their mother said, hugging her.

Lorna was left to grapple with the reality of her sister's

manipulative actions, imprisoned by their lies, she watched her sister's smug satisfaction. Paying for a new window made a further dint in her savings.

Weeks passed without incident, Lorna worked tirelessly, saving every cent for her long-awaited trip to meet Wendy. Each deposit brought her closer to her dream, and now, as the day of departure neared, her excitement was at its peak. She'd managed to save enough to ensure an unforgettable experience. But as her bank balance grew, so did Cara's apparent jealousy. The snide remarks and seeds of doubt Cara planted in Lorna's mind were becoming more frequent and vicious.

"Why would someone want to meet you?" Cara sneered. "Maybe you'll get over there, and her family will be murderers. They'll kill you in your sleep, take your body to a forest, and bury you. What happens if you get there, and they don't like you?"

Lorna tried to shake off her sister's words, refusing to let them dampen her spirits. "It's not going to happen. I'm going to have a great time." She remained focused, taking every shift and overtime opportunity to increase her savings. When it finally came time to buy her ticket, her excitement peaked. She made the necessary withdrawal and asked for her bank balance, expecting it to reflect her hard work and dedication. Instead, confusion set in. The balance was wrong. She asked the teller to repeat it, but the answer remained the same.

"How could this be?" Lorna wondered aloud.

The teller printed out a list of transactions, and Lorna scanned them quickly. Deposit, deposit, deposit…everything seemed correct until she noticed a single withdrawal. It had been made the week after the window incident.

"I don't recall making that withdrawal," she said, pointing to the paper.

"I can get you a copy of the withdrawal slip," the teller

replied.

Lorna nodded and stepped back, her mind racing. When the teller returned with the slip, Lorna's heart sank. The amount wasn't huge, but the fact money had been taken without her knowledge was monumental.

"Can I get a copy of this?" she asked.

"Sure," the teller said, handing over the slip.

As Lorna left the bank, emotions overwhelmed her. She knew exactly who had taken the money. Cara. There was only one person who could walk into a bank, look like her and sign her name. Fury and betrayal bubbled up inside her.

When Cara walked through the front door later that evening, Lorna didn't hesitate. "You took money from my bank account," she said, flapping the copy of the withdrawal in her hand.

Cara didn't even bother to deny it this time. "So what? It was only twenty dollars. You have lots more."

Lorna couldn't believe what she was hearing. "You had no right. It was my money."

"And I'm your sister," Cara shot back. "I needed it. Surely you wouldn't expect me to suffer." She paused; her tone softened. "Lorna, surely you'd help your sister. I mean, I'd have no issue helping you."

Tears welled in Lorna's eyes. Of course, she'd help her sister. She never wanted Cara to suffer, but stealing? It was a betrayal she hadn't expected. She felt sick to her stomach. If she reported Cara's actions, it could involve the police, and she couldn't bear the thought of being responsible for her sister going to jail.

"Don't you ever do that again," she snapped. "Don't ever take my money without my permission."

"Okay, okay," Cara said, rolling her eyes. "Don't get your knickers in a knot. I was going to tell you. I just forgot. I thought you'd understand. Like I said, I thought you wouldn't have an issue helping me. I know I wouldn't hesitate to help you."

Lorna turned away, unable to look at her sister any longer. The disappointment and betrayal cut deeper than any physical wound. As she retreated to her bedroom, she couldn't help but wonder how many more times Cara would betray her, but for now, she would have to focus on her trip and try to push the pain of her sister's actions to the back of her mind.

Nine

Tuesday, 12th March, 2024
New Discoveries

Lorna's phone buzzed, pulling her from her book. Jakob's message was brief: he would soon be at her house. It had been three days since he first appeared on her doorstep with the shocking news about Cara. Lorna's mind boggled as she wondered why the sudden silence. She knew her initial reaction had thrown Jakob, but she'd promised to consider his request. With time and space, she decided the least she could do was explore the possibility of his request. After all, nothing in life should be closed off without at least an initial exploration and an open mind.

A knock at the door interrupted her reading. Lorna opened it to find Jakob standing there, looking flushed and apologetic. "I'm sorry for not contacting you sooner, Aunt Lorna," he said. "I wanted to stay for a few days and catch up, but time got away from me. I've been working on a university assignment and now I have to return to Sydney."

Lorna gave him a small smile. "That's okay, Jakob. I understand." She paused, then added, "I've been to the doctor."

Jakob's eyes widened. "Oh wow! So, you're going to help Mum?"

"It's not that easy, Jakob. I want to find out what I'm getting myself into. It's a huge thing. I have to protect myself."

Jakob's phone rang, cutting Lorna short. He turned and walked a few steps away, speaking quietly into the phone. Lorna could catch snippets of his conversation but not enough to understand it fully. "I know, yes, I know. I've been away studying with my study group. Yes, I will be there. Thanks." He ended the call and looked at his watch. "I'm really sorry, Aunt Lorna. I'd love to stay and chat, but I have to go. Do you mind if I use your bathroom before I leave? I've got a long drive ahead."

Lorna nodded. "It's down the hallway, third door to the left."

Jakob dropped his bag on the lounge room floor and dashed down the hallway. As he disappeared, his bag fell to the side, spilling its contents. Lorna gasped and knelt to gather the scattered items. "What the heck?" she whispered to herself. As she examined the paper, she noted the date. It was recent. Her mind raced with suspicion.

Was Jakob telling her the truth? Was his visit solely about asking her to be a living kidney donor for Cara, or was there a hidden agenda? Did Cara even need a kidney? Jakob was old enough to understand his mother's feelings. Cara had been extremely vocal in the past; Lorna could call her until the cows came home, but there was no way Cara would answer her call. A wave of nausea swept over Lorna. Was she being played? Had Jakob inherited his mother's manipulative tendencies?

Memories of Jakob's manipulative ways as a youngster flashed through her mind. She recalled how he'd convinced his younger brother, Henry, to hand over his pocket money for the sake of brotherly love. Jakob had always had expensive tastes and a knack for getting what he wanted.

UNDER THE COVER OF CLOSENESS

A sense of urgency gripped Lorna. She grabbed Jakob's bag to return the papers before he came back. Opening the top flap, she noticed a strange bundle of documents held together by a band. She glanced towards the hallway. Silence. Did she have time? Another quick glance. Silence. She grabbed the bundle and began to read. "What the..." A noise from the hallway startled her. Lorna shoved the contents back into Jakob's bag, her mind swirling with the implications of what she'd seen. Should she tell him? Should she confront him?

Jakob returned, looking concerned. "Are you okay, Aunt Lorna? I'm sorry I have to run, but I'll call you in a couple of days, when I get some things sorted."

Lorna forced a smile. "I'm fine."

"Are you sure? You look like you've seen a ghost," Jakob said, collecting his bag from the floor and slinging it over his shoulder.

Lorna stepped aside to let him pass. "I'm fine, really. I'm just a bit overwhelmed by everything. Maybe a nice cup of tea is in order."

"Okay, well, I'd better run. Oh, here, that's my mobile number just in case you need to contact me," he said, handing her a piece of paper. "But I'd prefer it if we kept things on the quiet for now... I'll phone you," he said, indicating a phone call with his hand.

Lorna watched Jakob dash down to her front gate. She couldn't shake what she had seen. It was shocking, deeply personal, and deceitful on a new level. It changed everything.

Ten

1985
Excuses And Denials

Lorna sat by the window, staring at the gentle sway of the trees in her garden as she drank her cup of tea, memories flooding back to 1985, a time when life felt simpler. She smiled as she remembered her adventures in New Zealand with Wendy. She could still hear Cara's voice echoing from that day at the airport. It was years ago now, but the memory was still vivid. Cara had driven her to the airport, a rare display of sisterly affection. As they stood by the departure gate, she smirked and said, "I hope your plane doesn't crash. Maybe you should hold onto the biscuits they give you on the plane just in case you do crash, or if your little pen pal's family doesn't feed you."

Lorna rolled her eyes. "Thanks for the vote of confidence, Cara, I'm sure to have a great time. Don't miss me too much."

As she boarded the plane and settled into her seat, her excitement grew and she pushed her sister's words to the side. The flight seemed to stretch on forever, the anticipation of meeting Wendy kept Lorna's spirits high.

When the plane finally touched down in Auckland, she felt a rush of adrenaline. This was it. Stepping into the arrivals area, Lorna scanned the crowd and spotted Wendy holding a sign with her name on it.

UNDER THE COVER OF CLOSENESS

"Welcome to the Land of the Long White Cloud!" Wendy exclaimed, hugging Lorna tightly. "It's so good to finally meet you in person, we've got so much to explore!"

"I feel like I've known you all my life," Lorna replied.

The days that followed were a whirlwind of adventure and laughter. Wendy was everything Lorna had hoped for, honest, caring, and delightfully enthusiastic about sharing every experience equally. Unlike Cara, Wendy seemed to have no trace of jealousy. Instead, she wanted to explore and experience everything together, with equal contribution from both sides. Lorna wondered if her appreciation of their friendship was due to Wendy being an only child, whatever the reason she didn't care, she was free and would embrace the experience with open arms. The two had planned a road trip around the North Island, their adventure began in Auckland, a city bustling with life and energy. They explored the local sites, took a drive by Wendy's old school, and shared stories late into the night. Their first destination on their road trip was the Coromandel Peninsula, famous for its golden beaches. They stood in awe at Cathedral Cove, with its majestic limestone archway framing the turquoise water. They wandered along the shore, soaking in the beauty of the landscape, while taking countless photos.

"This is incredible," Lorna said, breathing in the salt water air.

"Wait until we get to Hot Water Beach," Wendy replied. "You're going to love it."

At Hot Water Beach, they rented a spade and joined other visitors in digging their own spa pools in the sand, letting the naturally heated mineral water bubble up around them. Lying in the warm water just meters from the ocean was a surreal experience, and Lorna couldn't help but laugh at the sheer delight of it.

"Can you believe this?" Wendy asked.

"It's like a dream."

The two giggled as they splashed and soaked in the warmth.

From there they travelled to Tauranga and the coastline of the Bay of Plenty, then on to Rotorua, where the geothermal activity and Maori culture left Lorna in awe. She felt alive and unhindered, a stark contrast to how she often felt around Cara.

"Oh my god, rotten eggs," Lorna said, covering her nose.

Wendy laughed. "It's the sulphur, you'll get used to it."

There were so many wonderful moments, one of the highlights was driving south to Mt Ruapehu, where they stayed at the Grand Chateau Tongariro Hotel. The hotel exuded class and elegance, a perfect prelude to their hike on the Tongariro Alpine Crossing. The 19km trek through the Tongariro National Park was awe-inspiring, with its cold mountain springs, ancient lava flows, steam vents, and the spectacular Emerald Lakes.

"I can't believe we're doing this," Lorna said, taking in the views. "This place is magical."

"We're taking on the world together, remember?" Wendy replied.

On their way back to Auckland, they stopped at the Waitomo Caves for some thrill-seeking. Black water rafting in the Black Labyrinth was an adrenaline rush like no other. Floating down an underground river on rubber tubes, jumping off subterranean waterfalls, and admiring the glowworm-studded cave interior was exhilarating. Their final stop was Hamilton, where they spent a few relaxing days. One evening, as they relaxed, Lorna shared a memory from her past. "You know, when I started working,

UNDER THE COVER OF CLOSENESS

I used to call in sick, claiming to be Cara," she said, with a chuckle. "But on the flip side, I'd get so annoyed when people mistook me for Cara and I had to show my driver's licence to prove I wasn't lying about my identity."

Wendy laughed. "Oh wow! Twins really do have it rough sometimes, don't they?"

Lorna laughed. "Yes, I believe we do, but it's the only thing I know and I wouldn't have it any other way."

Meeting Wendy and exploring New Zealand had been a dream come true, Lorna was grateful for the experience. The four weeks of absolute enjoyment made her feel alive, unhindered, and appreciated for who she was. For the first time in a long time, she rarely thought of Cara.

Eleven

Tuesday, 12th March, 2024
Big Brother Byron

Lorna stood at her kitchen sink washing her tea cup. She thought of Byron, her older brother. Should she phone him? Ask for his advice? They hadn't seen each other in years, although they occasionally spoke on the phone. Byron was six years older than the girls and hadn't had much to do with them growing up. The age difference had created a natural distance. By the time Lorna and Cara were in school, Byron had moved on to another stage in life. Growing up, their relationship with Byron was distant and hadn't changed much through adolescence to adulthood. Lorna remembered how Byron would frequently complain to their parents. His accusations were regular: they were too noisy, too whiny, they entered his room without permission, nagged him, got in his way, or simply ruined what had been his domain.

Lorna believed her brother viewed her and Cara as one entity, always referring to them as "they," "the girls," "the twins," or "you two." She wished he could look beyond their identical appearance and see she was different from Cara. But Byron's attitude started to shift when their father fell ill. One incident stood out vividly in her memory: Byron overheard Cara's rage as she berated Lorna, yelling, screaming, and threatening her. It had been an emotional and extremely embarrassing exchange for Lorna, but at last, others had witnessed her sister's fury. For the first time, Cara had been exposed.

Silently, Lorna cheered. It was the speaker button on Lorna's phone that had worked a treat. Cara had been so enraged she hadn't given thought to the possibility of Lorna being near others, let alone that she'd attempt to stand up to her and make her abusive behaviour public knowledge. Heads turned, faces flushed with embarrassment, and Lorna heard distant gasps beyond the wrath of Cara. The message had been received loud and clear. A lifeline. "Maybe now, they'll believe me," Lorna said silently to herself. *Surely, they'll have to believe.* Everyone else had been on the receiving end of Cara's rage, her lies, and manipulation, but they'd naively or foolishly been led to believe Lorna was immune and for the most part they were right, Lorna would defend her sister, but not when it came to certain principles, not when Cara was crossing the line. Cara was out of control.

The speaker button had shed new light on truths. Byron, her father, a handful of family members, and a close family friend had been astounded. They'd all asked if Lorna was okay. They finally listened and heard when Lorna told them she'd been subjected to Cara's rage for years. Cara would hate it if she knew she'd been exposed. She'd probably hate being exposed as much as she despised Byron. There had been a time when the two got along, but their brother had seen through Cara's lies. Cara hated Byron, she'd made that point abundantly clear to Lorna when they were younger, and from all accounts, Byron didn't have much time for her. He'd witnessed things he said he'd rather not talk about. Lorna sighed, her mind returning to the present. For now, she thought it best to keep the news of Jakob's visit and Cara's illness to herself. Why worry others when she wasn't even sure about the donation? She had promised to consider Jakob's request, and she intended to follow through on that promise. As she mulled over her next steps, her phone buzzed, it was a reminder from Dr Cornelius about her next appointment. Lorna's heart raced as she thought about the implications of what lay ahead. Should she share her concerns with Byron, seek his guidance, or continue on her own?

The memories of Byron's growing empathy after witnessing Cara's outburst played in her mind. Perhaps he could offer some much-needed perspective, or possibly her mother, should she tell her what was happening? The fear of rekindling old tensions held her back. She decided to wait and see how things unfolded at her doctor's appointment before making any decisions about involving anyone else. For now, she needed to focus on the present and the choices she had to make. With a deep breath, Lorna resolved to take things one step at a time. She needed to be sure about her decision regarding the kidney donation before bringing anyone else into the equation. Outside interference, bigotry and personal opinions would get her nowhere moving forward, this situation required clarity and objective thought. Her sister's life was at stake.

Twelve

1987
Jealousy

Time flew by at an amazing rate. The trip to New Zealand became a distant memory as Lorna and Wendy began planning new adventures. 1987 was the year Wendy would visit Australia, and Lorna was eager to return the hospitality and show her the sights. The countdown began, Lorna could hardly contain her excitement. When Wendy finally arrived in Australia, Lorna welcomed her with open arms. Cara was there to witness the reunion. Lorna saw her sister watching as they laughed and caught up. As they walked towards the exit, Cara strolled next to Wendy spinning the car keys on her finger. "Have you realised what she is yet?" Cara said.

Lorna turned to her sister, shocked. "Cara, what are you talking about?"

Without giving Wendy a chance to reply, Cara smirked. "So, you haven't worked out she's a bitch?" She laughed and walked off, leaving Lorna fuming and Wendy bewildered.

Lorna took a deep breath and turned to Wendy. "I'm so sorry about that. Cara can be... difficult."

Wendy nodded, though appeared a bit taken aback. "I'm here to see you, not to deal with her drama."

Lorna was relieved to leave Cara behind as she and

Wendy set off on their adventure around the sights of Australia. Their first destination was central Australia, home to the magical Ayers Rock. Anticipation built as they approached the massive red monolith.

"Ready for the climb?" Wendy asked, eyes wide with excitement.

"Absolutely," Lorna replied.

The climb to the top was a magnificent feat, with many stopping at Chicken Rock, too afraid of the heights. But Lorna and Wendy took every step with enthusiasm, determined to reach the summit. As the sun rose, the huge red stone transformed into a magical, vibrant pink.

"Look at that," Lorna whispered, awestruck by the sight.

"It's like something out of a dream," Wendy said, snapping pictures with her camera.

During the day, the rock appeared bright red, and they took in all the highlights, learning about local culture, flora, fauna, geology, and the European history of the area from their knowledgeable guide. In the afternoon, they enjoyed the magical sunset, watching in awe as the shades of orange turned to yellow.

"Let's have an authentic desert adventure," Lorna said, pointing to a sign.

Wendy jumped at the opportunity and they mounted up for a thrilling circuit along red sand tracks and forest trails, they spotted wild kangaroos and wallabies from their unique vantage point on top of a camel.

"This is amazing!" Lorna exclaimed, holding on tight as her camel trotted along.

"Every day here is wonderful," Wendy said.

Their journey then took them to Cairns, where they fulfilled Wendy's dream of diving on the Great Barrier Reef. The vibrant underwater world left them both in awe.

UNDER THE COVER OF CLOSENESS

"This is absolutely stunning," Wendy exclaimed as they surfaced from their dive.

"I've never seen anything like it," Lorna agreed. "I'm so glad we did this. It's even more beautiful than I imagined."

When they returned home, Cara's annoyance and jealousy was visible. She made several attempts to cut them down with derogatory comments, but Lorna and Wendy laughed it off.

"Had a good time playing tourists?" Cara sneered.

"Actually, we had the time of our lives," Lorna replied. Wendy laughed.

In a quiet moment, Cara cornered Lorna. "How dare you embarrass me. You'll pay for that. You mark my words. When you least expect it. No one makes me out to be a fool and gets away with it."

Lorna shrugged off her sister's threat. "I don't have time for your games, Cara. I'm enjoying my time with Wendy."

For the remainder of the holiday, Lorna refused to let Cara's bitterness overshadow her joy. She and Wendy continued to explore, laugh, and create unforgettable memories. As Wendy's departure neared, they both felt a twinge of sadness but also a sense of fulfillment. They'd shared another adventure and proven no amount of negativity from Cara could overshadow their friendship.

On the day Wendy left, Lorna hugged her tightly at the airport. "Safe travels, my dear friend."

"And remember, don't let Cara get to you. You're stronger than that," Wendy replied.

Lorna nodded, she'd learned to shrug off Cara's bitterness and focus on what truly mattered. Cara's words would no longer dictate her actions.

Thirteen

Wednesday, 13th March, 2024
Catching Words

Lorna's phone buzzed, gone were the thoughts of Wendy, her heart skipped a beat. Cara's name flash on the screen. Taking a deep breath, she answered, hoping for a moment of connection. She'd imagined the prospect of donating her kidney might change something between Cara and herself, she hoped the sacrifice, the pain, and the fear of surgery would forge a bond, create a bridge between them.

"Hello, Cara," Lorna said.

"You think you're so righteous, don't you, Lorna?" Cara snapped. "Always the saint, always the one who saves the day. I just heard from Jakob about what you're planning. You really think this will make everything better? You think I want your pity? I don't need your help. I don't need you."

Lorna's heart sank. She'd envisioned a different conversation, one filled with gratitude and understanding. Instead, all she felt was the sting of her sister's tongue. "Don't be so ridiculous, you need a kidney, Cara. You need a chance to live. I could possibly give you that."

"Out of guilt? Obligation?" Cara spat. "You're not doing it for me, Lorna. You're doing it to make yourself feel better. To play the hero. You think a surgery will erase the past? Will make up for everything?"

Lorna's eyes welled with tears. "I'm doing this because

you're my sister. I thought it might mean something. Because despite everything, I love you."

"Love?" Cara scoffed. "You don't know the meaning of the word. You with your antinatalism beliefs, wanting to get into the good books with MY boys. Wanting to turn them against me because you couldn't be bothered to have your own."

"You have no idea about my beliefs and you're being ridiculous." Lorna shook her head; she could see in Cara's twisted logic she believed what she said. Her world had always been one where manipulation and deceit were the only currencies that mattered. Love and selflessness, was a concept beyond her grasp. "You're right," Lorna said softly, her voice breaking. "I'm doing this for Jakob and Henry, as for you... I don't even know how to reach you anymore."

"Bitch!" Cara snapped before the line went dead.

Lorna sat there, the phone still pressed to her ear, it wasn't the first time she'd heard Cara call her names but today it felt like a huge blow, the chasm between them feeling wider than ever.

Fourteen

1988
The Great Divide

Life was forever changing, as the months passed, Lorna's life took a positive turn. She started dating, her social life blossomed, and she felt a renewed sense of happiness. Cara, too, seemed to have found her own circle of friends, and when they were together at home, things were amicable. Cara appeared genuinely happy for Lorna, but soon Lorna noticed a shift. Cara began showing up at places Lorna had discovered with her friends, infiltrating her inner circle, and dropping snide remarks that left Lorna bewildered. One afternoon, as Lorna sat on the lounge, Cara entered the room with a smug expression. "I didn't think you'd be into a snorer," Cara said, her voice tinged with sarcasm.

Lorna looked up, confused by her sister's remark. "What do you mean?"

"I popped over last night, but you weren't there."

"What are you talking about? I was here. You knew I was here."

"Not here," Cara smirked. "I thought you were with your little lover."

Lorna straightened on the lounge; her curiosity piqued. "No… You knew I was here. You knew I was staying home."

"Oops, my mistake. I must have forgotten." Cara

flicked her hair over her shoulder and smirked. "Although I must say little lover is very accommodating." She chuckled and crossed her arms over her chest. "Likes to make sure a girl is comfortable."

"What?"

"Oh, don't be jealous now. I know you don't like jealousy." Cara jammed her hands in her front pockets and raised her chin. "Maybe you need to have a little chat about loyalty. I know how you think about loyalty."

Lorna tightened her fists. What the heck was Cara alluding to? Had she committed the ultimate betrayal?

Cara stepped closer and lowered her voice. "It's terrible when someone makes you feel like a fool," she laughed. "Oh well, life goes on."

Lorna had seen the way Cara looked, heard her flirtatious comments, but she refused to give Cara the satisfaction of knowing she'd gotten to her. Had Cara stooped to a new low? Lorna wouldn't put anything past her, but her main priority was to ensure Cara felt no ripple from her nasty endeavour. She wouldn't allow her the satisfaction of knowing she'd finally gotten to her as she recalled her sister's words from when Wendy had visited: *How dare you embarrass me. You'll pay for that, you mark my words, when you least expect it. No one makes me out to be a fool and gets away with it.*

Was this her moment of revenge?

Getting up, Lorna shrugged off her sister's comment and left her standing in the room. Cara might have thought it possible to interfere and destroy, but that would only be possible if Lorna played into her hands. Lorna realised she had to stop being the cool girl, the one who ignored red flags, kept quiet in fear of rejection, and didn't put boundaries in place. Cara's words were a desperately needed wake-up call. If her sister had taught her anything, it was that all relationships should be respectful, and communication should be open and honest. Maybe she should look at her sister's comments as a blessing, a catalyst for quietly quitting a relationship that no longer served her. She deserved better than someone who thought it was acceptable to fool with her twin. Ending the relationship immediately would, however, send a signal to Cara. She'd know Lorna acted on what she'd said. For now, Lorna would stay silent. She'd allow herself time to deal with the situation, and then she'd decide the best course of action.

Rising tensions in the home were not confined to Lorna and Cara. Their parents began to argue more frequently, differences emerging that they could no longer reconcile. Lorna tried to dismiss these arguments as a temporary glitch, but it was clear their combined force was starting to splinter. Determined to maintain some form of stability, Lorna reduced the time she spent with friends to focus on work and study. Her aim was clear: work hard, achieve promotions, save diligently, and eventually buy her own place. Both her parents had been influential, Lorna regarded them as smart and sensible teachers. Her mother, a wise woman, often said, "The harder you work, the luckier you become." Her father, a successful self-employed businessman, believed in balance: "Work to live, don't live to work. Set yourself up and don't work for longer than you should. Life is to be enjoyed." Lorna adopted a strategy that combined both philosophies, she believed this would enable her to achieve her dreams. She wanted to be a daughter her parents were proud of, a successful and happy individual, a free thinker who would ultimately relax into an early retirement where she could enjoy the fruits of her labour. As for Cara, Lorna believed everyone in life made choices, and with those choices came consequences.

Sadly, just before Christmas 1988, her parents announced their separation. Lorna was shocked, though she could see things weren't working out and realised life was too short to stay where happiness had left. Immersed in her studies, she decided to stay with her mother in the family home. For Lorna, it wasn't about choosing sides; it was about being practical. Cara moved out and in with their father. The evening of the announcement was tense. Lorna sat at the dining table, her books spread out before her, trying to focus on her studies. Her parents stood in the living room, their voices carrying into the kitchen.

"This isn't working anymore," her mother said, her voice trembling with emotion.

"We've tried, but it's time to move on," her father replied.

Lorna looked up from her books, her heart filled with sadness by the finality of their decision. Cara, who had been listening from the bedroom, entered the room. "So, this is it?" she asked, her tone sharp. "You're just giving up?"

"It's not about giving up," their mother said. "It's about being happy."

Cara scoffed, rolling her eyes. "Whatever. I'm moving in with Dad."

Lorna watched her sister storm out of the room, a mix of anger and relief washing over her. At last, she could breathe. With Cara moving out, Lorna wouldn't have to worry about her sister's constant interference. Cara would no longer know the ins and outs of Lorna's personal life; she would be restricted from the knowledge she required to gatecrash. As the weeks passed, Lorna settled into a new routine, she felt a newfound sense of clarity and purpose. No longer living in the shadows of her sister's actions, her determination to succeed driving her forward. Cara, now living with their father, seemed distant. The physical and emotional space between them grew, giving Lorna the breathing room she desperately needed.

One afternoon, while sorting through some papers, Lorna's phone buzzed. It was a text from an old friend inviting her to a small gathering. For the first time in a long while, Lorna felt the urge to reconnect with her social life. She decided to go, realising she needed balance in her life, just as her father had always preached.

At the gathering, surrounded by friends and laughter, Lorna felt a renewed sense of hope. She chatted and laughed, momentarily forgetting the stresses of her family life and study commitments.

Returning home, her phone buzzed. It was a message from Cara.
"How's it going, sis? Settling in with Mum?"
Lorna sighed, her fingers hovering over the keypad. She decided to keep it brief. "Yes. All good. How about you?"
Cara's response was quick. "Fine. Dad's place is nice. Actually, things couldn't be better. I'm settling in really well. Working things out. Looking at the big picture. Working towards the future."
Lorna put down her phone, feeling a mix of relief and sadness. She missed the closeness she once had with Cara but was pleased her sister appeared happy and was looking towards the future, she knew their distance was necessary for her own peace of mind.

Fifteen

Thursday, 14th March, 2024
Reconnection Request

Lorna sat in her sunlit kitchen, a cup of tea growing cold in her hands, when her phone rang. Jakob's name flashed on the screen. Taking a deep breath, she answered. "Jakob, is everything okay?" she asked, trying to keep her voice steady. Lorna had been concerned that Jakob could have been subject to the wrath of Cara, she'd been uneasy in making contact, fearing if Cara found out it would only inflame the situation.

"Hi, Aunt Lorna. Yes, everything's fine," Jakob reassured her. "I mean well…um… well… mum hit the roof when I told her I'd seen you. I expected that. But I'm calling because Henry told me about a phone call mum made yesterday, he said she was yelling and mentioned your name, he said mum was furious and when she hung up, she threw her phone at the wall." Jakob drew in a long breath. "I hadn't told Henry I'd met up with you and asked you to be a living kidney donor for our mum. I didn't want to build up any hopes, but since he heard her… well since he heard her being harsh, he's been really upset. Henry has been asking about you and he wants to meet you."

Lorna's heart leapt. "Really? Henry wants to meet me?" she repeated, her voice trembling. Memories flooded back, like Jakob, Henry had been just a little boy the last time she saw him. She recalled how they would sing songs together, the favourite being the opening theme to Fraggle Rock, Henry would sit on Lorna's lap being bounced on her knees while waving his hands in the air. In the mornings, Henry would crawl into her bed, eagerly awaiting the made-up stories she would weave just for him and Jakob, incorporating their names into magical tales and exciting adventures.

"Does he remember me?" she asked.

"He remembers bits and pieces, and he really wants to reconnect."

Lorna felt a surge of happiness, but mixed with this joy was a sense of apprehension. Years had passed. So much had changed. What if Henry didn't remember her as fondly as she remembered him? "That's wonderful, Jakob. I'd love to see him," she said, her voice steady despite her swirling emotions. She closed her eyes for a moment, picturing Henry as he was back then... an outdoorsy child who loved getting dirt on his hands and under his nails. Henry loved being in the country, collecting eggs from the chickens, picking beans and tomatoes from the garden, and spending endless hours by the lake. They enjoyed long picnics in the sun, hiking through the bush and feeding the ducks. In contrast, Jakob had always preferred the indoors, reading books and playing with his electrical gadgets, fascinated by the virtual worlds they offered. Lorna remembered the joy in Henry's eyes as he explored nature, his laughter echoing as they joked. She recalled the warmth of his small hand in hers as they walked through the garden, his excitement as he discovered new plants and creatures. Those memories were like treasures and the thought of seeing Henry filled her with hope. "Henry has always loved the outdoors," Lorna said finally. "I remember how he would get up at a sparrow fart to help with the chickens."

Jakob laughed. "A sparrow fart, yes well he's still an early riser and he still loves nature," Jakob said. "He's never lost that part of himself. I think he really misses those days."

Lorna's heart swelled. "I miss them too, Jakob. I miss you both."

There was a pause, Lorna felt a sense of anticipation, a glimmer of hope that maybe, just maybe, they could rebuild what had been lost.

"Let's arrange a time for us to meet," Jakob suggested. "I think it would mean a lot to Henry... and to me too."

Lorna smiled, a tear slipping down her cheek. "I'd love that, Jakob. I really would."

"No worries, Aunt Lorna. I'll sort something out... I'll talk with Henry and get back to you with a date?"

As she hung up the phone, Lorna felt a renewed sense of purpose. Henry remembered her, wanted to see her. She was over the moon with excitement, but also apprehensive about the reunion. Deep down, she knew reconnecting with Henry and Jakob was the first step towards healing, but what would Cara think? Would she try to put a stop to their plans?

Sixteen

1992
The Reunion

Where had time gone? Lorna stood in her bedroom, staring at the invitation in her hand. The years had flown by so quickly, it seemed like just yesterday when she and Cara were inseparable. Now, she'd received an invitation to a high school reunion. She felt a mixture of curiosity and hesitation. Ten years had passed since she'd finished school. How should she respond? Should she respond? Life had moved on. She'd moved on. Although she still lived with her mother and frequently saw old friends, things were very different. She was different. In many ways, she'd risen beyond the world of twinship. Over the years she'd completed her studies, worked hard, achieved promotions, and gained prominence in her field of business. She was a success in her own right. With success came money. Lorna was close to taking the leap into the world of homeownership, not interested in a mansion, just a modest house she'd call her home. Maybe she should attend. It would be a proud moment to tell others of her achievements, not to gloat, but just to state facts to those who appeared interested. There was nothing wrong with letting others know how commitment could result in success.

Cara was carving her own path in life, she still lived

UNDER THE COVER OF CLOSENESS

with her father and seemed content to plod along, enjoying being the life of the party. Friends came and went for Cara. Whenever Lorna spoke with her sister, her best friend had changed, as if on a revolving door, the life of the friendship determined by Cara's needs.

Lorna wondered if Cara would accept the invitation. She picked up her phone, dialling Cara's number. "Hey, Cara. Did you get the invitation to the reunion?"

Cara's voice was unexpectedly enthusiastic. "I did! I think it would be so much fun to go together. What do you think?"

"Yeah, it could be nice," Lorna replied, surprised by her sister's excitement.

The two arrived together, Lorna felt a flutter of nerves, but after recognizing some familiar faces, she relaxed and grabbed a drink. Everyone was chatting, reminiscing about old times and discussing achievements and the paths their lives had taken since school. The news that two fellow students had passed away shocked her. Jane Davis had been found in a toilet cubicle at Central Station, drugs her demise. Suzanne Webber had been killed in a car accident. Two lives taken far too soon. Their loss was a reminder of the importance of living life to the fullest, to never take things for granted. Life was fragile. As Lorna sat and watched, her thoughts hit home. What did she want out of life? Where did she want to be? Where did she want to live? By the time the food arrived, her fears of cattiness disappeared, and Lorna relaxed into the evening. Cara had wandered off and was mingling leaving Lorna momentarily alone at the table.

Alison Cartwright approached, looking as preened as ever. Lorna was sure she'd undergone Botox. Alison's face remained straight even when she laughed, her lips pouted like she'd been sucking on far too many lollipops. "You must be so thrilled. Cara's such a success," Alison said, as she sat next to Lorna.

Lorna gave a blank stare and tilted her head. "What success?"

Without a chance to respond, Alison continued. "So do you own a house too?"

"Sorry, a house?"

"Cara told us all about her house. We couldn't believe she'd be one of the first to buy one in the suburb where we grew up. It's such an achievement."

Heat rose in Lorna's cheeks. Cara didn't own a house; she lived with their father, just as Lorna lived with their mother. Why was Cara claiming to be a homeowner?

"So… do you own your own home too?" Alison pressed.

"Um…no… No, I don't own a house."

"Oh, okay," Alison said, her interest waning. "Well, I guess I'll catch up with you later."

Lorna watched as Alison walked away, on the other side of the room Cara was acting the centre of attention. What had her sister been saying? Owning her own home? Why was she telling people she owned a home? Did she think it made her appear successful? Her rise in status certainly had everyone talking about her. Cara's lie also had everyone questioning Lorna's living arrangements of still residing with her mother. Cara's reported achievement far outshone Lorna's. Lorna's eyes hardened as she watched from a distance.

Why does Cara have to constantly lie? Is it a compulsion? She wouldn't know how to lie straight in bed, she thought as she scanned the exit, looking for a way out of the room. *She's not going to get away with it. I'm going to tell Dad what she's saying. How dare she tell people she's allowed him to move in with her, into her house?*

The next morning, Lorna was still fuming. She'd decided to cut the reunion short. While it had been lovely to catch up, the night was ruined by Cara's lie. Lorna was determined to stop her sister. Their father would soon learn what she'd been saying behind his back. Cara making out he was a charity case allowed to live under her roof was insulting. Determined to stop her sister, she went straight to their father.

"Dad, you won't believe what Cara's been telling people. She's saying she owns this house and you're living with her because you need her support."

Lorna's father laughed. "Don't worry, love. You worry about far too many things. There's no need to upset yourself. Sometimes we have to let things go in one ear and out the other. You know how your sister can be."

As she left her father's house, Lorna felt a swell of frustration. His dismissive attitude and lack of concern only fuelled her irritation.

In her bedroom she paced back and forth, picking up her phone she dialled her sister's number, ready for a confrontation. "Why are you telling people you own a house and Dad is living with you?" Lorna demanded.

"Mind your own business," Cara snapped. "I can tell anyone anything I want. You don't control me."

The line went dead as Cara hung up.

Lorna paced her bedroom, phone still clutched tightly in her hand, her mind racing, she threw her phone to her bed. *How can she spin such blatant lies?*

What did Cara's latest lie mean for their relationship, for their family? Ever since Cara had chosen to move in with their father things had appeared more relaxed at home, there was no more blame for things Cara had done. Cara claimed the reason she moved was because their father was less strict, allowing her more freedom, whereas their mother's rules felt suffocating. Was the truth more insidious? Cara had always known how to manipulate their parents, playing on their emotions to get what she wanted. It left Lorna feeling upset and powerless. She'd always tried to stay neutral, not wanting to take sides, but Cara's actions were making it increasingly difficult. How could she continue to watch from the sidelines while her sister spun lies and manipulated those around her?

Lorna sat on the edge of her bed, her thoughts swirling. Cara's decision to live with their father had been a calculated move. She remembered the arguments, the tears, and the way Cara had painted their mother as the villain, all to get what she wanted. Their father, eager to keep the peace, had let Cara have her way, creating a rift Lorna now found herself in the middle of.

"Why does she do this?" Lorna muttered to herself. "Why does she feel the need to lie?" Taking a deep breath, she decided to focus on what she could control. She couldn't change Cara or her father's reactions, but she could make choices that were right for her. She would continue to work hard, save for her own home, and build a life that wasn't defined by her sister's actions.

Six hours later, Lorna was still seething about her conversation with Cara. No matter how hard she tried she couldn't get the thoughts to leave her mind. And now, her mother sat opposite at the kitchen table; would it help to talk? The claim Cara had made about owning a house and their fathers denials churned to the point where she felt ill. She needed to talk, to vent, to make sense of her sister's latest lie.

"Mum," she said.

UNDER THE COVER OF CLOSENESS

Her mother looked up and raised an eyebrow. "What's the matter?"

Lorna hesitated for a moment, took a deep breath then plunged in. "Cara told everyone at the school reunion she owns a house and Dad lives with her. It's not true, and it makes Dad look like he's reliant on her."

"Lorna, you know how Cara can be. She likes to make herself look good in front of others."

"But it's not true and when I spoke to Dad, he just brushed it off."

Her mother sighed. "Lorna, you're making an issue out of nothing. How your father chooses to respond is his business. You need to stop."

"What?" Lorna's voice rose slightly in disbelief.

"You heard me. I've told you time and time again to stop," her mother said.

"Stop what?" Lorna felt a familiar frustration bubbling up.

"Giving in to her. From the time you were little, you always gave in to her. Your toys, your pocket money... she'd spend hers on lollies and then come back asking for yours, and you foolishly handed it over."

"Not all the time."

"Too many times. You created her greed. You encouraged her appetite by giving in to her, making her believe she could have whatever she wanted."

"And if I hadn't... what then?" Lorna snapped. "I know what then. I would have been in trouble. Cara would have cried, said I wasn't being fair, and we would have both been in trouble...her for whinging and me for annoying her. That's how it was, that's how it still is. You can't see me." Lorna's voice rose, her frustration turning to despair. "Why can't you see me? Here I am. I'm not Cara. I'm me. I'm not a package deal. What happens with one doesn't automatically roll on to the other. Why can't you see me?"

76

"Why are you screaming, Lorna?" her mother replied, her tone disapproving. "I simply said your actions are what made Cara behave as she does. There's no need for hysterics."

Lorna shook her head, tears of frustration welling in her eyes. "I can't do this. You can't see, and it doesn't matter what I say."

"Because you don't say, Lorna. I keep telling you, it's not what you say, it's the way you say it. You get all emotional and then you start attacking. You attack me, just like your sister. I don't need these raised voices."

"And there you go again, comparing me... 'Just like your sister!' That's my point. I'm not my sister. I didn't ask to be labelled the same as her."

She stormed out of the room, her mother's words echoing in her mind. Every conversation seemed to circle back to the same place, leaving her feeling unheard and invisible.

For now, there was nothing Lorna could do except watch from the sidelines. Cara had always been the more bullish twin, the one who took what she wanted without regard for the consequences. Lorna, on the other hand, had always been the peacemaker, the one who tried to keep everything together. But this latest lie felt like a tipping point. Lorna knew she had to distance herself from Cara's toxic influence and let go of what she couldn't control, focusing instead on the future she wanted.

Tomorrow was a new day.

Seventeen

Monday, 18th March, 2024
Tomorrow Is Another Day

Tomorrow is another day, Lorna thought to herself. *Breathe, just breathe.* She steadied her nerves as she prepared for her second visit to Dr Cornelius. This was it. The first real step in finding out if she could be a suitable candidate for a live kidney transplant for her twin sister, Cara. As she entered Dr Cornelius's office, the familiar scent of antiseptic greeted her. The doctor, with his calm and reassuring presence, invited her to sit down.

"Lorna, it's good to see you again," he said warmly. "How have you been feeling?"

"Nervous," Lorna replied. "But determined. I've been doing a lot of reading since my last visit, and to be honest, I feel overwhelmed. But I want to proceed with the investigations."

Dr Cornelius nodded. "That's perfectly normal. Let's go over the process again. In Australia, all screening tests, inpatient services, and follow-up costs related to live kidney donation are covered by Medicare. Preliminary screening includes a thorough physical examination, confirmation of normal blood pressure and BMI. This screening ensures unsuitable donors are identified early without significant resource expenditure."

Lorna absorbed the information, her mind racing. "At this stage, I'd like to proceed anonymously," she said. "I've read about others being rejected as candidates due to underlying health issues, and I don't want to upset anyone if I can't donate."

"Understood," Dr Cornelius said, making a note in her file. "We'll keep your request for anonymity. I'll contact Sydney Hospital and request they send you a donor questionnaire. This will be the first step in the screening process."

"Thank you," Lorna said, feeling a slight ease in her anxiety.

Dr Cornelius continued. "Today, we'll complete the first stage of basic testing. This includes a thorough physical examination, checking your blood pressure, and confirming your BMI. Based on your results, we'll be able to proceed with contacting the Sydney Renal Ward where you will have to go for blood and urine tests to assess iron levels, kidney function, liver levels, and cholesterol. It's there that you'll be assign a transplant co-ordinator who will guide you through your journey and assist with appointments."

The physical examination was thorough but uneventful. Dr Cornelius noted Lorna's results appeared good. "Your blood pressure and BMI are within normal ranges," he said, handing her a referral for the next set of tests. "You're off to a promising start, now let me make a phone call to the Sydney Renal Ward where we can make an appointment for those first tests."

Lorna smiled. "Thank you, thank you so much."

With the referral in hand and her appointment booked at Sydney Hospital Lorna felt a mixture of relief and apprehension. The anxious wait had begun, but she knew she'd taken an essential step forward. As she left the clinic, the weight of the situation pressed down on her. She tried to focus on the immediate tasks of staying healthy, and managing her stress.

Tomorrow is another day, she reminded herself. *One step at a time.*

Eighteen

1992
Distance

Lorna lay in bed, staring at the ceiling, thoughts swirling through her mind. She reflected on the path she'd travelled and the one still to be journeyed. Her thoughts drifted to her two school friends, gone too soon, their lives cut short before they could explore the vast possibilities the world had to offer. The fragility of life weighed heavily on her. What did she want out of life? What path would she choose? Her mind inevitably turned to Cara, her twin, whose propensity for lying had once again stirred the waters of their family. Was it expected that people settled in the area where they were born, settling for what was safe and known? The world offered endless opportunities, and she couldn't help but wonder if she would be restricting her possibilities if she didn't at least explore them. Her childhood had been one of privilege, filled with holidays exploring the vastness of Australia. Why not take that spirit of adventure further?

Her father's words echoed in her mind: "You should live to work, not work to live." With a newfound determination, Lorna sprang out of bed and dashed to the shower. Today would be the first day of changing her life, a positive move to define her independence and individuality. Not north or south, those paths had been extensively travelled. She would head west, over the mountains and beyond. This was her life. She was responsible for her actions, and contrary to what others thought, she wasn't to blame for how her sister behaved nor should she be compared. They were two separate entities, and this move would ensure she was treated as one.

With her mind set, Lorna packed herself some lunch, snacks, and drinks before jumping into her car. Always practical, she preferred bringing her own food to save money for bigger and better things. Both her parents had taught her the importance of saving. Her brother Byron had long moved out, having bought a lovely little house not too far from where they lived. While at school, Lorna had watched as others bought their lunch, but she was content with a Vegemite or peanut butter sandwich. She couldn't believe how many people at work ate a large portion of their pay on lunch and coffee every day, then complained about their inability to save for a house or holiday.

Lorna travelled from one town to the next, meeting with real estate agents and viewing properties of differing appearances until she found one. It was perfect, absolutely perfect. The house required some work, but she was confident she could complete most of it. The yard needed a lot of tidying, the lawn was overgrown, old sheds were collapsing, and the house was musty from being closed up. The floor covering needed replacing, the bathroom was mould-infested, and the kitchen was in disrepair. Lorna remembered her mother's advice about buying a house: "Don't buy the best house in the worst street, buy the worst house in the best street." *Could this rough diamond be my perfect forever home?* Lorna smiled at the possibilities. She could do it. She would barter with the owner. The real estate agent mentioned it had been on the market for a long while. If she ordered a building and pest inspection, she'd know what she was dealing with. She kept her excitement hidden from the agent, pointing out all the negative aspects that could potentially increase her repair costs. Driving home, she hoped the reports wouldn't reveal anything too adverse. If they didn't, she'd put in an offer.

With butterflies in her stomach, Lorna thought of her wonderful new adventure. Her dream of being a homeowner was so close. A new beginning where people would meet and know her as an individual.

Within a week, the building and pest reports came back. The required repairs were manageable. She made a low offer, hoping the owner would accept it but knowing she had a buffer to increase the purchase price if needed. To her amazement, her initial offer was accepted. Lorna jumped around with excitement. She informed her employer about her plans, and they agreed to transfer her to their regional office. Lorna accepted the transfer with open arms, taking a few weeks annual leave to move and settle in. Everything was full steam ahead.

Cara was, as usual, unsupportive. "Going to be a country hick," she sneered. Lorna's mother wished her all the best, knowing all birds eventually flew the coop. Her father, relaxed and non-judgmental, believed it was her decision. Lorna appreciated his attitude but was still concerned about his lack of reaction to Cara's lie about his house. His words came to mind: "Don't worry, Love." For now, she'd try not to worry. She'd focus on being a first-time homebuyer and exploring her new surroundings. With luck, she'd meet some wonderful new people.

Lorna's tree change made her feel freer than ever before. In the initial stages of moving in, her house was scarcely furnished. She stripped the kitchen of its cupboards, stripped the bathroom of all tiles, painted through, and had new kitchen and bathroom installations. For furniture, she was happy to use second-hand items. As long as they were clean and comfortable, it didn't matter if they had been preloved. New things could come later. Months passed, seasons changed, and her first winter was shocking. She'd never experienced the coldness of country life, where you could see your breath at midday. But she embraced the change, even her first snowfall. Life in her own house was coming together, and the house she purchased was becoming the home she loved.

Jubilation however, turned to sadness as she celebrated her first birthday without her sister and family. Lorna wondered if she'd made the right decision in moving to the country. "Happy birthday to me, happy birthday to me, happy birthday, dear Lorna, happy birthday to me." Lorna picked up the cupcake and blew out her candle, then returned the cake to the table. It was the first year she celebrated her birthday alone. Twenty-five. Moving to the country had seemed exciting, but being so busy with renovations and settling into work it meant friends were hard to find. For the most part, she enjoyed her new life. She understood it would take time to meet and develop new friendships, but old friends who'd congratulated her on her tree change had gone silent. They seemed to think the trip from the country to Sydney was shorter than the same road from Sydney to the country, so face-to-face contact was only initiated by Lorna.

Seeing Cara less frequently, keeping conversations brief, and avoiding topics that tended to lead to conflict had improved things. Cara's tendency to explode like a firecracker was better managed from a distance. Lorna's tree change afforded her the time for some self-care. It was important to manage her expectations and accept the possibility she might not be able to change Cara's toxic ways. Maybe the only thing she could control was the way she responded to it.

Nineteen

Tuesday, 19th March, 2024
Three Crazy Emus

Lorna picked up the picture from the mantel and read the words, "Friends are the family we choose for ourselves." She smiled; the words were so true. The photo was of her and her two dearest friends, Jamie and Jill, along with their two dogs, Daisy and Billy. It had been taken during a holiday together in Merimbula. Their friendship had endured for decades, forged through work and strengthened by shared experiences, the highs and lows of life, births, deaths, unions, and separations. Jamie and Jill were the most loving, kind, and caring friends she could have hoped for. The three of them had weathered many storms, facing health issues head-on, offering supporting words, comforting hugs, and reassuring love. They were the three crazy emus and two wombats, an affectionate title they'd bestowed upon themselves. Lorna chuckled at the memory.

It was time to tell them what had happened. She wanted to hear their thoughts and, if she was to go ahead, she would need their support. Glancing at the clock, Lorna returned the picture to the mantel and went to the kitchen to prepare morning tea. Her friends would arrive soon, now in the quiet she could almost hear her heart racing, apprehensive as to how her dear friends would react.

UNDER THE COVER OF CLOSENESS

The doorbell rang. Lorna opened the door to find Jamie and Jill standing there with Daisy and Billy, their much-adored toy poodles.

"Are you okay, Lorna?" Jamie asked as she stepped inside.

"Yes, you sounded as if something was wrong," Jill added before Lorna could answer.

Lorna bit her top lip and looked at her friends. "I'm okay... I have something I need to tell you."

Tears formed in her eyes as her two friends leaned closer, their voices softening. "What is it? What's wrong?" they asked in unison.

"I had a visitor. I've been asked..." She paused, worried about their reaction. Over the years, she'd told her friends about her twin sister, Cara. They'd witnessed Cara's antics at their father's funeral and supported Lorna when Cara disappeared with Jakob and Henry over a decade ago. They'd seen the love and affection Lorna shared with her nephews and heard Cara's venomous words.

"Well, come on then, don't keep us in suspense. Who?" Jamie asked.

"And what? What have you been asked?" Jill continued.

"Jakob."

"Jakob... who?" Jamie asked, her eyes meeting Lorna's. Her hand rose to her mouth as she realised who Jakob was. "Oh my... Jakob... little Jakob."

Tears rolled down Lorna's face as she nodded, acknowledging who.

"Are you serious? After all this time? Oh my gosh, I'm in shock. I can't believe it... after all this time. Are you okay?" Jamie stepped towards Lorna. "Here, let me give you a hug. You must be in shock. I know I am."

Jill moved closer, holding their hands. "I can't believe it either. I don't know if I'd recognise him... he wouldn't be a little boy anymore. Oh my gosh, he'd be a man now, a young man."

Lorna nodded. "He is."

"What did he want? You said he asked something," Jill said.

"Yes, and why are we only hearing about this now? I would have loved to see him again," Jamie said.

"He wasn't here for long... maybe we should all go to the lounge and sit, and I'll explain."

The three sat on the lounge, Daisy and Billy rummaged through the basket of dog's toys Lorna had stowed away in the corner of the room. Lorna knew her friends would react strongly to Jakob's request. They were protective and loyal. She hoped they would see the request for what it was and from whom it had come. Cara hadn't made the request; Jakob had. He was a scared son, afraid of losing his mother. While he had been absent from Lorna's life, this was not his decision. He, too, had been a victim of his mother's actions. A boy went where his mother instructed.

"Jakob told me Cara's sick, really sick."

"And what's that got to do with you? She wiped you," Jamie snapped.

Lorna nodded and looked at her two friends. Jill picked up her coffee and took a sip, returning the cup to the table. "So, what's that got to do with you?" she repeated Jamie's question.

"She needs a kidney transplant."

"Are you kidding? And she wants you to give her one? No way. After everything she's done? After how she made you feel, disappearing without a word, taking the boys with her when she knew how much you loved them? I'm sorry, but there's no way in hell... you'd be risking your life." Jamie was not backward in saying what she thought.

Jill sat on the lounge, looking dumbfounded, tears

streaming down her face. "Surely, you're not going to risk your life. I'm not sure if I would, but then again, you would be saving a life."

"But what about all the things she's done? Why did she send Jakob to do the grovelling? What did she say?" Jamie asked.

"I haven't said yes. To be honest, the thought terrifies me. But Cara didn't send Jakob. Jakob came out of concern. He wanted to help his mum."

"And what does Cara say?" Jill asked.

"When Cara found out she phoned me and blew my head off. She says she doesn't need me."

"Good. Let her work it out herself. No need to get you involved. She didn't want you involved before," Jamie said.

"But she's, my sister."

"Yep. And think about everything she's done. What she did to you, her disgusting posts on social media, the derogatory accusations she made about you, the thieving. What about the advertisement? Surely you can't forget the despicable behaviour. And your parents... what she did to them, to your father. What would your mother think?"

"I don't know. I don't know what anyone will think. I don't know what I think. I feel so... so overwhelmed. It doesn't feel real, but I know it is, and I can't just ignore Jakob. There's so much I need to get my head around. Maybe we should finish our coffee, and I'll explain things from the start."

The three drank their coffee. Lorna could see concern etched on her friends' faces. She thought of her mother, what would she think about the request? What would Byron think? At the end of the day, she knew the decision was hers and hers alone, but she also knew she'd require support. Relaxing into the softness of the cushions, she told her friends how Jakob had shown up late on a Saturday evening. On the following Monday, just over one week ago she took herself to the doctor to ask for information. Jakob had returned a few days later on the Tuesday and apologised for disappearing.

"Why didn't you call us and why didn't he go to the doctors with you?" Jamie asked.

"I needed to get my head around things before I could actually talk about it. I don't know why he disappeared; I had no way of contacting him. When he returned, he said he'd been studying, but his return visit was cut short, he received a phone call and said he had to get back to Sydney."

"Who called him? Cara?" Jill asked.

"It was probably a set up," Jamie mumbled.

"I don't know, I don't know who called him... all I know is he said he had to go. He asked to use the bathroom, and when he left the room, his bag fell to the side and opened, and something fell out. I saw something that made me... worry. I don't know what to think."

"What?" the friends questioned.

"Some papers. I didn't have time to see them all, but I need to speak with Jakob."

"Oh Lorna, this is too much. You don't need all this stress after everything she put you through. I know you were devastated when she disappeared, but things settled. What do you want to do?" Jamie asked.

"Yes, yes... what do you want to do?" Jill repeated. "I know we both came on strong with our initial reactions, but it's you we care about."

"That's right. We love and care about you. We'll respect and support your decision. That's what we do, but the decision has to be yours."

"Thank you. Thank you so much. I knew I could count on you."

"Of course. Come on, let's get up. This calls for a group hug," Jill said.

The three friends embraced each other. Lorna could

feel their warmth and love. Tears rolled down her cheeks. Challenging times were made less challenging with beautiful, loving friends by her side. No matter how things went, she knew she'd stand tall. *Three crazy emus and two wombats,* she thought. Friendship was one of the greatest things a person could offer; it cost nothing. Giving a live kidney would take a lot of thought. The process wouldn't happen overnight, and she was sure the three would have many more conversations about it.

After all the things Cara had said and done, would she be willing to save her sister's life?

Twenty

1996
Coming Together

Time and distance had worked wonders for Cara and Lorna, both were enjoying their separate lives. Cara had moved out from her father's house and ventured into homeownership and, by all reports, was settled. A family tradition had formed over the years, where different family members hosted the Christmas party. Grandparents, aunts, uncles, and cousins would gather, each adult contributing a part to the Christmas feast. This year, Cara insisted the party be held at her home. Christmas 1996 would mark the rekindling of their relationship.

In the months that followed, Lorna made several trips to Sydney to catch up with family, including Cara. For the first time in years, they celebrated their birthday together. Lorna embraced this new, more mature, and somewhat relaxed version of her sister, although she silently wondered what had happened to the explosive version and what it would take for her to reappear. For now, all was good. Cara even made return trips to Lorna's house, meeting her two best friends, Jamie and Jill, and becoming acquainted with the area.

One evening, while Cara was visiting, Lorna invited Jamie and Jill out for dinner. They decided on the local

UNDER THE COVER OF CLOSENESS

Indian restaurant, which Lorna had previously praised as the best in the west. Over dinner, their conversation turned to the meal. Cara took a bite and wrinkled her nose. "This is disgusting," she declared, loud enough for nearby tables to hear. "Lorna, you must have lost your taste since moving to the country. Good food and great restaurants are obviously only found in Sydney."

Lorna felt her cheeks flush with embarrassment. "Cara, can you keep it down, please?"

Cara's voice only grew louder. "I'll speak how I want."

The waitress approached, a concerned look on her face. "How is everything?"

Cara didn't hesitate. "Disgusting," she said, loud and clear.

Lorna, Jamie, and Jill exchanged embarrassed glances as they quickly finished their meal. Outside, Lorna took a deep breath and tried to reason with her sister. "Cara, there's a time and place for everything. I live in this town and frequent that restaurant."

"Well, that's not my problem," Cara snapped. "I certainly wouldn't eat there again."

Later, when Cara had returned to Sydney, Jamie and Jill spoke with Lorna. They still couldn't believe Cara's behaviour. "That was so embarrassing, Lorna," Jamie said, shaking her head. "She couldn't have just quietly commented? It was as if she was trying to make a situation out of nothing."

Lorna sighed. "I know. I thought things had changed."

"It's like she was waiting for an opportunity to cause a scene," Jill added, her voice tinged with disbelief.

Lorna nodded, her mind spinning with thoughts. "I just hoped we could have a nice evening. I wanted you all to get along."

Jamie put a comforting hand on Lorna's shoulder. "We

know you did. And we'll always support you. But maybe it's a reminder to be cautious. She hasn't completely changed."

As the evening wore on, Lorna couldn't shake the unease Cara's outburst had left. It was a stark reminder that while time and distance had worked wonders, some things might never change. She had to navigate this rekindled relationship carefully, balancing her desire for a peaceful life with the unpredictable nature of her twin sister.

Twenty-One

Monday, 1st April, 2024
April Fools

Lorna's phone buzzed on the kitchen counter, a welcome interruption to her thoughts. She glanced at the screen, her heart skipping a beat when she saw Jakob's name. It had been over two weeks since their last conversation, and she'd been wondering if he'd forgotten about her. She wiped her hands on a towel and swiped to answer, bringing the phone to her ear. "Hello, Jakob," she greeted warmly, trying to mask her surprise.

"Hi, Aunt Lorna, I wanted to let you know that Henry and I will be visiting soon."

Lorna blinked, momentarily taken aback. "Are you serious? This isn't an April Fool's joke, is it?" The possibility of finally seeing Henry after so long seemed too good to be true.

"100%... I'm serious...it's not a joke," Jakob assured her with a chuckle. "I know it's been a little while since we last spoke, and I didn't want you to think we'd abandoned you, especially after everything. Showing up out of nowhere after all these years and then asking you to… you know… donate a kidney."

"I never thought that, Jakob. I understand. You both have busy lives."

"We do," Jakob agreed. "But I've talked to Henry, and we're going to make time. We hope to see you within the month."

"That's wonderful. I've missed you both so much. And Jakob… How's Uncle Bernard doing? It's been so long since we've spoken, I've been worried…"

Jakob cut her off, his tone suddenly tight. "I'm sorry, Aunt Lorna, but I've got to go. I can't talk anymore right now."

"Wait, Jakob…" Before she could protest, the line went dead. Lorna stared at the phone in her hand, frustration bubbling inside her. It seemed every time they spoke, their conversations were cut short, and not by her doing. And then there was the issue of Jakob's bag, what she'd seen inside, it still haunted her. But every time she tried to talk; Jakob shut her down. *What is it? Why does it feel like he's hiding something?* Lorna sighed, setting the phone down. It was beginning to feel like she was the only one putting in the effort to build this relationship. It reminded her too much of her relationship with Cara, a one-sided affair where she was always the one reaching out, trying to keep things together, while Cara pushed her away.

As she walked to the sink and looked out the window, she thought of the long days ahead. The appointments in Sydney loomed on her calendar, long hours of travel and medical assessments. But she wasn't alone. She smiled, thinking about Jamie and Jill, her steadfast friends who'd been her rock through all of this. Jamie's words echoed in her mind: "This is your journey, Lorna. Don't let anyone else steer you off your path." Jamie's encouragement was like a beacon, guiding her through the uncertainty. And Jill, always the practical one, had made arrangements with her dog sitter to take care of both Billy and Daisy when the time came. "Even at short notice," Jill had assured her. "We'll turn one of those appointments into a girls' weekend. We'll be there by your side, no matter what."

UNDER THE COVER OF CLOSENESS

The idea of a girls' weekend in Sydney, turning one of her daunting medical appointments into something fun, was a comfort Lorna hadn't known she needed. The thought of laughter, of shared meals and warm conversations with her two closest friends, made the prospect of those long, sterile hospital corridors seem a little less bleak. Lorna smiled to herself, feeling a surge of gratitude. She wasn't alone in this, she had her friends, her chosen family, who would stand by her no matter what. Yet, beneath the comfort of their friendship, a gnawing worry persisted. She hadn't told her mother or brother about the contact with Jakob, about Cara's illness, or the request for a kidney donation. The weight of that secret pressed on her chest like a stone. She knew she couldn't keep it hidden forever, but the thought of unveiling it, of exposing herself to their opinions and judgments, made her hesitate.

Later that evening as she lay in bed, staring at the ceiling, Lorna couldn't shake the feeling that everything was coming to a head. She tried to push the worries away. But the questions kept coming: Was she doing the right thing? Was she being fair by keeping this from her family? And most of all, was she strong enough to see this through? Uncertainty gnawed, and the shadows of doubt crept closer. But somewhere in the darkness, Lorna clung to the belief she was making the right choices. For herself. For her sister. For her family.

Tomorrow would bring new challenges, but she would face them head-on.

Twenty-Two

1997
Moving Forward

Winter of 1997 was exceptionally cold, and Lorna decided a weekend escape to Sydney would be the perfect antidote. She could catch up with her parents and friends, leaving behind the chill that seemed to seep into her bones. Despite the distance and time apart, one thought nagged at her… Cara's claims about owning their father's house. It had bugged Lorna for years, and now seemed like the ideal time to finally address it. Settling into her father's cosy living room, she watched him read the newspaper, the flicker of the fireplace casting a warm glow. She took a deep breath, steeling herself for the conversation she'd been dreading. "Dad," she began cautiously, "remember years ago when we had our school reunion?"

"Yes," he replied, not looking up from his paper.

"Remember how I said Cara told the girls she owned this house?"

He glanced at her over his glasses. "Yes, and I said not to worry, Love."

"Yes, you did. But why does Cara continue to tell people she owns this house?"

He put the paper down, his eyes meeting hers. "Why do you let things worry you?"

"I'm not. I just want to know why. Please, Dad?"

Her father sighed and dropped the newspaper to his lap.

"Oh, okay."

Finally, some answers.

"When your mother and I separated, I needed to buy a place and sort some things out with my business," he began.

"Yes," Lorna nodded. "I remember you asked me about the title on houses and some issues related to business structures."

"Yes, but you were living with your mother. Cara had moved in with me. I was asset-rich, but cash-poor for a short period, and your sister kindly offered to help."

"How? She didn't have the money to buy a place. What's that got to do with her owning this house?"

"I needed a short-term loan to secure the house purchase until I could convert some of my assets into cash. Your sister put her name on the paperwork to help with the loan process. She knew someone in the loans department at the bank and worked everything out."

"So, she does own the house?" Lorna snapped.

"No, no, she doesn't. She never paid off any of the loan. She simply had her name on it because I didn't have enough time to produce paperwork supporting my ability to complete the repayments. I was the only one who paid the loan with proceeds from my employment, and the loan only existed for a short period until I could sell a property and finalise the divorce. Cara moved in with me and continued to pay board as she had done before, with your mother and I, and we split the bills equally."

Lorna shook her head. "Nope, something doesn't add up. Why does she still insist she owns this house? Something isn't right. I paid board and shared bills equally with Mum after you left. I certainly don't go around claiming to own her house."

"Well…" He shifted in his seat, his fingers tapping lightly on the armrest as his eyes darted to the floor. Lorna watched in silence as he took a deep breath, rubbing the back of his neck before speaking again. "Cara's name went onto the property title and the loan."

"Are you serious?" Lorna jumped to her feet. "You asked me about property titles, and she never paid a cent into the house except for board, yet her name is on the title? Are you mad? What were you thinking?"

"I was thinking I didn't want to miss out on buying the place. Your sister said she was helping so I could get the house. I liked it and didn't want to lose it while waiting for things to be finalised."

The colour drained from Lorna's face as her eyes widened in disbelief. She swallowed hard, her gaze fixed on her father, her mouth slightly open but unable to form words. Cara's claims, shocking as they were, had substance. If her name was on the property title, then legally she owned it, at least a portion of it, despite contributing nothing financially.

"What title do you have?" she asked.

"What do you mean?"

"Is the title Joint Tenants or Tenants in Common?"

"Joint, I think. It was years ago. Cara said she was helping."

Lorna scoffed. "Of course she was, helping herself to a free house. You do realise if you were to pass away, she owns this place. I knew there was more to it. I knew you were lying. That's why she was so smug in her comments. I can't believe you would do that. Why not tell the truth?"

"I didn't want to upset you. I worked out a way that everyone would be happy."

"But it's not right, Dad. You always told us how important it was to work hard for what we had. When we were growing up, we'd sit around the dinner table discussing our day, and we'd be reminded how the harder you worked, the luckier you became. And yet, here's Cara, she hasn't paid a cent into this house… your home… and now you've handed her the title free of charge. No wonder she's sitting back laughing. You can't change a title, Dad, not without the other party on the title agreeing to the change."

"Calm down, Lorna. I don't like it when you're upset. I'll talk with your sister. I know a way we can work all this out. Please let me explain."

"I'm listening. And I can tell you now, Cara isn't going to sign the house back over to you."

"I'm sure she'll be reasonable. I paid her all her money back when she bought her own place."

"What money? Don't tell me this gets worse."

"Let me explain. Things became tense with your sister. She didn't like my rules, and we had words about her bringing things into the house. She said she didn't want to live here anymore, that she didn't agree with my rules."

"What's that got to do with you giving her money?"

"Well, she needed money to buy her own place, so I agreed to repay her the board she had been giving me."

"But that was board. I paid board to Mum. I didn't get it paid back when I decided to move out and buy my own place. Board is a living expense."

"I know, love, but I just wanted to help. I didn't want to argue. I had the money to help her, and with Cara moving out, I had my place back and peace and quiet."

Lorna shook her head, calculating how much money her father would have given her sister. "You would have given her thousands, tens of thousands... based on the board I paid Mum and the time Cara lived with you."

Her father nodded. "Yes, just over $30,000."

"Oh my God, I feel sick. I can't believe this."

"I'll fix things. Let me fix it. I'll talk with Cara. I'll work out a way to make it right."

The next morning, Lorna returned home with her father's reassurance he'd make things right. She promised to keep their discussion quiet.

Two weeks later, her father phoned to say he'd spoken with Cara. Cara had sought legal advice and, while she refused to sign over the property, she agreed to a property title agreement. In this agreement Cara would acknowledge she'd received just over $30,000 in cash from their father when she moved out, in addition to this money she would ultimately want to receive another $60,000, arguing the property had tripled in value while she was living there and she could have invested her board money elsewhere for similar gains. If their father sold the property at a later date, he would give Cara the $60,000. If he passed away, the property would be sold, Cara would receive $60,000 and the balance of the sale price would be split in accordance to their fathers Will.

Cara believed this was fair as she no longer lived with her father nor did she contribute to any bills or maintenance of the property. Lorna found her sister's logic absurd; at the time of Cara moving in with their father, Cara didn't have the money to buy a house, and she'd already received her board money back, she'd effectively been living for free. Her father while being naive in his actions had been extremely generous.

A family meeting was called by their father. Byron, Cara, and Lorna sat down with him, and he explained what had occurred all those years ago when he first separated from their mother. Cara produced the property agreement she had created, it outlined how she refused to sign the property back over to their father and how she believed she should be compensated for living with their father. They all read and signed the property agreement. Byron took Lorna aside and quietly expressed his annoyance with his sister. "I can't believe the audacity, she's greedy and she doesn't seem to care. I'm sorry, from now on I have no time for her."

Before signing the agreement, their father suggested another possible solution: if their mother left her property to Lorna and Cara received his, Byron could inherit all the other assets and cash. This suggestion was quickly dismissed. Lorna was furious. How could their father assume what their mother would do with her Will? Their mother had always believed in treating her children equally, regardless of circumstance.

Lorna left the meeting disgusted by her sister's greed but relieved the truth behind the ownership issue had been revealed and finally settled. Before returning home, she visited her mother and told her what had happened. Her mother was equally unimpressed by their father's suggestion regarding her Will. As Lorna drove back to the country, she felt a mix of emotions, relief, frustration, and a lingering sense of betrayal.

At least everything's out in the open now and Cara's greed has hit a limit.

Twenty-Three

Wednesday, 3rd April, 2024
Hello Sue

Lorna was a bundle of nerves as she arrived at Sydney Hospital for the first time. Today was a significant day, she was meeting her transplant coordinator, Sue Edwards, who would guide her through the complex process of becoming a live kidney donor. This day also marked the beginning of the medical evaluations, with the first of three blood and urine tests that would determine if she was a compatible donor for her twin sister, Cara. As she walked through the hospital corridors, Lorna couldn't help but recall all the things she'd read online. *Doctor Google can be your friend or your worst nightmare*, she thought, remembering the stories that had fuelled her anxiety. Some said eating too much meat could skew the results by increasing creatinine levels, a key indicator of kidney function. Others warned against excessive exercise, advising instead to drink copious amounts of water. Walking was Lorna's main mode of exercise, and she worried her usual routine might somehow sabotage the tests. She'd read every excuse under the sun as to why potential donors had failed their workup tests. But when she finally sat down with Sue Edwards, all those fears began to dissipate.

"You need to eat and exercise as you would in your normal daily life," Sue said reassuringly, her voice calm and authoritative. "Everything in moderation. There's no need to try and influence the results; you won't be doing anyone a favour. Reading up on the process is great, but don't let fear carry you away. Keep both feet on the ground and focus on moving through your testing without getting caught up in all the hype and mind-boggling hysteria."

Lorna nodded, absorbing Sue's words. She'd let fear carry her away, allowing it to dictate her actions in a way that now seemed unnecessary. "I hope I haven't messed things up with all the changes I made to my routine," she said.

But Sue's reassurance helped her push those worries aside.

The testing itself went smoothly, much to Lorna's relief. It was over in no time. Just one needle, multiple vials of blood taken, a pleasant chat with the nurse, and finally, a quick trip to the bathroom to supply the required urine sample. Simple. Done.

As she prepared to leave, Sue informed her the results from the blood and urine tests would generally take about two weeks. "In the meantime, here's some additional reading material that may help with understanding the process, you'll have to return to your doctor, who will be sent a copy of all results. Your GP will have to issue you with a referral to see a nephrologist who is a doctor with expertise in the care of kidneys, they will examine your medical history, order tests and answer any questions," Sue added. "Just focus on eating healthy, staying hydrated, getting as fit as possible. Lose weight if you need to, reduce alcohol, and cease smoking."

Lorna felt a wave of relief; she was already in a healthy weight range, rarely drank, and had quit smoking years ago.

On the journey home, she felt a sense of accomplishment. The first appointment in Sydney was behind her, and she was grateful to have found an instant connection with Sue. *The next round of tests will be far less stressful*, she thought.

"I can do this," she told herself, her nerves finally starting to settle.

Twenty-Four

2002
A Private Affair

With the house issue behind them, life moved forward in a way that felt almost ordinary. Lorna felt a sense of happiness, and continued to see Cara, but there was always a part of her that remained vigilant, she was careful in what she said and how she said it. As Lorna navigated this new normal, memories of their childhood would often surface. Growing up, their family hadn't had much involvement with their father's siblings. Aunt Victoria, their father's sister, lived in England, while his older brother Bernard preferred a quiet, private life with his wife, Sally. The two would occasionally join in family celebrations, but for the most part, they kept to themselves. Lorna remembered those rare gatherings with a mix of curiosity and awkwardness. She remembered how, as a child, she had once asked Aunt Sally if she didn't like children. There had been no malice in her question, just the simple curiosity of a young girl trying to understand the world around her.

Aunt Sally, who had always struck Lorna as a reserved woman, had surprised her with an unexpected honesty. "Oh, Lorna, it's not that I don't like children," she had said gently. "I was an only child myself. It was a lonely existence, really. I was also a chubby child, and the taunts from others were cruel. It made me decide, at a very young age, I didn't want to bring a child into a world that could be so unkind. I never wanted to subject anyone to that kind of cruelty."

Lorna had appreciated her aunt's candour; it seemed so rare for an adult to speak so openly with a child. It was a refreshing moment of connection that lingered in her memory, even as the years passed. Tragically, Aunt Sally's life was cut short before she'd even reached retirement age. She was fatally struck by a car, an event that shocked the entire family. Lorna's father had delivered the devastating news, his voice trembling with grief. Uncle Bernard was shattered, his world collapsing in the blink of an eye.

Lorna felt helpless, unable to go to her uncle's side due to the distance and her work commitments. She'd done what she could, phoning him to express her condolences and sending a heartfelt sympathy card. She hoped her words might bring some small comfort, though she knew they could never truly ease his pain. Cara, too, had expressed her sadness and reassured Lorna she would pass on her kind words when she saw him.

Their father wasn't well at the time, so Cara had taken it upon herself to visit Uncle Bernard, find out what arrangements had been made, and keep everyone informed. Lorna had been grateful for her sister's willingness to step in, trusting she would handle everything with care.

The next day, Lorna received an update from Cara. Uncle Bernard, too distraught to face a large funeral, had told Cara he wished for a private cremation. Lorna had been shocked by her uncle's request, it seemed so final, so stark. But she understood it was his decision. It was a wish that should be quietly respected, no matter how difficult it was for the rest of the family to accept.

"Could you let Mum, Dad, and Byron know?" Cara had asked. "I just don't think I can go through explaining it all again."

Lorna had agreed, and later that evening, she relayed the information to her parents and brother. She could sense the shock and sadness in their voices as she broke the news. It wasn't the way she'd envisioned saying goodbye to Aunt Sally, but she understood and trusted her sister had done what was best, they would all honour Uncle Bernard's wishes.

Twenty-Five

Wednesday, 17th April, 2024
Relief

Lorna sat in the quiet waiting room, her heart pounding in her chest. The air was thick with the scent of lavender, meant to calm, but Lorna didn't really like the scent of lavender and she couldn't shake her gnawing unease. She'd been waiting, anxiously, for the results of her first blood and urine tests. It was these tests that would tell her if she was compatible to donate a kidney to Cara. Every tick of the clock seemed to echo in her mind, reminding her that these results could change everything. She tried to distract herself by focusing on her life, her friends, and her general routines but the thought of those tests lingered in the back of her mind. She hadn't told anyone else about the testing, except for Jamie and Jill, not even her mother. *Why worry her if there's nothing to tell?* It was only hearsay from Jakob, after all. Cara still refused to speak to her directly, except for one explosive and extremely brief phone call. *What if it turns out to be nothing?* Partial information could only lead to unnecessary worry, and she didn't want to burden her mother. But the thought of keeping this from her weighed heavy. Their relationship was built on honesty and trust. How would her mother feel if she knew Lorna was hiding this from her? No doubt she'd be annoyed Lorna thought, no doubt she'd see it as a negative in their relationship. Lorna sighed, running a hand through her hair

UNDER THE COVER OF CLOSENESS

as she waited for her appointment. She thought back to her conversation with Dr Cornelius, who'd suggested she see a counsellor. He'd been right, she needed to talk to someone about her feelings, about the estrangement with Cara, and about the overwhelming request to donate a kidney. That's why she was here, waiting to meet Lorraine Doran, a local counsellor who came highly recommended.

When Lorraine finally greeted her, Lorna was struck by how warm and welcoming she was. As they settled into the session, Lorna explained her situation, the estrangement from Cara, the sudden reappearance of Jakob after so many years, and the monumental request he'd made.

"It's a big request," Lorraine said, her voice gentle. "And support, do you have support?"

Lorna nodded, grateful for the opportunity to talk it out. "Oh yes, most definitely. I've got my two best friends, Jamie and Jill. They're the only ones I've told so far…then there's Jakob and Henry, Cara's boys. I haven't reunited with Henry yet, but it was Jakob who told me about his mother's illness. They've said they'll visit soon. And then there's my mother and brother, although…I haven't mentioned anything to them yet. That's the quandary I'm in. When do I tell them?"

Lorraine listened intently as Lorna continued. "I had the first of my blood and urine tests two weeks ago. They'll confirm if I'm compatible, which my coordinator believes I should be, given that Cara and I are identical twins. But it's still an anxious wait. I'd like to know for sure that I've passed the first hurdle before saying anything."

"I'm sure you'll be fine," Lorraine said, offering a reassuring smile. "And your sister, have you spoken with her?"

Lorna hesitated, her mind flashing back to the brief, explosive phone call with Cara. "Not really," she admitted, her voice quiet. "She called for a moment when she found out I was considering being her kidney donor, but…she's got a lot on her plate right now."

"And how do you feel about that?"

"Well," Lorna began, choosing her words carefully. "We haven't spoken for years, and I've survived. My life is wonderful. Hearing from her or not is irrelevant."

"But you're willing to give her a kidney?"

"For the moment," Lorna replied, meeting Lorraine's gaze. "I'm investigating the possibility of becoming a donor, yes."

Lorraine nodded. "Let's move on to your family. You mentioned you haven't told them. Why?"

Lorna sighed; this was an issue she'd been wrestling with. "I try to be a practical person. Why would I want to burden someone with worry when there are still so many unknowns? I don't know the specifics of Cara's condition. I only have limited details from Jakob. I don't know if Cara will agree to the procedure, if she'll be an acceptable recipient, or if I'll be eligible to donate. So why upset the apple cart?"

"You don't think they could offer support?"

"Of course, they could, and no doubt they would," Lorna replied. "But it's about weighing when support is needed versus when it's not. I don't believe the potential upset and anxiety this could cause warrants my opening my mouth, not just yet. And I know I'll probably upset some by not saying anything, but this decision to keep quiet isn't about secrecy, it's about protecting them, silently."

Lorraine listened; her expression thoughtful. "You'll know when the time is right to share. Just don't underestimate the listening ability of others. There's another saying, a problem shared is a problem halved."

Lorna chuckled softly. "Yes, there is."

Lorraine looked puzzled for a moment, then asked, "I

must admit, I'm not too certain about the specifics of being a live kidney donor. Do you know if donating a kidney can reduce your lifespan?"

Lorna straightened in her chair, her eyes narrowing slightly. "Well, let me ask you...do you know how long I'm going to live?"

Lorraine looked taken aback by the question. "Of course not, no."

"Well, that's good," Lorna said. "As for your question, no.... there is no evidence to suggest donating a kidney reduces an individual's lifespan. But that makes me wonder, if it's unknown when I will die, then how would anyone know if I'm shortening my lifespan? I may get a disease later on, or have a car accident. Who knows what may happen? All I care about is right now, my kidney could potentially save my sister's life."

Lorraine smiled; she appeared impressed by Lorna's conviction. "Great answer."

Just then, Lorna's phone rang. She excused herself and answered it, her heart pounding. As she listened, a smile spread across her face. "Oh, that's wonderful news!" she exclaimed, her voice filled with relief and joy. The results from her initial blood and urine tests were back, they were positive. She was compatible. She could continue with the work-up tests. As Lorna ended the call, she felt a wave of emotion wash over her. The anxiety, the uncertainty, the fear, they were still there, but now there was also hope. She was one step closer to possibly helping Cara, one step closer to finding out what the future would hold.

Twenty-Six

2003
Here He Comes

Lorna rolled over in bed, clutching her stomach as nausea swirled within her. *What on earth did I eat last night?* she wondered; her mind foggy with discomfort. She lay still, hoping the sensation would pass, and allow her to fall asleep again. But morning came too quickly, and as soon as her feet touched the cool floor, the nausea returned with a vengeance. Lorna clutched her stomach, trying to steady herself against the bed. *Maybe it was the seafood I had*, she thought, forcing herself to move through the waves of queasiness.

The next morning, she was met with the same unwelcome sensation. From the moment her feet hit the floor, nausea swirled. Lorna shook her head, convincing herself it was just a lingering bug, something she would soon shake off. But as the day wore on and the nausea decreased, she began to feel an increased concern creeping in. *It's probably just a virus*, she told herself, but the persistent nausea continued to gnaw at the back of her mind. She mentally retraced her steps, her meals, her interactions, there was nothing out of the ordinary. Yet, each morning brought the same unsettling sensation, and soon, she couldn't dismiss it any longer.

One night, she was jolted awake by sharp stomach

cramps. Waves of nausea swirled and she barely made it to the bathroom before she was hunched over the toilet, dizzy and disoriented. She sank to the floor, her body trembling from the sudden onslaught. *What's happening to me?* Her hands pushed firmly against the cold tiles. She was sick again and again, exhausted she lay there, feeling utterly defeated. *This isn't normal*, she thought as she pulled herself up, her legs shaky as she made her way back to bed. Her body felt foreign, her breasts tender, her abdomen sensitive, and a constant bloated feeling lingered. *I need to see Dr Cornelius*, the worry too great to ignore. Lorna feared what might be lurking beneath these symptoms, she hoped there was nothing too serious happening.

The next day, she dragged herself to the doctor's office, her nerves on edge. The nausea had momentarily subsided, but the pain in her breasts and the uneasy feeling in her stomach were still there. Dr Cornelius examined her records, noting her good health and the fact at thirty-six, she hadn't yet needed a mammogram. As he flipped through her details, he looked up, a slight frown creasing his brow. "Lorna, I have to ask, there's no chance you might be pregnant, is there?"

Lorna couldn't help it. She burst out laughing, the sound echoing in the sterile room. "Oh, God, no. Things down there closed up long ago. You'd probably find cobwebs if you looked."

Dr Cornelius chuckled, shaking his head. "Oh, Lorna, it's nice to see you haven't lost your sense of humour."

Lorna smiled, but inside, she couldn't shake the worry.

"Let's have a look," he said gently, guiding her to the examination table. Lorna's anxiety spiked as he touched her abdomen, then moved to her breasts, his touch light but probing. The tenderness was undeniable, and when Dr Cornelius asked if anyone in her family had ever had breast cancer, a cold fear gripped her.

Breast cancer?

Lorna's mind raced, desperately searching her memories. "No, no one." The thought of cancer lodged in her mind, an unwelcome and terrifying possibility. Dr Cornelius must have seen the panic in her eyes because he quickly added, "Let's not get ahead of ourselves, Lorna. There are many reasons you might feel this way, hormonal imbalances, for example. I'll have you do some blood tests and an ultrasound of your breasts to be thorough."

Cancer, the word echoed in Lorna's mind as she left the doctors surgery. Her hands trembled as she retrieved her car keys, she fumbled for her phone, calling Jamie. As soon as she heard her friend's voice, Lorna burst into tears, her fear spilling out uncontrollably.

Jamie's voice was calm and soothing. "You're young, you're fit, you're healthy, Lorna. I'm sure the results will be fine. But even if they aren't, we'll deal with it together. Don't let your mind run away with this. Don't go down that rabbit hole. You have to focus on what's in front of you, not the 'what ifs.'"

Lorna clung to Jamie's words, grateful for her friend's unwavering support. She's right, Lorna told herself, trying to calm her racing thoughts.

One step at a time.

The next morning, Lorna went to the pathology clinic for the blood tests, her heart pounding as the nurse drew the samples. The kind nurse told her the results would be back by the next morning, but the waiting felt unbearable. Two days later, she had her ultrasound, the cold gel on her skin adding to the chill in her bones.

By the end of the week, Lorna was back in Dr

UNDER THE COVER OF CLOSENESS

Cornelius's office, the anxiety tightening her chest. But this time, she wasn't the only one with new information. As she sat down, Dr Cornelius reviewed her results. "Everything looks normal," he said, a small smile on his face. "Your blood results are within the acceptable ranges, and the ultrasound didn't show any abnormalities."

Lorna let out a breath she didn't realise she'd been holding. *Normal*, the word felt like a lifeline, but there was still something she needed to say. "Cara's pregnant," she blurted.

Dr Cornelius leaned back in his chair, his brow furrowing as he scratched his head. "I'm sorry?"

"My twin sister, Cara," Lorna explained. "She called me, and when I mentioned I'd been feeling sick, she told me she's pregnant. I can hardly believe it, but I think that's what I have. I'm having my sister's morning sickness. I can't believe it, Cara says she feels great, she hasn't been sick at all."

His gaze shifted from Lorna to the papers on his desk, lingering for a moment before returning to her, a faint crease forming between his brows as he rubbed his chin. "I've heard about this before, sympathetic pregnancy symptoms. But I must say, I've never seen it personally. Given your results, it might be best to hold off on further testing for now. But if your symptoms worsen, I want you to come back immediately."

Lorna nodded, feeling a strange mix of relief and irritation. *It has to be Cara's pregnancy. If only she'd told me sooner, I wouldn't have gone through all this panic.*

As the weeks passed and Cara's pregnancy progressed, Lorna's morning sickness gradually faded. She reflected on her sister's criticisms. Cara had insisted Lorna should have called her earlier, but Lorna couldn't understand why Cara hadn't mentioned the pregnancy in the first place. *We'll just have to agree to disagree*, Lorna thought, trying to push away the lingering annoyance. At least now she knew what was wrong, and she was grateful for Jamie's unwavering support.

Cara's sarcasm cut through the phone line. "Oh yes, you and Jamie are thick as thieves. Or maybe just thick."

Lorna chose to let the remark slide, not wanting to fuel another pointless argument. *Some things just aren't worth it*, she reminded herself. Instead, she focused on the excitement of becoming an aunt, looking forward to meeting her surprise niece or nephew.

Months later, Lorna found herself standing beside Cara's hospital bed, trying to keep her sister calm as the contractions came closer together. The room buzzed with tension, and suddenly, a gut-wrenching spasm gripped Lorna's abdomen. She gasped, doubling over as pain shot through her.

"What are you doing? This isn't about you. I'm the one having a baby!" Cara snapped.

Lorna stared at her sister, feeling the pain intensify. "I'm sorry, but I don't know what's happening," she groaned, clutching her stomach. The stabbing sensation was unbearable, and dizziness washed over her.

"Stop it," Cara spat. "You're not having a baby, I am!"

The nurse rushed to Cara's side, gently reminding her to focus on her breathing and suggesting Lorna take a seat. The contractions seemed endless, Cara's blood pressure rose as she demanded attention and drugs to ease her pain. Her baby wasn't turning and the doctor feared it was becoming distressed. Cara would need an emergency caesarean. Lorna was left alone to wait, the pain in her abdomen continued to persist. Just under an hour later Lorna's pain subsided as quickly as it had come, a sudden wave of relief washed over her. The pain was gone. *Cara must have had the baby*, she thought, tears of joy welling in her eyes as she anxiously awaited the news.

Finally, a nurse appeared, a warm smile on her face. "Congratulations, Auntie Lorna," she said. "You'll be able to see your sister shortly. Both mum and bub are doing well."

"What did she have? Please, tell me," Lorna pleaded, her heart racing with anticipation.

"A little boy," the nurse replied, her smile widening. "A healthy little boy."

Lorna's excitement bubbled over, and she couldn't contain herself as she paced the room, waiting to see Cara, waiting to meet her beautiful nephew. When Cara was finally brought back to the room, Lorna rushed to her side, her eyes filling with tears at the sight of the tiny bundle in her sister's arms. Cara looked exhausted but proud as she glanced at Lorna. "Say hello to your Auntie Lorna," she whispered, gently pulling back the blanket to reveal the baby's tiny face. "Say hello to my gorgeous little boy, Jakob."

Lorna's heart swelled with love as she gazed at her nephew. "Welcome to the world, little Jakob."

Twenty-Seven

Sunday, 28th April, 2024
Emotions

Lorna moved through her house, tidying things that were already in place, her hands trembling as she smoothed out cushions and aligned picture frames. Her home was always tidy, but today it had to be perfect. It wasn't just about cleanliness; it was about creating a space that was warm and inviting, a place where walls could come down and where honesty could flourish. Today, Jakob and Henry were coming. She'd waited so long for this moment. A chance to reconnect, to bridge the years of silence, to explain, to listen, to forgive. Every detail had to be right. Her house needed to feel like a safe haven, where they could begin to mend what had been broken.

She glanced at her watch. *They should be here any minute.* Her heart raced with a mixture of excitement and dread. She knew she had to be patient, not to let her eagerness overwhelm them. The last thing she wanted was to rush them into conversations they weren't ready for, to scare them away before they could even begin to open up. She had no idea what Cara had told them, how they might see her after all this time.

Lorna's mind spun with the weight of what she needed to say, the responsibility she felt to own her part in the years they'd lost. It had been so long since she'd seen them. She thought about the move, the abrupt separation that had ripped them from her life. *Had they understood what was happening all those years ago, or had they been blindsided like me? Were they unsure of where they belonged in the world? Were they confused and hurt?* Lorna's heart ached at the thought that the boys might have felt abandoned, left to deal with the upheaval without the comfort of explanation. She could only imagine the shock and bewilderment they must have experienced, not knowing why everything had changed so suddenly.

She thought of all the adjustments they had to make, new house, new school, new friends. How hard it must have been for them, ripped away from everything familiar. She wasn't the only one who had been affected. They, too, had likely struggled to make sense of it all. She needed to understand their feelings, to be sensitive to what they'd gone through.

A knock at the door startled her out of her thoughts. This was it. She hesitated, torn between checking on the food in the oven and rushing to the door. *The oven can wait.* She took a deep breath and hurried to the door, her hands trembling as she reached for the handle. She swung the door open, her smile bright but nervous. "Jakob," she said with a smile. "It's so good to see you." Her eyes darted past him, looking down the front path. Searching. She turned towards Jakob. "Where's Henry?"

"He's...um... he's." Jakob turned looking over his shoulder.

"Here I am," Henry said appearing from around the corner. He dashed up the stairs wrapping his arms around his aunt. "Aunt Lorna, oh aunt Lorna... I've missed you so much."

All the fear and tension melted away as she embraced her loving nephew, her own tears brimming. "I've missed you too, Henry. I've missed both of you more than words can say."

Inside, the three of them settled into the lounge room, Lorna offered them drinks, remembering how they used to love the club soda she'd sometimes give them as a treat. She smiled as Henry's eyes lit up at the familiar taste. "I was going to add a scoop of ice cream, but I thought that might be a bit too much before lunch," she said.

"There's no such thing as too early for ice cream," Jakob chuckled.

The years of separation seemed to melt away; tears welled in Lorna's eyes. This was what she'd missed… the easy laughter, the small, shared moments. Emotions she'd been holding back finally overwhelmed her. "I've missed you so much," she choked out, her voice trembling. "I'm so sorry I wasn't there for you. I'm sorry I let things get so bad with your mum. I never wanted to hurt you, to make you feel like I abandoned you. I hope you know how much I missed you."

Jakob was at her side in an instant, his arm around her shoulders. "We know, Aunt Lorna," he whispered, his voice thick with emotion. "We missed you too."

Henry's sobs filled the room, and Lorna held him close, her heart breaking at the sight of his tears. "I feel so foolish, I'm supposed to be the strong one," she murmured, wiping her eyes. "The adult who can keep it together," she spluttered.

Jakob shook his head. "We love you, Aunt Lorna, just the way you are. We wouldn't be here if we didn't love you."

Taking a deep breath, Lorna tried to regain her composure. Henry leaned back into his chair as Lorna leaned forward to take a sip of her drink, grateful for the boys' concern. "Thank you," she said softly. "I knew this would be emotional, but I never expected it to be this hard."

Henry nodded; his eyes still red from crying. "We've got a lot to talk about, Aunt Lorna," he said. "A lot to catch up on."

And they did. The hours slipped by as they talked, the years of separation slowly dissolving in the warmth of their reunion. Lorna listened as they told her about their new lives, their school, their friends, their employment, their mother's illness. Jakob spoke quietly about their hope that Cara would get her transplant before needing dialysis, and Henry echoed his brother's wishes.

Lorna was careful not to press too much, sensing some details were better left unexplored for now. She didn't ask for their new address, knowing it might feel intrusive. For now, she was content just to have them here; to know they still cared about her, they hadn't forgotten her. Henry made sure she had his mobile number, sending her a sweet message she saved immediately. "I love you, Aunt Lorna," he had written. "I missed you and I'm so happy to see you."

Before Lorna knew it, it was time for lunch, she'd once again cast her mind back to what the boys had enjoyed. Tacos were a great option, she recalled how they'd all sit around the table, everyone making their own creations. Henry licking the juices that had run down his hands and arms. The laughter and giggling when someone's taco shell snapped resulting in the contents collapsing to their plate. Lorna being called a chicken when she decided to make a deconstructed version, where she snapped her taco shells in half and piled the toppings on, more like an open sandwich. They were fun times she hoped to recreate.

As they moved to the dining room, Lorna marvelled at how easily they fell back into the rhythm of their old traditions. Tacos had been and still were a favourite. Their meal full of laughter and messes, of broken taco shells, shared joy and memories as they recounted stories from when they were younger. Lorna was surprised by their recollections.

As lunch wound down, Henry pushed his plate aside and asked, almost hesitantly, "Do you mind if I take a walk around the dam, Aunt Lorna? Just to clear my head a bit."

Lorna studied his face. There was something off, he suddenly appeared sad. He'd always been sensitive, more so than Jakob. They'd started lunch with a balanced conversation, easily picking up where they'd left off all those years ago. But then, suddenly, Henry had gone quiet. She feared he was upset, and it made her highly concerned. "Of course, Henry," Lorna replied, giving him a smile. "I'll get started on dessert while you're gone. Take your time." She watched him walk out the door, his shoulders slightly hunched. *A walk might do him good*, she thought, *give him a moment to gather himself.* It also gave her a moment, a perfect moment. With Henry outside, Lorna turned to Jakob, who was still sitting at the table, seemingly lost in thought. She took a deep breath, her heart thudding in her chest.

It was now or never.

"Jakob," she began, her voice trembling slightly, "I need to ask you something. I have a couple of questions... three, actually. But with two of them, I'm hoping they can be settled easily."

Jakob shifted in his seat, eyebrows furrowing as he leaned back. "What is it, Aunt Lorna?"

She hesitated, sensing his sudden defensiveness. "I don't want you to take this the wrong way, Jakob. I just need a few answers."

His expression hardened as he crossed his arms. "What answers?"

Lorna bit her lip, nerves knotting in her stomach. Maybe this wasn't the right time. But she had to know. "Um..."

"What?" he prompted, "What is it?"

Gathering her courage, Lorna leaned forward. "The bundle... I saw the bundle in your bag when you were here... your bag fell over and open." She paused; her mouth dry as sand. Reaching for her glass, she took a gulp of water. "I'm sorry, Jakob. I don't mean to upset things, but I need to know. I need to know about the bundle?"

Jakob's eyes widened for a moment before he shook his head, sitting up straighter. "Yes, I know... I was hoping you'd tell me."

Lorna frowned. "Me? What do you want me to tell you?"

"The truth," Jakob said.

"The truth?" Lorna repeated, more baffled than ever. "Me?"

"Yes, you, Aunt Lorna. Why would you do that?"

"Do what? I've got no idea what you're talking about."

Jakob's eyes were glassy with unshed tears as he uncrossed his arms and reached into his bag. With a thud, he dropped a bundle of papers onto the table between them.

Lorna gasped, her heart pounding in her chest. "What... I never... I never... that's not true. I've never seen these before!"

Jakob's stared towards her, his voice trembling. "Really?"

"Really," Lorna insisted, picking up the bundle with shaking hands. "I swear, Jakob, I've never seen these before. I promise you, on my life. If I'd received letters from you, there's no way I would've returned them. You have no idea how much I missed you, how much I missed

Henry." Tears welled in her eyes as her voice broke. "I was devastated when you left. Heartbroken."

Jakob's expression softened, and suddenly, the tension between them shattered. He reached out, and together, they cried... years of pain and misunderstanding pouring out in a flood of tears.

When the sobs subsided, Lorna wiped her eyes, taking another sip of water to steady herself. "And the paper?" she asked, her voice still shaky.

Jakob looked puzzled. "What paper?"

"The one with the details of my property," Lorna said. "It showed how much my place is worth."

"Oh, that... The printout? I just googled your address. When I found the letters, I wanted to make sure I had the right address before coming to ask about donating a kidney to Mum. It was just a property search. I didn't even notice it had a price. I promise, Aunt Lorna, it wasn't anything more. Please believe me. You have to believe me."

Lorna studied his face, searching for any hint of deceit, but found none. "I believe you, Jakob," she finally said.

Just then, Henry returned from his walk, his steps slower, more measured. Lorna's mind raced. She had one more question, the one that had been gnawing at her for so long. But could she bring herself to ask it now? As she cleared the plates from the table, she decided it would have to wait a little longer. She couldn't risk breaking the fragile peace that had just been restored. But as she sliced the cheesecake, determination returned. She couldn't leave it unasked. Not this time. She'd waited too long already.

After dessert, as they moved to the lounge, Lorna knew the moment had come. She couldn't hold back any longer. "I need to know," she said, her voice trembling with a mix of fear and urgency. "What happened to Uncle Bernard?"

UNDER THE COVER OF CLOSENESS

Jakob and Henry exchanged a glance, their expressions suddenly tense. Lorna's heart skipped a beat. She could see the hesitation in their eyes, the reluctance to answer.

"Is he still with us?" she pressed.

Jakob shook his head, and Henry looked down at the floor.

A deep sense of betrayal and disgust filled Lorna as she realised the truth. Cara had played the situation perfectly, her actions had denied Lorna yet again the ability to say goodbye to another relative, this time it was her beloved uncle. The prawns versus pawns conversation they'd had, Cara's opinion of the elderly, her cold, calculating demeanour... it all made sense now. Unable to bear it any longer, Lorna jumped from the lounge and dashed to the bathroom. She barely made it to the sink before the bile rose in her throat. The truth of her sister's actions was more than she could stomach.

When Lorna returned to the lounge room she could sense a shift in mood. Jakob subtly glanced at his watch. Lorna knew the moment was coming, the inevitable goodbye she wasn't ready for but had to accept.

"Aunt Lorna, we should probably head off. We've got a long drive ahead, and we want to get home before it gets too dark," Jakob said.

Henry nodded in agreement, his expression mirroring Jakob's mix of reluctance and practicality. "Yeah, it's a long drive. We should get going."

Lorna's chest tightened. She didn't want to let them go, not yet. The house had felt so full with them here, filled with laughter, with stories, with the possibility of healing. But she couldn't keep them, couldn't hold them back from their lives. "I understand," she said softly. "I'm so grateful you both came. It means more to me than you know."

Jakob smiled. "It was really good to see you, Aunt

Lorna. We've missed you."

Henry, still quiet, stepped forward and wrapped his arms around her in a hug that was both tender and reassuring. "We'll text you when we get home," he promised.

Lorna held onto him for a moment longer, savouring his embrace. When they finally pulled apart, she looked at both of them. "I hope this is just the beginning," she said, her voice almost a whisper. "The start of us rebuilding… everything."

Jakob nodded. "We hope so too."

They lingered for a moment at the door, Lorna knew she couldn't ask for more, couldn't push them to stay or ask them to promise more than they were ready to give.

"Drive safe," she said, trying to keep her voice steady. "I'll be waiting to hear from you."

"We will," Jakob assured her, and with a final wave, they stepped outside, the door closing gently behind them.

Lorna stood there for a moment, her hand resting on the doorframe, listening as their footsteps faded away. She wanted to believe this visit was a turning point, they would find their way back to each other, that time could heal what had been broken. But as she stood in the now-quiet house, the echoes of their presence still lingering, she couldn't shake the nagging doubt. The fear that despite their promises, the distance between them might grow again, that life would pull them in different directions, and she would be left waiting, hoping for something that might never fully return.

Only time would tell if things would continue in a positive way, she hoped with all her heart they would.

Twenty-Eight

2004
I'll Stand by You

Lorna sat on the lounge, staring at the ceiling, trying to clear her mind. No sooner had Jakob entered the world than Cara's relationship began to crumble. The past months had been a whirlwind of emotions, joy, fear, anxiety, and now, relief. Jakob had brought so much happiness into her life, and every moment she spent with him was wonderful. But Cara's world began to unravel. Lorna remembered her sister's phone call like it was yesterday, Cara's voice trembling. "Alex is trying to take Jakob from me," Cara had whispered. "I can't... I can't lose my baby."

Lorna had felt the pit in her stomach drop. "What? Who?"

"Alex. Alex wants custody. We've split and now I'm being accused of being an unfit mother," Cara cried.

Lorna couldn't believe what she was hearing, she knew her sister's relationship had been volatile at times but she never thought it would come to this. She loved Jakob and she knew how much her sister loved him. The thought of her losing him was unbearable. "It'll be okay, Cara. We'll get through this. I'll help you. You're not alone. You won't lose him, Cara. I promise." Those words had come out so easily, but now, as she sat in her quiet lounge room, the weight of that promise pressed down on her.

Each fortnight, Lorna had packed her bags and travelled to Sydney to care for Jakob while Cara worked. Cara's work hours included alternate Saturdays, and the thought of leaving Jakob with a stranger terrified her. Lorna didn't mind, it was worth it to see his little face light up when she walked through the door. Every visit revealed new milestones, and Lorna cherished every moment she spent with her nephew.

At three months, Jakob's smiles were no longer random; they were directed at her. At six months, he was babbling, making sounds that almost resembled words. Lorna had laughed with him, playing peekaboo and watching as he tried to grab at her hair with his chubby little hands. By nine months, he was crawling all over the place, exploring every corner of the house. And now, as he approached his first birthday, he was starting to take those first wobbly steps, his tiny hands clutching at the furniture for support. Jakob was growing so fast, and Lorna marvelled at how much he'd changed in such a short time. But amidst the joy, there was always the underlying fear of what might happen if Cara lost the custody battle.

The solicitor's office had become a second home for them. Lorna sat through each meeting, watching as Cara's confidence slowly eroded with every new piece of bad news. The legal fees were spiralling into numbers neither of them had ever imagined and Cara had been on the verge of a breakdown more than once. "I don't know how I'm going to pay for this, Lorna," Cara had said. "I don't have that kind of money. I'll lose everything."

Lorna knew she had to step in. She couldn't bear to see her sister suffer like this. "You won't," she had replied. "I'll help you. We'll figure it out."

Cara looked at her in shock. "I'll pay you back, every

cent, no matter how long it takes."

"Yes, you will, I'm sorry but I can't afford to give it to you, but we will get through this together. I mean it." And so, they did. Lorna paid the legal fees, even though it meant dipping into her savings and Cara had promised to pay her back. All Lorna wanted was for her sister to win this fight, for Jakob to stay with his mother. Helping her sister was the right thing to do.

Family should help family, Lorna thought.

The mediation sessions were gruelling, filled with accusations and counter-accusations. Lorna could see the toll it was taking on Cara, the dark circles under her eyes, the way her hands trembled whenever she talked about the possibility of losing Jakob. Then, out of nowhere, Cara's ex suddenly dropped everything, no longer interested in fighting for custody. The papers were drawn up quickly, the signatures collected without hesitation. Cara's ex was voluntarily relinquishing all parental rights and responsibilities. Jakob was Cara's, and hers alone.

Lorna had been stunned when she got the call from Cara, her voice filled with disbelief. "Alex has given up," Cara had said. "The papers have been signed. Jakob is mine, all mine." Relief had washed over Lorna; happy her nephew would no longer be subject to a battle between two warring adults. At last, it was over. Jakob was safe. He would stay with Cara, where he belonged.

Now, sitting in her lounge room, Lorna let out a long breath. It was hard to believe that just a few weeks ago, they'd been preparing for a court battle, and now, Jakob was officially Cara's, with no more threats looming over them. But it wasn't just relief she felt, it was also exhaustion. The emotional rollercoaster of the past year had taken its toll on her, too. She loved her sister and nephew dearly, but the constant worry, the trips to Sydney, the financial strain, it had all added up. As she sat there, her phone buzzed. It was a message from Cara. "Thank you for everything, Lorna. I couldn't have done this without you. Jakob is lucky to have an aunt like you." Lorna smile. Despite everything, it was moments like this that made it all worth it. Putting her phone down, she leaned back and closed her eyes, letting herself enjoy this brief moment of peace. The future was uncertain, but for now, at least, they were all okay.

Twenty-Nine

Friday, 24th May, 2024
Verification

Lorna sat in the waiting room; her hands clasped tightly together in her lap. A knot of nerves twisting in her belly, and her heart pounding with anticipation. She'd spent countless nights rehearsing the conversation in her mind, bracing herself for what might come. Today was the day she'd meet with Dr Angela Brothers, her renal specialist and transplant Nephrologist who would guide her through the complex and daunting process of potentially donating a kidney to her sister, Cara.

Can I really do this? Am I healthy enough? Will Cara even accept? And what about Cara, is she well enough?

Before her thoughts could spiral further, the door to the consultation room opened, and a warm, inviting voice called her name. Lorna looked up to see her renal specialist, standing with a gentle smile. "Lorna, it's good to meet you," Dr Brothers said as she gestured for her to enter. The doctor's presence was calming, her demeanour professional yet compassionate, putting Lorna at ease almost immediately.

"Thank you," Lorna replied, returning the smile as she stepped into the room. It was bright and clean, with large windows that let in the afternoon light. Dr Brothers motioned for her to take a seat, and as Lorna settled into the chair, the tension in her shoulders began to ease. After a few moments of small talk, Dr Brothers got down to business, reviewing the paperwork Lorna had brought with her and carefully considering the details of her case. Lorna watched as the doctor's eyes moved swiftly over the documents.

"Lorna," Dr Brothers began, "I understand you have a lot of questions about becoming a living kidney donor, and I want to make sure you're fully informed before making any decisions."

Lorna nodded; her throat suddenly dry. "Yes, I do. I want to know everything, what it involves, the risks, and if I'm even a suitable candidate, and to be honest, I'm pretty nervous."

Dr Brothers leaned forward; her hands folded neatly on the desk. "That's completely understandable. Let's start by going over the process. I want you to feel informed and supported every step of the way."

Lorna nodded again, feeling a flicker of hope.

"The work-up process for a potential living kidney donor is extensive," she explained. "It typically takes anywhere from three to twelve months, depending on various factors. The goal is to ensure you're medically and psychologically suitable to donate one of your kidneys. This process will involve a team of healthcare professionals, including your GP, a transplant coordinator, a nephrologist – that's me of course, a surgeon, psychologist or psychiatrist, and possibly a social worker."

Lorna listened intently, absorbing the information. Dr Brothers continued, outlining the steps ahead. "You'll undergo a series of tests to assess your overall health, and your eligibility will be evaluated by multiple specialists. It's essential you're fully informed about the risks and benefits before making a decision."

Lorna nodded again, her mind racing with questions. "And what about Cara? What does she need to do?"

Dr Brothers' expression softened. "For Cara, it's also a complex process. A kidney transplant is a treatment for end-stage kidney disease, but it's not a cure. Cara will need to undergo her own assessments, as the risks can sometimes be too high for a transplant. Her overall health will be evaluated, and she'll need to agree to the procedure, understanding the potential risks involved."

Lorna's thoughts drifted to Cara as Dr Brothers talked about the recipient's role. Would Cara want to go through with this? Lorna couldn't shake the memory of her sister's cold refusal to engage in conversation, the way she had shut Lorna out. But this was different. This was life and death. Would Cara be able to put aside her pride, her anger, and accept the help that was being offered?

"Would a transplant mean she wouldn't need dialysis?" Lorna asked.

"In many cases, yes," Dr Brothers replied. "If the transplant is done early enough, it can be considered pre-emptive, which means Cara could avoid dialysis altogether. The surgery would be planned in advance, and this could improve the chances of success, especially since the time between removing the kidney and transplanting it would be shorter."

"What if…" Lorna paused, "what if…what if Cara doesn't want to go through with it? What if she refuses to even consider the transplant?"

Dr Brothers met her gaze with understanding. "That's a possibility we have to consider. The recipient has to agree to the transplant and be willing to undergo the necessary tests and surgery. If Cara isn't on board, then unfortunately, the process can't move forward."

Lorna swallowed hard, the reality of the situation sinking in. "But if she does agree…what then?"

"If she agrees, and both of you are found to be suitable,

the surgery could be scheduled," Dr Brothers explained. "Kidney transplants in Australia have a high success rate, and a pre-emptive transplant, done before the need for dialysis can offer the best outcomes. The surgery itself would likely be done laparoscopically, which means a quicker recovery and less pain for you. But again, it all depends on both you and Cara being ready and willing."

Lorna's heart swelled with a mixture of hope and fear. Dr Brothers reassurance helped ease her concern. The doctor continued to explain the aftercare, the potential risks, both physical and emotional, and the support available to donors. By the time the appointment concluded, Lorna felt overwhelmed, but she also felt a strange sense of resolve. This wasn't going to be easy, but it was the right thing to do.

As she left the clinic, Lorna reached for her phone, her fingers trembling slightly as she dialled Jakob's number. It rang only twice before he picked up. "Jakob, it's Aunt Lorna," she said, her voice steady despite the whirlwind of emotions inside her. "I just came from my appointment with the nephrologist. I've decided to go ahead with all the testing. But Jakob…your mother has to agree to this. She has to start the process, or there's nothing I can do."

There was a pause on the other end, then a breath of relief. "Thank you, Aunt Lorna," Jakob said quietly. "Thank you so much. I'll talk to her. I'll make her see sense."

Lorna ended the call, her thoughts returning to Cara. Was Cara definite in rejecting her sisters help? Or would Cara agree to completing the assessment? If so, would the kidney transplant team consider her medically suitable? And would Lorna be well enough? Or did she have a condition that would prevent donation?

Glancing at her watch, Lorna made her way down the

long, sterile corridor to her next appointment, the click of her shoes echoing faintly off the walls. The hospital felt more familiar now and with these tests she felt a little more prepared. Sue, her transplant coordinator, had arranged for the second series of blood and urine tests, the verification stage. Lorna had done her research, spoken with Sue and Dr Brothers, and tried to absorb as much information as she could. The nerves were still there, but they were quieter, more manageable than the first time she'd sat in one of those uncomfortable waiting room chairs.

She remembered the anxiety she experienced only a few weeks ago with the initial round of tests. The fear of the unknown, each blood draw and scan feeling like a step into uncharted territory. But now, with the knowledge she'd gained, this second round felt different. It was less about fear and more about determination. The tests themselves were over in a blur of routine procedures and clinical efficiency. Lorna watched the nurse label vials of her blood with a strange detachment, as if this was happening to someone else. The urine test was quick, unremarkable. As she left the hospital, a small part of her was relieved to have this part over with.

As she drove home, Lorna's thoughts wandered to the future, the testing, the waiting, the endless uncertainty. Would she even be a viable donor? What if the tests showed she wasn't? What if she had the same undiagnosed condition as her sister? And even if she was viable, what if Cara refused her help entirely? Cara had been so distant, so resistant to any real communication. The fear her sister might reject her offer to help, after everything, gnawed at her.

But Lorna couldn't let herself spiral. She had to focus on what she could control, what she could do. The tests were a step forward, a necessary part of the process. Whether or not she would be a viable donor wasn't something she could decide, it was up to the results, to biology, to fate. She let out a slow breath as she pulled into her driveway, the quiet of the countryside a stark contrast to the bustling hospital. There was still so much she didn't know, so much that was out of her hands. But for now, she could only take things one step at a time, one day at a time. The rest, she would face when it came.

Thirty

2005
Tappers Disease

Lorna sat at her kitchen table, the faint hum of the refrigerator the only sound in her otherwise quiet house. Bills and bank statements were scattered in front of her, a stark reminder of the financial strain she was under. She'd always been careful with her money, but helping Cara with her custody battle had taken a toll. Lorna had never hesitated when Cara needed her. It wasn't just about the money; it was about standing by her sister when she needed it most. But now, with maintenance issues in her home piling up and no sign of the money Cara owed her, Lorna was beginning to worry. Every time she tried to bring up the loan, Cara became defensive, as if Lorna were the one at fault for wanting her money back. Lorna sighed, rubbing her temples. She'd been more than happy to help, ecstatic even, when Cara's legal battles were over. But now, her own finances were stretched thin, and the prospect of taking on more overtime loomed over her. She hoped Cara would continue repaying her sooner rather than later; the idea of going to the bank to take out a loan filled her with dread.

The sudden ring of the phone startled Lorna from her thoughts. She picked up, hearing Cara's voice on the other end, bursting with excitement. "I'm pregnant! Lorna, I'm pregnant! Little Jakob's going to have a new brother or sister!"

Lorna's heart skipped a beat. Silence filled the line as she struggled to find the right words. *Pregnant?* How could Cara afford to have another child when she was still paying off her legal expenses in dribs and drabs? It was a nice thought, Jakob having a sibling, but raising a child was expensive, and Cara already seemed to be drowning with debt.

"Well, aren't you going to congratulate me?" Cara's voice cut through the silence, a tinge of irritation creeping in.

"Of course, I am. Congratulations," Lorna replied, trying to mask her concern.

"Well, you could say it as if you meant it."

"Of course, I mean it, Cara. Jakob would love to have a little brother or sister." Lorna forced enthusiasm into her voice, though doubt lingered. How could she make Cara understand the gravity of the situation without ruining her joy?

In the months that followed, Lorna found herself both relieved and worried. Unlike Cara's first pregnancy with Jakob, which had been fraught with complications, this time was smooth. Little Henry arrived healthy, and Jakob was over the moon to have a baby brother. Lorna couldn't help but smile as she watched Jakob dote on Henry, eagerly helping his mother with small tasks, like setting the table or preparing Henry's high chair.

Lorna would sit with them, reading stories and weaving their names into the characters, creating a magical world where they were the heroes. Jakob would sit beside his brother, gently patting him, always asking if he was okay. The sight filled Lorna with a bittersweet joy; she loved these boys deeply, but the strain on Cara's finances, and by extension, her own, was impossible to ignore.

As the months passed, Lorna quietly hoped Cara would find a partner, someone stable who could help her settle down. Her past relationships seemed purely transactional, lacking any real emotion or empathy. Cara would lavish attention and affection on those she deemed worthy, only to discard them when they no longer served her purpose. To her, love was merely a tool to manipulate and control others in her relentless pursuit of dominance.

Cara's party lifestyle showed no signs of slowing down, and when Lorna cautiously suggested she spend more time focusing on her boys, Cara snapped. "You're not a mother, so you don't understand," Cara said, her voice sharp with frustration. "I love my boys, but I need a social life too."

Lorna bit back her retort, swallowing the words she wanted to say. Yes, she wasn't a mother, but that didn't mean she lacked common sense. You didn't need to have children to recognise when someone was making reckless choices.

She couldn't help but marvel at how different they were, despite being identical twins. To others, Cara was innocent and playful, but Lorna saw desperation behind the facade. Cara was someone who knew what she wanted and didn't hesitate to use her charms, among other things, to get it. Lorna often thought of it as "Tapper's disease." All she needed was a tap on her head, and her pants fell down, legs springing open, ready for the next conquest. Cara was all too willing to fall for sweet words and empty promises. But what really left Lorna feeling disgusted was Cara's ability to twist words and spin any situation to her advantage. She remembered a conversation they'd had with their mother about the complications during their birth. Their mother had mentioned how Cara, the smaller twin and a breech birth, had nearly died at birth. Somehow, Cara had taken those words and told others, "My mother said I should have died at birth," completely altering the meaning and turning it into a pitiful narrative for herself.

Lorna had been mortified then, but nothing could prepare her for what came next. Cara, annoyed with their parents, decided to place an advertisement on social media. The criteria were strict, the reasoning an absolute fabrication. The ad read: "Looking for grandparents."

Lorna saw red when she found out. She grabbed the phone, hands shaking, and dialled Cara's number. "What the hell is this?" Lorna demanded the moment Cara picked up.

"What do you mean?" Cara's voice was laced with annoyance.

"The ad, Cara! Take it down! Now!"

Cara's anger flared in an instant. "Why should I? Maybe I'll put up an ad to replace your role too, Lorna."

Lorna was stunned. There was no reasoning with Cara when she was like this, no way to make her see how wrong she was. Weeks later, Cara casually mentioned she'd found a nice older couple willing to take on the role of Jakob and Henry's grandparents, Lorna felt sick to her stomach.

"That's disgusting," Lorna said, her voice trembling with disbelief. "Our parents would be mortified if they knew."

"You're overreacting, as usual," Cara shot back, dismissing Lorna's concern. "It's great for Jakob and Henry to have multiple older role models."

Lorna hung up the phone, dread pooling in her stomach.

How far would her sister go? What would she do next?

Thirty-One

Friday, 31st May, 2024
Highs And Lows

Lorna sat in the passenger seat of Jamie's car; her stomach tight with nerves. The CT renal angiogram scheduled for today was just another step in the process, but it felt monumental, this scan would determine if she was a viable kidney donor for Cara. The overcast sky mirrored her mood as they drove through the familiar streets to the local PRP Imaging centre. Lorna stared out the window, lost in her thoughts.

"Are you sure you're okay with all this?" Jamie asked.

"As okay as I can be, I suppose. It's just… a lot to take in."

Jamie nodded. "I know. You'll be fine, you're doing something incredibly brave. Cara's lucky to have you."

Lorna didn't respond immediately. It wasn't just the scan that weighed on her. It was everything else, the past, the present, and the uncertain future. The conversation with Jakob replayed in her mind, his voice so keen as he told her they would visit her again soon. She wanted to believe in those words, but doubt crept into her mind. Would this really be the beginning of something new with Jakob and Henry, or was she setting herself up for disappointment?

As they pulled into the parking lot, Jamie reached over and gave Lorna's hand a reassuring squeeze. "You're doing something incredible, Lorna. Don't forget that."

Lorna forced a smile and squeezed back. "Thanks, Jamie. I just hope it's enough."

In the waiting room, Lorna's stomach churned, the soft murmur of voices and the occasional clatter of medical equipment only heightened her anxiety. She glanced at Jamie, who sat beside her, flipping through an old magazine. "You don't have to stay, you know," Lorna whispered, though the truth was she didn't want to be alone.

Jamie looked up. "I'm not going anywhere. We'll grab some lunch after this, okay?"

Lorna nodded, grateful for her friend's support.

A nurse appeared at the door, clipboard in hand. "Lorna? We're ready for you."

Lorna stood, smoothing down the front of her shirt before following the nurse into the clinical room where she followed the nurse's instructions, and changed into a hospital gown. She'd been told about the scan in detail, how it would visualise the arteries supplying her kidneys with blood, ensuring everything was in place for a potential transplant. Her renal specialist, Dr Brothers, had explained the importance of this test.

The scan would provide the medical team with an accurate assessment of the number, size and position of her renal arteries and veins. It also assessed the status of her kidneys and included renal stones, the ureters and bladder. It allowed the surgeon to select the kidney that was most suitable for donation. Most people had one or two arteries that supply blood to each kidney. Occasionally some people had extra blood vessels, which are normal for them but could make the transplant operation technically very difficult. Such variations in structure could exclude a potential donor, Lorna knew the test was crucial as were positive results. But the idea of lying on that cold bed, with a machine whirring around her, felt daunting.

"Just here, please," the nurse said, gesturing to the CT examination bed.

Lorna climbed onto the bed, the paper crinkling beneath her as she lay back. The nurse was gentle but efficient as she inserted the cannula into Lorna's arm. "This is for the contrast," she explained. "It'll help us see the blood vessels more clearly."

Lorna nodded, biting her lip as the needle slipped under her skin. She'd always hated needles, but this was something she had to endure. *It's for Cara*, she reminded herself, even though the thought didn't bring comfort.

The nurse adjusted Lorna's position, placing her arms above her head. "We're going to start now. You'll hear some instructions through the intercom. Just relax and try to stay as still as possible."

Relax. The word seemed almost ironic. Lorna took a deep breath, staring up at the ceiling as the machine hummed to life. The bed shifted, moving her in and out of the scanner as the machine clicked and whirred around her. She closed her eyes, focusing on her breathing.

"Take a deep breath in and hold," came the voice over the intercom.

She complied, holding her breath as instructed. The seconds dragged, her heart pounding in her chest. As the contrast was injected into her arm, she felt a warm sensation spreading through her body. It was strange, almost like a wave of heat washing over her. She held still, focusing on the end goal, the results that would determine if she could go through with the donation. As the machine continued its work, Lorna's thoughts drifted back to her family. To her father, who was no longer here to offer his steady advice. To her mother, who wished differences could be set aside and everyone could get along. And, of course, to Cara, the twin she hadn't spoken to in years, the one who had taken Jakob and Henry away without so much as a goodbye. Could Lorna really do this for her?

The scan seemed to take forever, each passing moment intensifying the heaviness in her chest. She wanted to believe this was the right thing to do, that giving Cara a second chance at life was worth all the pain. But doubt lingered, as persistent as ever.

"Breathe normally," the voice instructed, pulling her back to the present.

Lorna exhaled slowly, feeling the bed shift as the scan neared its end. The nurse reappeared, removing the cannula from her arm and offering a warm smile. "All done. You did great. Make sure to drink plenty of fluids today to help flush out the contrast."

"Thank you," Lorna murmured, sitting up and rubbing her arm where the needle had been. Her mind was already racing ahead to the next step, waiting for the results, then waiting to hear from Dr Brothers and her transplant co-ordinator, Sue. As she changed back into her clothes, she couldn't shake the feeling of being in limbo, stuck between what was and what could be. She needed to get out, to breathe fresh air.

When she returned to the waiting room, Jamie was there, all smiles. "How'd it go?"

"It was fine," Lorna replied. "They said I should have the results in a few days."

"Great, let's get you out of here and grab some lunch. You must be starving."

Outside, the sky was a dull grey, the air heavy with the threat of rain. Lorna wrapped her coat tighter around herself, standing by the entrance as she fished her phone out of her bag. She stared at the screen, her finger hovering over Jakob's number. She wanted to call him, to tell him how the scan went, to hear his voice reassuring her everything would be okay. But she hesitated. What would she even say? Would he care? With a sigh, she slipped the phone back into her bag and started walking with Jamie towards her car. The results would come soon enough, and with them, more decisions, more uncertainties. All she could do now was wait and hope when the time came, she would have the strength to face whatever lay ahead.

Jamie drove them to a small café, and they settled into the cosy seats ordering toasted sandwiches, but Lorna barely tasted hers. Her thoughts were still back at the clinic, spinning with what-ifs and worst-case scenarios.

"Lorna, it's going to be fine," Jamie said softly, reaching across the table to squeeze her hand.

Lorna smiled, appreciating the gesture. "I hope so. It's just... hard not to worry."

Jamie nodded. They talked about other things, anything to keep Lorna's mind off the looming results. Jill was unable to join them for lunch due to work commitments, but she texted Lorna, apologising and promising to meet up later. Lorna appreciated the thought, though she wished her friend could have been there. The three of them had been a tight-knit group for years, and Jill's absence was felt.

As their meal continued so did their conversation, laughter slowly replacing the anxiety of the morning. But as the day wore on, Lorna couldn't quite shake the sense of unease. After lunch, Jamie suggested they meet Jill at a local wine bar once she finished work. Lorna agreed, knowing the company of her friends would help keep her grounded. They strolled leisurely to the wine bar, Jamie chattering away while Lorna tried to relax.

Jill had rushed over as soon as she finished work meeting them at the bar. She hugged Lorna tightly before they all settled into a quiet corner. "Sorry I couldn't come earlier," Jill said, looking genuinely upset. "I hated that I couldn't be there with you today."

"It's okay, really," Lorna reassured her, though she couldn't help but wish Jill had been there. Jill always knew how to lighten her mood.

They chatted about their days, trying to keep things light. Lorna almost started to relax, the tension in her shoulders easing as they laughed over something trivial Jill said. But just as she took a sip of her Merlot, her phone buzzed on the table. She glanced at the screen and froze.

Jakob.

Her heart leapt as she quickly picked up the phone, her voice barely steady. "Hello?"

"Aunt Lorna," Jakob's voice was tense, and Lorna immediately knew this wasn't a whimsical call.

"What's wrong?" she asked.

There was a pause on the other end, then Jakob sighed heavily. "We can't see you anymore. Not until after the transplant."

"What?" Lorna whispered. She gripped the phone tighter, her knuckles white. "Why?"

"Mum's worried," Jakob said, his voice strained. "She thinks our visits might be seen as... pressure to donate."

Lorna almost laughed; the idea was so absurd. "Pressure to donate? That's ridiculous!"

"I know," Jakob said. "But she's insistent. She doesn't want any misunderstandings."

Lorna felt like the floor had dropped out from under her. She could hardly process what he was saying. "So, what? I just don't get to see you until then?"

"I'm sorry, it's not what I want."

UNDER THE COVER OF CLOSENESS

The call ended, leaving Lorna staring at the phone in disbelief. A tear slipped down her cheek, quickly followed by another. She wiped them away, but it was too late, Jamie and Jill were already looking at her, concern etched on their faces.

"Lorna, are you okay?" Jamie asked.

"It wasn't about the tests, was it?" Jill added, her voice laced with worry.

Lorna shook her head, trying to find her voice. "No... it was Jakob. He said... he said they can't see me until after the transplant. Cara thinks... it might look like they're pressuring me to donate."

"Pressuring you?" Jamie echoed, her eyes widening. "That's insane!"

Lorna nodded. "It's just an excuse to keep them away. She's just trying to control everything. She knows how much I love those boys…"

Jill slid closer, wrapping an arm around Lorna's shoulders. "I'm so sorry. That's so unfair. But you know we're here for you, right? Whatever happens, you've got us."

Lorna looked up, meeting her friends' concerned gazes. "I know. Thank you. I just… I don't know how much more of this I can take."

Jamie reached across the table and took Lorna's hand. "We're here for you, okay? You don't have to go through this alone. We won't let you."

Lorna gave a half smile. They sat in silence for a moment, the weight of the conversation settling around them. Finally, Jamie broke the tension. "How about we get out of here? Maybe a walk around the lake will clear our heads, we could pick up Daisy and Billy on the way."

Lorna nodded, grateful for the distraction.

As they left the wine bar and headed towards the lake,

she tried to push the conversation with Jakob out of her mind. But the truth was, Cara's influence was stronger than ever, and Lorna couldn't shake the feeling she could possibly lose her nephews all over again.

The afternoon breeze was cool, and as they walked along the bank, Lorna let the sound of the wind within the trees calm her racing thoughts. She didn't have all the answers, and she knew the road ahead would be challenging. But with her friends by her side, she felt just a little bit stronger, a little more ready to face whatever came next.

Thirty-Two

2008
The Puppet

Lorna sat by the pool, her feet gently stirring the cool water as she watched Henry and Jakob play. The sun was beginning its descent, casting a long shadow across the water, but the boys were still full of energy, splashing and laughing as if the day would never end. Lorna smiled, savouring the peace of the moment. Over the years, things had finally settled. The animosity that once defined her relationship with Cara had faded, replaced by something that resembled an amicable bond. It was hard to believe, really. Cara and the boys would visit Lorna in the country, and she, in turn, would make the journey to Sydney. It felt good, this peace between them, even if it was built on a foundation that still had a few cracks. They were a family again, or at least as close to one as they'd ever been.

Lorna sighed, her thoughts drifting to the boys. Where had the time gone? Jakob had just celebrated his fifth birthday with a dinosaur-themed party, he was going to start school soon. And Henry, now three, was busy mastering the social complexities of preschool. How had they grown so fast? Lorna marvelled at how quickly these once-tiny babies had turned into little boys with their own personalities and preferences. She found herself chuckling as she remembered the chaos of Jakob's birthday party. Children running and screaming everywhere... Fairy bread, cordial, and lollies, the magic potion for hyperactive kids.

At least things were finally steady. Cara had finished paying back the money she borrowed during her messy custody battle over Jakob, and she'd curbed her wild partying days. Now, she was all about parenting groups and being the involved mother. Lorna had even managed to save up enough to do some small renovations on her own home. Through time, effort, and hard-earned money, Lorna had turned her house into a true haven, a place where she found a profound sense of contentment and peace.

As she watched the boys, Lorna marvelled at how far they'd come since their first swimming lessons. Cara had insisted the boys start lessons at six months, and Lorna had been there to witness those first splash and sputter moments. Back then, both boys were terrified of getting their faces wet. Jakob had clung to his mother like an octopus, refusing to let go. Lorna chuckled, remembering those early days.

Jakob, especially, had taken to the water like he was born for it. Lorna often thought he must wish he was an octopus, able to live and breathe underwater. He loved diving to the bottom to retrieve toys, his little body cutting through the water with ease. Henry, on the other hand, preferred the safety of the steps, splashing about while Jakob tried to coax him into deeper water. But both boys were confident in their abilities, and that gave Lorna peace of mind as she supervised them. She loved these moments with her nephews. They were water babies, and they adored it when their Aunt Lorna joined them in the pool for cannonball contests or games of Marco Polo. But today, she was content to watch, to just be there with them, soaking in the joy of the present moment.

UNDER THE COVER OF CLOSENESS

The shadows had shifted, the sails no longer providing the shade they once did. It was getting late. Lorna glanced at her watch; Cara would be home soon. Her job had once again required her to work alternating weekends for a few months, and Lorna had happily agreed to help by coming to Sydney to watch the boys. It gave her an excuse to spend time with them and catch up with her family and friends. Lorna treasured this time with her nephews. Long walks, trips to the skate park, and their favourite cosy mornings with story time or watching Fraggle Rock. They'd even given themselves character names from the show, a little tradition that never failed to bring a smile to Lorna's face.

The scent of nearby barbecues filled the air as Cara walked through the back door, freshly changed from work. Without a word, she opened the pool gate and jumped in, joining the boys in their fun. Laughter bubbled up from the pool as they recounted their day at the park.

Later, as they sat under the pergola, enjoying a barbecue dinner, Cara pointed towards the sails overhead. "Look, do you think that sail is starting to fray?" she asked.

Lorna looked up, squinting at the fabric. "It's not too bad," she replied, "I don't think it's going to break. They're just a bit faded."

"Yeah, but it would look better if I could get new sails. These ones are looking a bit shabby."

Lorna laughed. "Oh yeah, and it would be lovely if I had a pool too, but sometimes we just can't have everything we want. Why waste money on new ones when these still have a few years left?"

Cara shrugged. "But it would be better if they were new. I wonder if I could put them up myself?"

Lorna looked at the poles, assessing the task. One was near the roof of the house, possibly reachable, but the others stood alone, with clips in precarious spots. "I certainly wouldn't try it. You'd have to span the sail across the pool, lift it to the clips, and tension it. It's too dangerous, you could fall and break your neck."

"Then how can I get new sails?"

"Just wait and save up," Lorna suggested. "Get a professional to fit them."

"I don't want to wait. Maybe I could ask Uncle Bernard. I'm sure he'd help. Maybe you could ask him for me?"

"I'm not asking him to buy you pool sails."

"Why not? He'll listen to you, and I won't feel like a scab asking for money. You wouldn't want me to fall and get hurt, would you? Besides, Uncle's loaded. He's always talking about his shares; he doesn't need all that money."

Irritation bubbled within Lorna and she shook her head, feeling a familiar knot of unease forming in her stomach. "I'm not asking him to buy you pool sails, it's his money, and he's our uncle, not a piggy bank," she repeated firmly.

But the conversation didn't end there. The next day, they visited Uncle Bernard, the conversation eventually circling back to the pool sails. As they sat together, Cara brought it up again. "Wasn't it so hot yesterday?" she began, her voice casual. "I'm so glad Lorna can look after the boys while I work. It must be nice not having to work weekends," she said, shooting Lorna a glance. "The boys love their time in the pool, but the sails… they're looking a little worse for wear."

"They aren't too bad," Lorna interjected, hoping to steer the conversation away from what she feared was coming.

"But the boys love the pool. It's something we can do together that doesn't cost much, and they need the shade to protect their skin. I wouldn't want the sails to fall."

Lorna felt her chest tighten. *She's setting this up*, she thought, realising too late where Cara was going. "They're not going to fall," Lorna said, trying to keep her voice steady and defuse the situation.

Cara sighed dramatically. "Maybe not, but I think I'll have to get new ones. I should be able to find some online and install them myself."

"Don't be ridiculous," Lorna snapped, "I told you it's too dangerous. You could fall and hurt yourself, or worse you could break your neck.

"Well, I can't afford to have someone replace them, and I need to take care of Jakob and Henry. I don't want them to get skin cancer," Cara said, her eyes welling up with tears.

Uncle Bernard, who'd been quietly listening straightened in his chair and looked alarmed. "Hang on, hang on. No one's going to get hurt. Cara, you can't go climbing ladders. It's too dangerous, you should listen to your sister."

Cara wiped her eyes, her voice trembling as she replied. "I just want to do what's best for my boys. I can't work more hours; I'd never see them. I just want to keep them safe."

Uncle Bernard softened; his concern evident. "Maybe I could help. How about you get some quotes for installers, and we'll see what we can do."

Cara nodded, her tears drying up as quickly as they had appeared. "I guess I could make some inquiries."

Lorna couldn't believe the audacity of her sister. The sails didn't need replacing, they weren't falling apart, they were just a little weathered from the sun and there was a tiny fray, barely noticeable. How could Cara live with herself, knowing she'd manipulated their uncle like that? Lorna felt sick, realising she'd been played, played like a puppet. Cara had turned her concern into an opportunity to scam their uncle, painting herself as the struggling single mother in need of his generosity. And worst of all, Lorna had unknowingly been part of it. *How could I have been so naive?* Lorna thought, her mind racing. Cara had once again used her to get what she wanted.

That night, as she lay in bed, Lorna vowed to herself that she would never let Cara use her like that again. She'd been a fool, but she wouldn't be fooled twice.

When the new sails were installed, Cara couldn't wait to show them off. She sent photos and called Lorna; her voice full of glee. "Look what I got! See, I told you he was loaded, and he was only too happy to pay for the more expensive ones."

Lorna felt her stomach churn as she looked at the photos of her sister's new sails. "It doesn't matter how much money he has, Cara. Like I said before, he's our uncle, not a piggy bank."

"He was happy to help," Cara shot back. "Uncle Bernard doesn't have much to make him happy these days so what I did was a good thing."

"But you lied. You didn't need new sails."

"You're just jealous because he bought them for me," Cara snapped. "You don't get it, do you? I have to do what I can for my boys. You have everything, money, time, freedom. I have to work my arse off just to keep things together. I told Uncle Bernard you're loaded, that you didn't even need to work. That's why you could help me with my legal fees for Jakob's custody."

Lorna stared in disbelief. "That's bullshit! I'm not jealous and what you told Uncle Bernard is a blatant lie. Why would you say such a thing, I work hard for what I have. I live in the country; my home wouldn't be worth half of your house price and your house is much larger than mine, and you have a pool. I can't believe you would say that, I went without to help you with Jakob's custody because that's what family does."

Cara sniggered. "And look where that got you. Don't pretend you're some martyr, Lorna. You'll always be fine… Get over it!"

The phone clicked. Cara had terminated the call.

Lorna felt something break inside her. She'd always known Cara was manipulative, but this… this was a new low.

Another weekend came quickly, and Lorna was up before dawn, ready to head to Sydney. She'd taken the Friday off work, her first stop was her mother's, where they'd planned to have lunch. It was always a joy to catch up with her mother, whose life was full of social events and activities. After spending the night, Lorna would see her father, who had also planned a lunch with his brother Bernard.

Lorna's father had been unwell, but that morning, he was feeling better, so they went ahead with their plans. They met Uncle Bernard at a local Chinese restaurant, where Cara, Jakob, and Henry joined them. Cara had taken a rostered day off work, it was a lovely meal, filled with laughter and conversation and no mention about the pool sails. But as the day wore on, Lorna couldn't shake the unease that had settled in her chest.

After lunch, Lorna dropped her father off at home and made her way back to Cara's. Though nothing was said about their recent phone call, Lorna could feel the tension lingering in the air. She was grateful for the presence of her nephews; they provided a much-needed distraction, and their playful energy allowed things to move forward without further conflict.

Another fortnight passed, and once again, Lorna made the trip to Sydney, ready for a weekend of minding Jakob and Henry. On Saturday morning, they visited their nanny, who doted on them and spoiled them with toys and treats. But their plans to visit Uncle Bernard with her father were interrupted when Lorna's father called, saying he was too unwell to go out. Cara called from her work insisting Lorna should wait for another time to catch up together but Lorna decided to take the boys to see their uncle anyway. As they sat in his living room, the conversation turned to his concerns about living alone and the possibility of having a fall.

"Maybe you should get one of those emergency devices, Dad has one," Lorna suggested, "or perhaps consider having someone stay with you for company."

Uncle Bernard shook his head. "I don't need one of those gadgets. I've got a good system in place with Cara. She looks after me. She says she's more than happy to call in and now she phones me every day."

Lorna felt her unease deepen. "But what if something happens and you can't reach the phone, maybe you could have someone stay with you for company.?"

"Oh, God no," Uncle Bernard replied. "The last time I had someone stay here was for Aunt Sally's funeral."

Lorna straightened in her seat, her heart skipping a beat. "Aunt Sally's funeral?" she echoed.

"Yes, her cousin Anne came down from Brisbane," Uncle Bernard continued, not noticing Lorna's sudden tension.

Lorna's mind raced. "Her cousin came down? But... Cara told me you wanted a closed funeral. She said you wanted a private affair, a private cremation."

Uncle Bernard's expression faltered, confusion creeping into his eyes. "No, Cara was kind enough to drive us all to the funeral."

UNDER THE COVER OF CLOSENESS

Lorna felt her stomach drop. "But...Cara said...I didn't know. I would have come if I'd known."

"It was very kind of Cara to take us," Uncle Bernard said slowly. "I don't remember why you weren't there."

Lorna's mind whirled with questions. She'd never been told about being able to attend the funeral, Cara had said it was private, that no one else had been invited. But now, hearing Cara had driven them to the funeral, Lorna felt like the ground was shifting beneath her feet. What else had Cara hidden from her? Her thoughts interrupted by Jakob, who tugged on her sleeve, asking for help with a puzzle. She forced a smile and turned her attention to him, but her mind remained on Uncle Bernard's words.

Later that night, as Lorna lay in bed, she couldn't stop thinking about what Uncle Bernard had said. Why would Cara lie to her about something so important? What else had she hidden? And more importantly, why? Lorna felt a deep sense of betrayal, and she knew she couldn't let it go. But she had to let her father know, Uncle Bernard's brother deserved to know the truth, no matter how painful it might be, everyone deserved the truth.

As she drove home, Lorna couldn't stop thinking about it. She loved her sister, but she couldn't ignore the pattern that was emerging, she hoped Uncle Bernard would see through Cara's facade.

Back at home, Lorna's thoughts raced with how she might approach the issue of Aunt Sally's funeral. It was a conversation she thought best done in person and so she made it a point to check in on her parents regularly, keeping quiet about the revelation. Their calls had become a routine source of comfort, especially with everything happening in their lives. She also made sure to keep an eye on Uncle

Bernard.

Her father continued to be unwell, and Lorna, always the caretaker, decided to bring him some homemade meals on her next visit to Sydney. Lasagna, curried prawns, and curried sausages, meals she knew he loved. It was a small way she could help, a way to ease her mind knowing he had something healthy and easy to heat up. As Lorna packed up the meals, her mind drifted back to the heated conversation she'd had with Cara about their father. The memory stung as she recalled how quickly things had escalated. She'd merely mentioned helping out, trying to do her part, when out of nowhere, Cara had launched into a scathing attack. "Dad doesn't want to feel controlled; he wants to be independent and do what he wants. He wants to be spoken to quietly; he's fragile. He hasn't asked you to do things… you're taking away his independence."

Cara's words stung deeply. Lorna wasn't trying to control him; she was just trying to help. "I'm not trying to control him," she'd insisted, but Cara wasn't having it.

"Yes, you are. You shouldn't do things for him unless he asks," Cara snapped, her voice sharp and unyielding.

Lorna had been taken aback by the accusation. Their father was unwell, and it was clear he needed help, not just when he asked, but when it was obvious he was struggling. "Cara, if the fridge needs cleaning, then it should be cleaned. If he doesn't have food and is too unwell to go to the shops, then we should get him food."

"Not unless he asks. You're taking away his independence."

"Don't be ridiculous," Lorna had replied, frustration bubbling up inside her. "He's too unwell, and you can't just let him go without healthy food. You can't let the food he has rot and go mouldy."

"Why not? It's his choice."

"If you were sick, I'd help you. I have in the past," Lorna said, trying to appeal to her sister's better nature.

"But that's different. You know I'd want your help."

"Come on, Cara... he's, our father." Lorna's voice had raised, unable to contain her frustration.

"You need to calm down, Lorna. You need anger management."

"I do not. I'm angry for a reason, because what you're saying is ridiculous." Lorna had paused, trying to regain her composure. "Cara, if I see our dad needs help, then I'm going to help. I don't care what you say. How can you be so selfish? You're happy to help Uncle Bernard."

Cara had merely shrugged and smirked. "Oh well, he thanks me. I know he's grateful."

"What? He pays you?" Lorna had asked, suspiciously. The realisation had hit her hard, making her question everything about her sister's motives.

Cara's smirk deepened, but she remained silent. There was no way to prove what Lorna believed, that Cara was taking advantage of their uncle, but the thought of it was deeply upsetting, especially when Cara seemed so dismissive about their father's well-being.

Lorna travelled to Sydney with the prepared meals in a cooler bag. Walking into her father's house, she found him relaxing on the lounge. He looked tired, and frail. It appeared he'd lost more weight.

"Hi, Dad," she said softly, placing the containers on the kitchen counter.

Gerald smiled up at her. "Lorna, love, you didn't have to do all this," he said, beginning to rise from his seat.

"It's no trouble, Dad," Lorna replied, moving to his side. "I just want to make sure you're eating well, especially since it looks like you've lost more weight."

Gerald nodded, but then he began to shuffle towards the

kitchen. "Let me get my wallet. How much do I owe you?"

Lorna stared at him; her mouth slightly open as she tried to process his words. "Dad, I don't want your money. I'm just making sure you're taking care of yourself."

He hesitated, his brow furrowing and eyes squinting slightly as he turned to her. "It's okay, love. I'm happy to pay for the meals you make. Your sister puts a price on each meal and adds it to my fortnightly account based on what ingredients she uses. I understand about the cost-of-living crisis."

Lorna tilted her head. "Fortnightly account? What fortnightly account?"

Gerald, oblivious to the growing rage within her, walked over to the kitchen bench and picked up a piece of paper. "The spreadsheet she created to help me, so I don't get confused," he explained, handing it to Lorna. "Cara's told me how I'm getting forgetful, so the spreadsheet lists the cost of all the meals she makes, the charges for her time in doing my housework, helping in the garden, all the incidentals like petrol and extra things she buys. Here, have a look."

Lorna's hand trembled as she took the paper from him. Her eyes scanned the list. "She charges you?"

"I don't mind paying," Gerald said with a small smile. "I've got the money, and I can afford it."

Lorna felt a wave of anger and sadness crash over her. "What you mind or what you should do are two different things. Byron helps you; I help you… we've never expected anything. You're our father."

"I know, but she's got the boys to take care of."

"And she gives you a plate of leftovers," Lorna snapped, flapping the piece of paper in the air. "Look at this! The price she's charging you for the leftovers is what it would cost for the complete meal. You're paying her food bill, Dad. You fund the total meal; she's eating for free."

UNDER THE COVER OF CLOSENESS

Gerald frowned, clearly uncomfortable. "Your sister's struggling, love."

"She's not struggling, Dad. She's a liar. A user. A manipulative thief."

"Oh, come on, Lorna. I've got the money. I can afford it... Here, I'll give you some money too. Like I said, I can afford it."

Lorna's heart broke. "It's not about what you can afford, Dad. It's the principle. It's your money, not hers. A person shouldn't charge someone when they offer to help, especially not their parent." She motioned for her father to sit back down on the lounge. "I think you should take a seat, Dad. There's something I need to tell you." Her voice was trembling, the weight of telling her father the truth about Aunt Sally's funeral pressing down on her. This was going to hurt, but it had to be said. Lorna hesitated for a moment before speaking. "Dad," she said gently, choosing her words carefully, "do you remember when Aunt Sally died?"

Her father's face softened with sadness. "Oh yeah, love. That would be about five years ago now."

Lorna nodded, confirming his memory. "Yep, in 2002. Do you remember how we didn't go to her funeral?"

"Of course I do," he replied, a hint of defensiveness in his tone. "I've been sick, but I haven't lost my marbles... Cara said Bernard wanted to have a private affair."

Lorna nodded. "Well, I told you that Cara had told me that's what he wanted," she reminded him.

"Yes, love, I know," her father said. "But I also spoke with your sister. She told me the same thing. She said she'd called in on Bernie, and he was upset, wanted space, so we respected his wishes."

Lorna took a deep breath, bracing herself. "But he didn't, Dad."

Her father's brow furrowed. "What do you mean?"

"Cara lied, Dad," Lorna said, pausing to study her

father's reaction. "She lied about it all. Cara went to the funeral."

His eyes widened. "She what?"

"I'm sorry, Dad," Lorna said, guilt washing over her.

"It's not for you to be sorry," her father said, his voice laced with disbelief and pain. "She lied and kept me from showing support... No wonder I thought Bernie had an issue with me. This explains it all." He paused, rubbing his chin as though deep in thought. Lorna could see the hurt in his eyes, the betrayal sinking in. But then, as if shaking off the weight of it all, he sighed. "Oh well, love, nothing we can do now. How about a nice cup of tea."

Lorna managed a small smile, admiring her father's resilience even as she felt his pain. "I'll make it," she offered, standing up. She knew her father was deeply upset, hurt by Cara's lies. But she also knew he was a man who didn't like confrontation. If something had happened and couldn't be changed, he saw no use in creating waves. Still, Lorna knew this wasn't something he would easily forget.

Would her father confront Cara about her lie? Was it worth stirring up things that couldn't be changed?

Thirty-Three

Monday, 3rd June, 2024
Vital Readings

In the quiet moments of the night, when the world was still and dark, Lorna often found herself awake, her thoughts drifting to the things that kept her up. It was a familiar pattern, these nighttime awakenings, where her mind would pick apart the threads of her life. Tonight was no different. She lay in bed, wrapped in the warmth of her blankets, the cool breeze from the open window brushing against her face. The stars outside seemed to watch over her, and she wondered if, somewhere under the same sky, Cara was thinking of her too.

Jakob and Henry had assured her they would keep their communications secret, hidden from their mother to avoid any additional strain. Their conversations had become a lifeline for Lorna, a connection to the family she was trying to help. The boys' positivity and encouragement eased her worry. They kept her updated on their lives and on how their mother was coping. For the most part, Cara was managing, but she was far from well. They'd, so far, avoided putting her on dialysis, and Lorna clung to the hope her sister could skip it altogether with the "just in time" transplant.

Lorna knew patients who received a kidney transplant before starting dialysis or after only a short period of it tended to have better outcomes. She wanted to give Cara the best possible chance to resume a normal life. While the transplant wouldn't be a cure and Cara would still face several restrictions, her overall quality of life would improve. These thoughts fuelled Lorna's determination to push forward with the testing requirements, the urgency of the situation never far from her mind.

Sue, her transplant coordinator, had been a steady source of reassurance. She couldn't guarantee what would happen with Cara since donors and recipients had separate medical teams, but she had promised to ensure Lorna's tests were completed as quickly as possible. Lorna appreciated Sue's dedication, though she couldn't help but feel the weight of the responsibility on her shoulders.

As the first light of dawn began to seep through the window, Lorna knew she had another long day ahead. Her diary had the letters "DTPA/GFR" scribbled in it, a reminder of the tests she was scheduled to undergo. Sue had explained these tests to her: the DTPA scan was a type of renal imaging that would measure the function of her kidneys, comparing how the left and right kidneys worked. The GFR, or glomerular filtration rate, would show how well her kidneys were filtering waste from her blood. These tests were crucial; without the results showing two healthy, functioning kidneys, the possibility of her donating one to Cara wouldn't even be on the table.

Walking into her local PRP Diagnostic Imaging Clinic, Lorna felt a gnawing emptiness in her stomach. She hadn't eaten since the night before, following the instructions to avoid food and drink except water for several hours before the test. Even the smell of food seemed to taunt her as she passed a café on her way inside. *Why is it that when you*

UNDER THE COVER OF CLOSENESS

can't eat, food is the only thing you can think about? she thought.

Lorna had learned more about kidneys in the past few months than she ever thought she would need to know. The kidneys filtered blood, removing waste and extra water to make urine. The GFR showed how well they were doing their job. Simple, yet so vital, Lorna thought as she checked in at the reception desk. The waiting room was quiet, the murmur of the television in the corner blending with the hushed conversations around her. With preparation requiring her to drink 1-1.5 litres of water within the hour prior to the test, Lorna sipped from her water bottle, trying to keep her mind occupied, but her thoughts kept drifting back to Cara. She pictured her sister, the way she used to be, full of life and energy. It was hard to reconcile that image with the fragile woman her nephews had described. The thought of her sister needing dialysis, of her life being tethered to a machine, was unbearable.

Finally, her name was called, and Lorna followed the nurse into the dimly lit room where the Gamma camera awaited. She felt a twinge of anxiety as she lay down, her mind racing. This is just one more step, she reminded herself. One more step towards helping Cara. The nurse was kind, explaining each part of the procedure as it happened. First, the small injection of the radioactive tracer, a necessary step that didn't hurt but felt strange nonetheless. Lorna watched as the nurse moved around the room, adjusting the equipment, while the camera began its slow, methodical scan of her kidneys.

As the minutes ticked by, Lorna focused on the ceiling, trying to push away the worries that kept creeping in. She thought of the conversations she'd had with Jakob and Henry, their voices full of hope and determination. She thought of Sue's reassurances, of the way her mother had looked at her when she told her what she was doing. She thought of her two best friends, Jamie and Jill with their beautiful toy poodles; three crazy emus and two wombats. She smiled, thankful for all the wonderful things in her life. This is worth it, she told herself. It has to be. Closing her eyes, Lorna's mind wandered again, this time to the future. What would life be like after the transplant? Would Cara finally appreciate the sacrifices she was making? Would they have a chance to repair their fractured relationship? Or would things remain as strained as they were now? The questions swirled in her mind, unanswered and unsettling.

After what felt like an eternity, the first part of the test was over, and the nurse instructed her to wait for the next hour before returning for the GFR assessment. Lorna was grateful she'd thought to bring some food, though the thought of eating still felt foreign after hours of fasting. As she sat in the waiting room, nibbling on a sandwich, Lorna let her mind wander back to the night before. She had stared up at those same stars, wondering about Cara, hoping somewhere, deep down, her sister understood why she was doing this. The urgency, the drive to push through these tests, it was all for her. For them. For their family. And as daunting as it all felt, Lorna knew she wouldn't stop until she had done everything she could.

By the time the tests were over, Lorna was exhausted, both physically and emotionally. The weight of the day settled heavily on her shoulders as she made her way home. But beneath the fatigue, a flicker of hope remained. She had done what was necessary, and now, all she could do was wait. Wait for the results, wait for the next step, and hope that in the end all would be okay.

Thirty-Four

2008
Unwell

Time was not kind to Mr Gerald Martin. Lorna watched with growing despair as her father's health declined. The vibrant man who'd once possessed boundless energy was now a shadow of himself. His rapid weight loss was alarming, and his once full face had become sunken, with hollow cheeks and tired eyes. Lorna's heart broke when she looked at him. This was not the father she knew, the man who ate well, never smoked or drank, and always seemed invincible. Now, he struggled to get out of bed, ate like a sparrow, and seemed to be fading before her eyes.

Lorna tried to hide her worry as she prepared meals for him, but it was impossible to ignore the evidence of his dwindling appetite. What used to be one serving size was now divided into halves, and then into quarters, served on a bread-and-butter plate. She noticed it all, the single slice of toast cut into four, the half-rasher of bacon with one egg, and the tiny cup of soup he called a large bowl. It was no wonder he was losing weight. "You need to eat more, Dad," she would tell him, trying to mask the worry in her voice. "You have to use energy to make energy. If you don't eat, your body can't function properly."

Gerald's response was always the same, a mix of frustration and resignation. "I'll make myself vomit if

I force in more food," he would say, "I know what I can handle," his voice tinged with aggravation.

Lorna would sigh inwardly, fighting back tears, it wasn't just about the food, it was about watching her father slowly give up, watching him slip further away from her. And then there was Cara, ever the voice of reason or so she thought. "You're doing too much, Lorna, he hasn't asked you to do things. You shouldn't do anything unless he specifically asks," she would insist, her tone tinged with frustration. "He's ignorant. I can't be bothered arguing with him. Let him do what he wants."

"Of course he's depressed," Lorna had said to Byron one day. "Who wouldn't be, when he can't do the things, he's always done? But there has to be more to it than that. The idea his exhaustion and weight loss could be cured with a pill seems absurd."

Byron had nodded, his expression weary. He'd been visiting their father regularly, only to find him in bed most of the time, too weak to do much of anything. The doctors' lack of answers only fuelled their frustration. Their father insisted he wasn't just depressed, he was angry. Angry his body was betraying him, angry and frustrated no one could give him a straight answer.

"Why don't you come and stay with me?" Lorna suggested one day, desperate to do something, anything, that might help. "A break away in the country might be good. Staying where you are isn't getting you anywhere. Maybe with new doctors you'll find some real answers instead of excuses." To her surprise, her father agreed.

It was strange at first, having him live with her. They were both set in their ways, Lorna liked things organised and orderly, while her father had always been more relaxed. But with his declining health, he'd almost given up on picking up after himself. They set some ground rules, hoping it

UNDER THE COVER OF CLOSENESS

would help things run smoothly. There was no time limit on his visit; they would play it by ear and see how things went.

Byron was pleased with the change in strategy. He agreed to maintain their father's yard and check in for mail. Cara, on the other hand, seemed annoyed. Lorna couldn't help but wonder if it was because she would no longer receive the extra money their father had been giving her. Despite the tension, Lorna felt a small flicker of hope. Maybe, just maybe, this change would help improve her father's health. Anything had to be better than the slippery slope he'd been on. But her hope was short-lived. Gerald hadn't been with Lorna for a day when he yelled from his bedroom. Lorna rushed in. Shock. Her father was lying on the bed, his face contorted, his nose twitching, and his eyes closed. His face appeared lopsided, and his voice was slurred. Fear gripped.

"Dad?" she whispered, panic rising in her throat. "Are you having a stroke?" Her mind raced as she grabbed her phone, instinctively hitting record to capture what was happening. She needed evidence, something to show the doctors. Within minutes, the contortion faded, and her father was able to speak. He explained, in a shaky voice, this wasn't the first time he'd experienced such an episode. But when he tried to explain it to the doctors, they'd been unable to figure out what was wrong.

"We're going to the hospital," Lorna said, her voice firm. "Now."

The video she'd taken proved invaluable. After an initial examination in the emergency room, Gerald was referred to a neurologist. And finally, after months of fear and uncertainty, they had an answer. Gerald wasn't depressed, he was having mini-seizures. Seizures that physically manifested only in his face and neck but drained his energy to the point of exhaustion. The neurologist explained these seizures, particularly the ones happening at night, were like running a marathon in his sleep.

Lorna felt a mix of relief and anger. Relief there was finally a diagnosis, her father hadn't been imagining things. But anger, too, at the time that had been lost, at the doctors who'd dismissed his symptoms as mere depression. Over the following months, they worked to adjust his medication, finding the right balance to control the frequency and intensity of the seizures. It was a slow process, but there was hope. Time, it all took time. Gerald had lost so much weight it was vital to rebuild his strength. The doctors gave strict instructions on what he should eat to help him regain weight and body strength. While his illness was diagnosed, there was no cure. It was imperative for him to be vigilant about his diet, medication, and lifestyle. One would affect the other.

Having her father live with her became a lesson in patience for Lorna. She thought about how she must have tested her parents' patience when she was growing up, and now, the roles were reversed. She was the carer, and her father was the one who needed looking after. As the months passed, Gerald's enthusiasm for life slowly returned. He began to gain weight, and with a regime of light exercise, his strength and endurance improved. With his health on the mend, Lorna insisted he start contributing more to the daily running of the house. They shared cooking duties, and when Lorna was at work, her father made his own lunch and took care of small jobs around the house. The spark returned to his eyes, and Lorna couldn't have been more relieved.

She welcomed Byron and Cara's visits, believing they should all come together to support their father, their parents had looked after them growing up, it was only right they should put any differences aside and look after their parents as they aged.

In the quiet moments, Gerald would open up to Lorna, sharing his fears and concerns. He admitted how scared he'd been, how he'd thought he wasn't long for this world. But now, with the seizures under control, he felt a renewed sense of purpose and he insisted on going to a solicitor.

"I just want to make sure everything is in order," he said.

Lorna nodded, understanding this was something he needed to do for his own peace of mind. Together, they went to her solicitor, where he had new power of attorney and enduring guardianship papers drawn up, listing all three children, Byron, Lorna, and Cara.

By the time he returned home, six months had passed. The new paperwork was signed by everyone, and Gerald assured them his Will was already in place, with everything divided equally among his children. Lorna felt a sense of closure, knowing they'd done everything they could to address his medical concerns and ensure his future care.

Byron tidied up their father's yard, and Lorna stocked his fridge with fresh food before leaving him at home. Her job was done, for now. Gerald was confident he could continue at his own pace, and Lorna was hopeful they'd turned a corner. As she drove away, she couldn't help but feel a weight lifting from her shoulders. Her father, the man who'd once been a mere shadow of himself was now standing tall, they were on the right path. At last, there was hope in his eyes.

Thirty-Five

Wednesday, 12th June, 2024
Geps and Friends

Lorna awoke with a burst of excitement, a feeling that had been rare these past months. Tomorrow would be a significant day, another step closer to her goal of becoming a kidney donor. Three more tests awaited her, each one bringing her nearer to the final confirmation. But today wasn't about needles, doctors, or waiting rooms. Today she would focus on something far more light hearted; joy, friendship, and a midweek escape with her two best friends Jamie and Jill. The three crazy emus, as they fondly called themselves, were about to take flight towards Sydney, leaving their worries behind, if only for a brief moment. Meanwhile, Jamie and Jill's two little wombats, their cherished pets, would have their own adventure with Jill's trusted pet sitter.

Lorna had packed the night before, her suitcase sitting by the door, ready to go. The most crucial item? The all-important GEPs, of course. Good Eating Pants... a genius invention, really. Over the years, the trio had built a collection of inside jokes, code words, and abbreviations, but none were as cherished as the GEPs. A girl's best friend, these pants were the ultimate example of comfort and style, they were versatile, coming in a range of colours but timeless black was a favourite. The elasticated waist and optional drawstring meant no restrictions, no discomfort, just pure, unadulterated ease. Whether dressed up or down, GEPs ensured no matter how much they indulged in good food and drink, they would never feel constrained. Perfect for wining, dining, and whatever adventures awaited them in Sydney.

A toot of a horn pulled Lorna from her daydreaming. Peeking out the window she spotted Jamie's car parked in the driveway. Jamie's infectious energy was already obvious as she leaned out of the driver's window, yelling, "Let's get ready to party!"

Jill jumped out of the passenger seat, waving her arms in the air. "Woohoo! I'm so excited! I booked us a fantastic hotel on the harbour, and Jamie scored us reservations at that fabulous Italian restaurant you were raving about."

Lorna felt a mix of gratitude and love for these two women. They always knew how to turn a daunting time into a celebration, and that was the true beauty of their friendship. Grabbing her suitcase, she stepped outside and shouted back, "I've got my GEPs on, and I'm ready to party!"

Jamie and Jill burst into laughter, their excitement bubbling over as they danced around the driveway. "And we've got ours too! Let's hit the road in style," Jamie replied, "and in comfort!" Jill added with a wink.

The drive to Sydney was filled with laughter and chatter, the kind of easy conversation only years of deep friendship could foster. They stopped for coffee along the way, stretching their legs and enjoying the warmth of the sun, which seemed unseasonably generous for the beginning of winter. By the time they arrived in Sydney, Lorna felt a deep sense of contentment. She took over the driving for the final stretch, guiding them smoothly to their hotel just in time for check-in. After a quick freshen-up, the three friends set out to explore Circular Quay, the iconic Sydney Opera House and Harbour Bridge providing the perfect backdrop for their group photos. Later, they dressed up in their evening GEPs and headed to the Italian restaurant, where they savoured every bite of their meal, the wine flowing as easily as their conversation.

As Lorna sat at the dinner table, twirling her fork in a plate of freshly made pasta, she felt a sense of calm wash over her. She hadn't felt this relaxed in months. Tomorrow would bring its challenges, more needles, more tests, but tonight, surrounded by friends, she felt invincible. It was as if the laughter and warmth of the evening had fortified her, wrapping her in a cocoon of positivity.

Morning arrived too soon, and with it, the flutter of nerves returned. Lorna lay in bed, staring at the ceiling, her thoughts racing. The tests ahead were necessary but intimidating. She knew all too well that sometimes, these tests uncovered hidden issues in donors. *What if something goes wrong? What if I'm not as healthy as I feel?*

Jill's voice cut through her spiralling thoughts. "Morning, Lorna! Ready for another day of adventure?"

Jamie added from the other room, "We've got our GEPs on, and we're with you all the way."

Lorna smiled. How did they always know exactly what to say? She got out of bed and joined her friends. They'd all agreed to fast in solidarity with Lorna until her glucose tolerance test was complete. The three of them showered and dressed, their GEPs giving them a sense of unity and comfort.

The hospital wasn't far from the hotel, and soon they were sitting in the waiting area. Lorna's stomach growled,

UNDER THE COVER OF CLOSENESS

Jamie and Jill sat on either side of her, chattering away to keep her mind off the test. When Lorna was finally called in, she took a deep breath and followed the nurse, her friends' words of encouragement echoing behind. The glucose tolerance test was as unpleasant as Lorna had feared. The needle pricks were minor, but the sugary drink was nauseating. She sat quietly as the minutes ticked by, her thoughts drifting in and out of focus. Jamie and Jill were there with her, cracking jokes and making her laugh until her sides hurt. At one point, they were laughing so hard a nurse shot them a stern look.

"Okay, you two," Lorna said through her giggles, "if you don't stop, they're going to kick us out of here!"

Jamie grinned. "What? We're just trying to keep things light."

"Shhh! we'd better behave," Jill chuckled putting her hand to her mouth.

Lorna was grateful beyond words for their support. After what felt like an eternity but was really just two hours of sitting, waiting, and trying not to think about the gnawing hunger in her stomach, Lorna was done with the glucose test. Next up was the ECG. The nurse attached the electrodes to her chest, arms, and legs, the cold patches causing her to shiver slightly. But even then, Jamie and Jill kept her distracted, talking about anything and everything, making sure she never felt alone.

Finally, it was time for the echocardiogram. Lorna was more prepared for this one, mentally at least, but it made her most uncomfortable. She hated the thought of stripping down and having gel smeared across her chest. As she lay on her side, the sonographer gently moved the ultrasound probe across her chest, the cool gel causing a brief shiver again. It was a strange sensation, hearing the soft whoosh of her heart through the machine, her eyes were fixed on the monitor, watching the rhythmic pulsing, the steady beat that had carried her through every moment of her life. It was a surreal experience, yet there was something deeply reassuring about it. Each beat on the screen was a reminder that her heart was strong, that she was strong. But as she lay there, her thoughts began to drift, carrying her back to a time when she'd sat in a similar room, but with a different purpose. She'd been there with Cara, who'd been experiencing chest pains. Lorna could still see the fear in Cara's eyes, the worry something could be terribly wrong. Cara had tried to stay composed, but the tension in her voice had betrayed her fear of what the tests might reveal. Lorna had stayed by her side, offering words of support and reassurance, doing everything she could to keep her sister calm.

Lorna's chest tightened at the memory. What would Cara say now, if she were here, standing next to her? Would she even care? The thought struck Lorna unexpectedly, bringing with it a pang of sadness. Cara had always been so focused on her own worries, her own struggles. Lorna knew this was her journey, her evaluation to undergo. Cara probably had too many concerns of her own to think about her right now.

But still, Lorna liked to imagine that maybe, just maybe, there was a slim chance her sister was thinking of her. That somewhere, Cara was wishing her well, hoping all would go smoothly. It was a comforting thought, even if it wasn't likely to be true. But it kept Lorna motivated, giving her the strength to face the next test, the next challenge.

As the sonographer continued the scan, Lorna took a deep breath, focusing on the rhythmic sound of her heart, steady and unyielding. She would get through this. And whether or not Cara was thinking of her, Lorna knew she had the strength to continue, driven by the hope that in the end, it would all be worth it.

When it was all over, Lorna felt a wave of exhaustion hit her. But it was a good kind of tired, the kind that comes after facing something difficult and coming out the other side. As they left the clinic, Lorna squeezed Jamie and Jill's hands. "Thank you. I couldn't have done this without you."

Jamie smiled, a knowing look in her eyes. "Of course you could have. But you don't have to do it alone."

The three friends spent the rest of the day with Lorna's mother, enjoying a late lunch and soaking in the last bit of their time together before heading back to Sydney for one final night of fun. The live music was the perfect ending to a whirlwind trip.

As they travelled back home the following morning, Lorna leaned her head against the car window, feeling the fatigue settle in. But she also felt relief. Another round of tests was behind her, and for now, she could focus on the present, on her friends, on the laughter, on the simple joy of being together.

Tomorrow would bring whatever it would bring, but today, she was grateful. The power of positive thought, bolstered by the love of true friends, was something that could never be underestimated.

Tomorrow would be another day, and with Jamie and Jill by her side, Lorna knew she could face anything.

Thirty-Six

2009
A Great Investment

Lorna's phone trembled in her hand as she dialled her father's number. Pressing the phone to her ear, she waited for her father to pick up. "Hi, Dad," Lorna began, trying to sound cheerful. "How are you feeling?"

There was a pause on the other end, then a sigh. "Hello." Her father's voice crackled over the line, a little weaker than the last time they'd spoken.

"Dad. Its Lorna. How are you?" she said a little louder.

"I've been better, love. I've been talking to your brother. We're thinking it's time I move into a nursing home. It's probably best for everyone."

Lorna's heart stopped for a moment. "A nursing home? This is the first I'm hearing about it."

"I know, love, I'm sorry. I thought Byron would've mentioned it to you."

"We haven't spoken, Byron hasn't said anything, why didn't you tell me about this sooner?"

"Byron's been good about it, helping me figure out the details. We thought it was best not to worry anyone until we had everything in place. But now...now I think it's time you knew. I want to sell the house, Lorna. I need to sell it to pay for the nursing home and to make sure all the loose ends are tied up. I need peace of mind."

Lorna stood frozen, wide eyed as a chill ran through

her, prickling her skin with goosebumps. Clenching the phone a little tighter, she caught her breath as the weight of the news settled over her. Moving into a nursing home was a big deal. Her father had appeared stronger since he'd stayed with her, more confident in his home environment. Hearing her father's words Lorna wondered if her father was just throwing in the towel.

"This is something I've been thinking about for a while, since I returned from your place but it's hard to accept, you know? I've also been trying to talk to Cara about it, but she's been refusing to speak to me."

Lorna felt a rush of sadness and anger, clenching her jaw she struggled to steady her breath. "She's not talking to you?"

"No," he said, "She won't even pick up the phone. I've decided if I'm going to move into a home, I need to sell the house to pay for it. I want to make sure everything's taken care of so I can have some peace of mind."

"I'll talk to Cara, see what's going on."

She hung up the phone and immediately called her sister. Cara answered on the second ring.

"What do you want, Lorna?"

Lorna took a breath, trying to steady herself. "I just spoke with Dad. He mentioned something about going into a nursing home. He wants to sell the house."

"A nursing home?" Cara snapped. "This is the first I'm hearing about it. He's lost it! He can't just sell the house! What if he changes his mind? Where would he go? His house would belong to someone else, a stranger. He's not thinking clearly! He's getting beyond it, Lorna. It's probably dementia, like his mother."

"Cara."

"No, I won't agree to the house being sold. I'm looking out for his best interests, unlike Byron, who's just trying to get his hands on the money. I've spoken with Uncle Bernard, I told him about dad losing the plot, I told him our brother wants to ship him off to a nursing home. Uncle Bernard is appalled, he says he doesn't even know if he wants to speak to him anymore. If the house stays where it is, Dad will always have the option to go back. That's my last word on it, Lorna. The house stays until Dad dies, and then we can sort things out."

There was no point in arguing. Cara was adamant, and nothing Lorna said would change her mind. "Alright, Cara. I'll talk to you later."

As Lorna hung up the phone, she couldn't shake the sickening feeling in her gut. She didn't want to believe it, but Cara's insistence on keeping the house was more than just concern for their father…it felt like something else, something darker.

Later that evening, Lorna called her father again, hoping to reassure him.

"Dad, I talked to Cara."

"And?"

"She's upset, Dad. She doesn't think you should sell the house. She's worried about what would happen if you changed your mind, she doesn't think you're thinking clearly."

Her father groaned. "I'm not changing my mind, Lorna. You know what I was like when I stayed with you. I wasn't well, but I wasn't forgetful or confused. Surely, you don't think I'm losing it?"

"Of course not, Dad," Lorna said. "I believe you. I'm just trying to keep the peace, I thought she'd listen to me. I just want what's best for you, Dad. You know that, right?"

"I do, love. Don't worry about arguing with your sister. This is between me and her. I've even been to a solicitor. They've tried to contact Cara, but she's ignoring them. She seems to think if she does nothing, nothing will happen. Well, she's got another thing coming. She won't take everything I own, not if I have anything to say about it."

Lorna hung up the phone, and sat in stunned silence. How far would Cara go? How could her twin, someone who looked exactly like her, be so different? Cara's behaviour was sickening, and the more Lorna thought about it, the more it became clear that her sister had a hidden agenda. The red flag was Cara's insistence on keeping the house, regardless of their father's wishes.

The next morning, Lorna phoned Cara again. She couldn't drop the issue. They were all adults, and they should be able to work things out.

"Cara," Lorna began, trying to keep her voice calm, "Dad told me about the solicitor trying to contact you. You should just talk to them and respect his wishes."

Cara's voice was sharp. "It's my house, Lorna. Byron just wants to get his hands on it."

"No, he doesn't. Dad wants to sell it. It's his house. This issue was settled years ago. You agreed, Cara. You even wrote up the property agreement. We all agreed and signed it. I've still got my copy."

"Oh! That's right. You're the bitch who keeps records," Cara spat.

"Why are you turning on me? I'm just saying what happened, what we agreed to. This is about what's right, Cara."

"Fuck off, Lorna. If you're not with me, you're against me. Fuck off. I don't need you, and this has nothing to do with you. It's my house."

"You know that's bullshit," Lorna's voice trembled with anger. "It's Dad's home, and he should be able to sell it. You need to do the right thing and work it out with him."

"Mind your own business, Lorna. I'm not going to be

forced into anything."

Lorna felt sick as she hung up the phone. Her father was rightfully distressed, all he wanted was to ensure he could live out his final years in peace. But Cara's greed was blinding her to everything else. She couldn't believe how far her sister had fallen. How could her own sister be so selfish? How had things gone so wrong between them?

A few weeks later, Lorna returned to Sydney to catch up with the family. She found herself alone with Cara, who seemed more composed than during their last conversation.

"So, since Dad wants to go to a nursing home, I've been thinking," Cara began casually. "What if we built townhouses on the block? We could demolish the old house and put up three townhouses. You could help pay for the build, and then we could split the profits when we sell. It's a way for you to build your wealth, and if Dad doesn't like the nursing home, he could have a new townhouse."

Lorna stared at her sister, unable to believe what she was hearing. "Cara, I don't think that's a good idea. I don't have the money for something like that, and besides, why not just let Dad sell the house?"

"You're no help. I thought you'd be interested in building your wealth."

Lorna shook her head. "I'm planning to visit Dad and Mum this afternoon. Want to come with Jakob and Henry?"

Cara's expression darkened. "No. I'm not interested in visiting them. I thought you'd help me, but instead, you're still on their side."

"This isn't about sides, Cara," Lorna said, straightening her posture while trying to keep her voice steady. "It's about doing what's right."

"Fine. Do whatever you want. Just don't expect me to be involved."

Lorna's posture straightened and a small but confident

smile pulled at the corners of her mouth. A newfound strength settled within her as she left to visit her parents. Cara was becoming more unrecognisable with each passing day.

That evening, they went out for a Chinese meal. Cara, eager to order another drink, raised her hand and clicked her fingers at the server.

Lorna was mortified. "Are you serious, Cara? Who do you think you are? That's so disrespectful."

The server approached, professional and composed, taking their order. But the damage was done. Cara glared at Lorna and kicked her under the table. "Shut it."

Jakob and Henry sat eating, oblivious to their disagreement.

Lorna rubbed her leg, fighting back tears. She didn't want to cause a scene, but she was seething inside. When they left the restaurant, Cara's anger boiled over. "How dare you embarrass and humiliate me like that in front of everyone?"

Lorna couldn't hold back any longer. "Your behaviour was disgusting and rude, it was your actions that were humiliating, not me."

"That's how you're supposed to treat servants," Cara retorted.

Lorna's jaw dropped. "She wasn't your servant, Cara. She was a professional doing her job. Next time, I won't sit in silence. Next time, I'll make sure everyone knows exactly what I think."

"You can't speak to me like that." Cara pointed towards her sister.

Lorna's chin lifted. "I just did."

Later that night, Lorna lay in the darkness, unable to sleep. Cara was on the phone, badmouthing her to someone.

Lorna's anger simmered as she listened to Cara's distorted version of events, knowing she was being painted as the villain.

The next morning, Jakob and Henry crept into her room, ready for story time. But their fun was short-lived when Cara came in, dragging the boys away and telling them they had to help her instead of playing with their aunt.

Lorna showered, letting the water hide her tears. She packed her bag, hugged the boys, and left. As she drove home, the realisation hit her: Cara was intent on shutting her out, simply because she didn't agree with her.

It was a bitter pill to swallow, but Lorna knew she couldn't force Cara to see reason. She had to protect herself from Cara, it was time to set boundaries, to stand up for herself and hold onto what she knew was right, even if it meant standing against her own twin sister.

Thirty-Seven

Friday, 14th June, 2024
Testing Times

One test after another, Lorna was exhausted, yet she never veered from the list of tests and tasks she was required to complete to ensure she was medically and psychologically suitable to be a living kidney donor for Cara. Days blurred together. Each step drained her, but she pushed forward, driven by a sense of duty and love.

Each donor was allocated a transplant coordinator to assist them on their journey, and Lorna had met with Sue at her very first appointment in Sydney Hospital. Sue's support had been unwavering, her knowledge invaluable, and her reassurances a godsend. To Lorna, Sue was nothing short of an angel. She guided Lorna through each step of the intricate and often overwhelming process, offering clarity where there was confusion and comfort where there was doubt.

As Lorna progressed through the series of medical evaluations, the scans, x-rays, and compatibility tests, Sue was always there, a steady presence, she explained the medical jargon in layman's terms, broke down complex procedures into understandable steps, and offered a listening ear whenever Lorna needed to vent her fears or frustrations.

"You're doing great, Lorna," Sue would say, her voice

soothing. "Remember, this is a marathon, not a sprint. Take it one step at a time."

Lorna clung to those words, especially during the more gruelling parts of the process. It was exhausting, both physically and emotionally. But knowing Sue was just a phone call away provided a sense of security Lorna desperately needed. Sue kept Lorna focused on the positive aspects of the journey. "You're doing this out of love," Sue reminded her. "This is about giving your sister a chance at a better life."

The unwavering support of Jamie and Jill had also become her lifeline through difficult days. They were always there with a comforting word, a reassuring smile, or a well-timed distraction when the weight of her decision threatened to overwhelm her. Their friendship was a constant source of strength, a reminder she wasn't alone in this.

Jamie had a way of cutting through the noise, offering a clear perspective Lorna desperately needed. "This is your journey, Lorna," Jamie had said during one of their long talks. "You can't let anyone steer you off course. This is about what you want, what you're willing to do."

Jill, on the other hand, was all warmth and practicality. "Don't worry about anything, I'm more than happy to make you some meals, to assist in any way I can, we've got it covered," Jill had reassured her. "You focus on taking care of yourself."

These gestures of support and care were an enormous help, each kind word and thoughtful action reminded her she was loved, that she had people in her corner. Jakob and Henry were doing their part too, sending her little messages of encouragement whenever they could. A photo of a meal they'd cooked together, a quick update on their lives, or even just a simple "Thinking of you" text. These moments of connection, however brief, always brought a smile to

Lorna's face, they were a reminder that she was still part of their lives, she hadn't lost them entirely to the past.

But then there was Byron, her brother, his well wishes had been brief, almost dismissive. "I wish you all the best, Lorna," he had said, "But I just don't get why you'd risk your own life for someone who wouldn't do the same for you." Byron's practical, no-nonsense approach was typical, but it left her with a nagging doubt. Was she being foolish? Was she risking too much for a sister who had been so distant, so unkind?

And her mother, with her gentle but firm wisdom. "I only want what's best for all my children," she had said, her eyes filled with the quiet concern only a mother could have. "This is your choice, Lorna. You have to live with whatever you decide. Just keep me in the loop, okay?"

Her mother's words echoed in Lorna's mind, a mixture of love and caution that left her feeling both supported and burdened. It was a reminder that her decision affected everyone around her, everyone she loved.

Despite the doubts, the questions, and the uncertainty, Lorna couldn't ignore the feeling that maybe, just maybe, Cara did appreciate her help. Jakob had hinted as much, suggesting Cara's silence might be rooted in worry, not indifference. Perhaps her sister was afraid reaching out might be seen as coercion, that any contact could be misinterpreted as pressure for Lorna to donate the kidney she so desperately needed.

What kept Lorna going was the thought of giving her sister a gift that couldn't be measured by any price, a gift offered without the expectation of anything in return. It was an act of pure altruism, a good deed done simply because it was the right thing to do. She often found herself daydreaming about Cara's reaction if the procedure was to occur. Would it bridge the gap that had formed between them over the years? Would it heal the wounds left by misunderstandings? Lorna didn't know the answers, but she clung to the hope that this selfless act would in the very least save Cara's life. Perhaps this would be the turning point, the moment they both needed to rediscover the bond they'd once shared. Each appointment brought her closer to the final decision. The medical professionals were meticulous, leaving no stone unturned to ensure the transplant would be successful and safe for both her and Cara. As exhausting as it was, Lorna appreciated their thoroughness. It reinforced the gravity of her choice, the weight of the commitment she was making.

There were moments of doubt, late at night when the house was quiet, and she was left alone with her thoughts. What if something went wrong? But then, she would think of Jakob and Henry, of the future they deserved with a healthy mother. She thought of Cara's smile, the one she hadn't seen in years but remembered.

Lorna's resolve hardened with each passing day. She knew she couldn't expect anything from Cara, too much time had passed, but this was her chance to do something truly meaningful, to give Cara the greatest gift imaginable. It wasn't about recognition or gratitude; it was about love, pure and simple. The love that had always been there, beneath the surface of their complicated relationship.

Returning home, Lorna was greeted by the comforting smell of a slow-cooked lamb roast. She felt a wave of nostalgia wash over her as she prepared her dinner. She recalled how she'd taught Cara the simple art of slow-cooker lamb. The memory was vivid: one lamb leg stabbed with a sharp knife, slivers of garlic poked inside, a sprig of rosemary placed on top. After eight hours on low, the succulent lamb leg would fall apart, its juices whipped together with a simple roux to make a wonderful rich gravy.

Lorna smiled as she remembered the first time, she showed Cara how to prepare the dish. Cara had been sceptical at first, uncertain about the slow cooker's magic. But as the hours passed and the house filled with the rich, savory aroma, her scepticism turned to excitement.
"See, it's easy," Lorna had said, pulling apart the tender meat with a fork. "Just let it cook slowly, and it does all the work for you."
Cara had laughed, "You make it look so simple," she'd replied, reaching for a piece of the perfectly cooked lamb.
Those cooking lessons had been more than just about food; they were about connection, about sharing a piece of herself with her sister. It was in those moments, standing side by side in the kitchen, that Lorna had felt closest to Cara. Lorna thought about those times, they seemed like a lifetime ago.

As she ate, her mind wandered to the lamb roasts she'd enjoyed with family, with Cara and the boys, with Uncle Bernard. Each memory brought a bittersweet smile to her face. The warmth of those moments, the laughter and love, the sense of belonging. Each memory a reminder of the connections that had once seemed unbreakable.

After dinner, she cleaned up and made her way to bed. As she lay down, the aroma of the roast still lingering in the air, she thought about the shared meals, the conversations, the joy. They were moments that had shaped her. She fell asleep thinking about those moments, each one a reminder of why she was doing this. For family. For love. For the hope of rekindling something despite the erosion caused by time and distance.

Thirty-Eight

2009
Playing For a Car

Lorna watched from the kitchen window as Cara sat opposite Uncle Bernard. The five of them had just finished a nice roast lamb lunch, a meal Cara had organised in honour of their uncle's 80th birthday. Lorna had come down from the country for the weekend because Cara needed to work and wanted to go out with friends on Saturday evening. It was now Sunday, and Lorna would leave later that afternoon to drive home, so she could return to work on Monday morning. The long drive and exhausting weekend were worth it, as Lorna cherished every chance to catch up with her nephews, Jakob and Henry. Saturday mornings were spent with them jumping into her bed, where they enjoyed stories, she created with them as the main characters. During the day they would go to the skate park or to the shops then prepare a nice Saturday dinner. Her weekend trips also helped Cara immensely, as they allowed her to earn weekend penalty rates and have days off during the week to relax.

Their lunchtime conversation on that day had been enjoyable. Jakob and Henry spoke about school, Henry was enthusiastic as ever talking about his insect collection and the vegetable plot his class had created, Jakob eager to explain his latest computer game strategies. As usual, Uncle

Bernard talked about the share market and his surging share prices. Lorna talked about life in the country, how she enjoyed the quietness and the simple things in life. Cara, on the other hand, focused on the struggles of being a single parent and her demanding work life. When Lorna mentioned the possibility of replacing her twenty-year-old car with a new one, she could see Cara's eyes glint. The sudden shift in her sister's behaviour was obvious. Cara straightened her back, rolled her eyes, then glared in Lorna's direction.

"Lorna, weren't you going to do the dishes since I prepared lunch for everyone?" she asked. "Then you could maybe bring out the cake I made for Uncle Bernard, if it's not too much trouble." Cara smiled and then turned her attention to Uncle Bernard. "I made such a lovely cake for you, Uncle. Your favourite, chocolate ripple. Homemade cakes are so much better than shop-bought ones; I think it's because they're made with love."

Uncle Bernard smiled with delight. "Oh, that's so nice of you, Cara. You're always looking after me. Always spoiling me."

"Well, of course, you are family and, well... Lorna just had to move so far away to the country. I love the closeness we share," she paused and smiled, "I wouldn't have it any other way. Family looks after family."

Cara picked up her plate and passed it across the table to Lorna. "Thanks so much, Lorna. When you finish the dishes, you'll find the candles in the bottom drawer. And maybe you boys could have a quick dip in the pool while Aunt Lorna cleans up."

Jakob and Henry jumped at the chance and dashed off.

From the kitchen window, Lorna's attention briefly turned to the boys playing in the pool. Suddenly, out of the corner of her eye she noticed Cara's head drop forward, her chin striking her chest. Her full attention returned to her sister and uncle. From all accounts it appeared Uncle Bernard had noticed Cara's swift movement too as she straightened in his chair, eyebrows raised. Lorna turned off the kitchen tap and leaned forward, watching intently. Cara began complaining about the age of her car, which wasn't as old as Lorna's and had far fewer kilometres on the odometer. Lorna heard her sister mention to their uncle her need for new tyres and how the car wouldn't pass its roadworthy check with the registration due. Cara included the boys in her discussion, stating how amazing they were and how she feared for their safety due to the tyres. The car also desperately needed a service. With all these expenses combined, she thought it would be better to maybe think about a new car, like her sister. After all, safety features in new cars were far superior to those in her old car.

Lorna couldn't believe what she was hearing. The audacity of her sister! When would her jealousy and scheming end?

"Lorna's so lucky, out in the country with no one else to worry about, living the easy life, all cashed up without a care in the world. She's so lucky," Cara said, her head lowered. "I really don't want to, but what's the alternative?" she continued, looking up from her brow. Uncle Bernard's eyebrows furrowed, and before he had a chance to respond, Cara continued. "I hate feeling like this, I just hate being in this predicament. I like to be independent; to feel I can make it on my own. I hear it all the time, we all hear it… the cost-of-living crisis. People not being able to afford the basics. I never thought I'd find myself in this position." She paused, inhaling a shuttered breath, and looked up from her brow as if to gauge Uncle Bernard's reaction. His face showed increasing concern, and then, sealing her deal, Cara burst into tears. "I'm just so worried, not about me, about the boys, about my family."

Lorna watched on, listening to her sister's manipulative words. In the distance, she could see Jakob and Henry swimming in the pool, under the shade of the pool sails that Uncle Bernard had paid for less than a year ago. Was there no end to her sister's scheming? Why couldn't their uncle see her manipulations? Was he that gullible? Lorna feared if she returned to the conversation with the cake and a side of concerns, she would be guaranteed an argument. Uncle Bernard, with his freshly stroked ego, could view her accusations as an insult to his intelligence. Her father was right; his brother couldn't help himself. Uncle Bernard had always viewed himself as a hero in pants to any damsel in distress. Cara had also remembered her father's description, only she was the one using his weakness for her gain. Or maybe they were using each other, Lorna thought. With her living so far away in the country and Uncle Bernard aging, he would need increasing assistance. He'd always stated he never wanted to go to a nursing home. Was Cara the means to his end? It was sickening. Why couldn't they just be honest with each other?

Lorna sighed, wiping her hands on a dish towel. She knew she had to pick her battles. As much as she wanted to call Cara out on her manipulations, she didn't want to ruin Uncle Bernard's birthday. Instead, she resolved to keep an eye on things and to protect her uncle in any way she could. As she brought out the cake, she plastered a smile on her face, determined to keep the peace for now, even if it meant swallowing her anger.

When Lorna returned to the table with the cake, candles flickering on top, Cara called the boys from the pool. Everyone sang "Happy Birthday" as Uncle Bernard blew out the candles, the boys yelling for him to make a wish. Lorna made her own wish, hoping her sister would stop with her incessant conniving.

With the cake finished, the boys returned to the pool, and Uncle Bernard left for home. Lorna took a deep breath and decided it was time to confront Cara about her underhanded behaviour.

"I heard you, making out to Uncle Bernard that I live an easy life, a life of luxury, free of financial concerns. That's wrong, Cara, and you know it. I have bills to pay, and I need to work just like you. The only difference is, if I want something, I save for it. Nothing has been given to me. I moved to the country so I could afford to buy a cheaper place, to enjoy a better quality of life. You could have done the same. You don't need to live in such a big house. Your house is twice the size of mine, and your mortgage was more than double, but it didn't need to be."

"Uncle Bernard will believe what he wants," Cara replied, ignoring Lorna's comments.

Lorna, annoyed at her sister's manipulating, pressed on. "I'm onto you. I see how you got me to be your puppet with the pool sails. What I said to Uncle Bernard made him concerned for your safety, and that's why he paid for your new sails. You manipulated me, and I fell into your hands because I too care about your safety. I didn't want you to climb the pole to fix the sails alone. I said I would have helped you, but that wasn't good enough. I foolishly went along with you, drawn into your conversation. And he fell for it, hook, line, and sinker. I know he paid for the sails and not for the basic ones, you gave him the quote for the most expensive ones. You didn't even need new sails, you could have waited and saved for them yourself and yet you got him to pay for everything, and you just sat back and took his money."

Cara laughed. "You're just jealous he gave me his money and not you."

"I'm not jealous. What you did was wrong. You had the quotes for the sails. I saw them, and you said you could even afford the better-quality ones if you saved a little longer. Yet, you took the money from Uncle Bernard."

"And... what's your point? He's got plenty of money."

"That's my point. It's his, NOT yours. You used me to get the sails, and now you're trying to get a new car out of him. That's wrong. It doesn't matter how much money he has. You don't use people. You don't lie to them."

Cara chuckled. "I didn't lie. My car is old; it needs new tyres; it needs a service and its due for a registration check soon. And we've all heard about the cost-of-living crisis, so if my uncle feels good because he buys me a new car, then I've done a good thing. I've made him feel happy, and there probably aren't many things that would make an 80-year-old happy. So there. I'd call that a win, win." Cara turned away from Lorna. "Boys, come on over and say goodbye to your aunt. She needs to leave now; she needs to get back to the country."

Turning to Lorna, she added, "Travel safe, sis."

Lorna stood there, speechless, watching as her nephews ran over to hug her goodbye. As she made her way to the car, she couldn't shake the feeling of disappointment and betrayal. She knew she had to find a way to protect Uncle Bernard without falling into Cara's schemes again. It was going to be a long drive back to the country, and she had a lot to think about.

Thirty-Nine

Friday, 28th June, 2024
Doubts Appear

Lorna sat in the waiting room of Dr Angela Brothers's office, her fingers nervously drumming against her knee as she replayed the events of the past few months in her mind, reuniting with Jakob and Henry, the endless tests, needles, scans, and the persistent anxiety that seemed to follow her every move. Today was the day they'd go over all the results. Sue Edwards, her transplant coordinator, sat beside her, offering a comforting presence. Sue had agreed to attend this meeting with Lorna after Lorna had said she felt anxious, and Lorna was grateful for it. Her friends, Jamie and Jill, couldn't make it due to work commitments, so having Sue by her side made the situation feel a little less daunting.

Her phone buzzed in her hand, and she smiled as she saw messages from Jamie and Jill pop up on the screen, filled with encouragement and love. But what truly lifted her spirits was a message from her nephews, Jakob and Henry. Their words were simple but filled with affection, and as she read their text, Lorna felt a twinge of added pressure. She'd promised Jakob and Henry, she would go through with the testing, but the reservations about donating a kidney to Cara hadn't lessened. If anything, they'd only grown stronger.

What happens if I fail the testing? Lorna thought, her mind racing as she waited for her name to be called. Or worse, what if I chicken out? Would Jakob and Henry understand? Would anyone?

Her thoughts interrupted when Dr Brothers appeared at the door. "Lorna, we're ready for you," she said gently, her presence immediately calming Lorna, just as it had during their first meeting. Dr Brothers had a way of making her patients feel seen and heard, and that had resonated with Lorna from the beginning.

With a deep breath, Lorna stood up, slipping her phone into her bag. Sue gave her a reassuring nod, and together they followed Dr Brothers into her office.

The room was as welcoming as the waiting area, filled with natural light and soft, neutral tones that created an atmosphere of calm.

"Please, take a seat," Dr Brothers said, gesturing to the chairs in front of her desk. Lorna and Sue sat down, and Dr Brothers took her place behind the desk, flipping open Lorna's file. "Okay let me have a look at your results."

Lorna nodded, trying to focus on the doctor's words, though her mind kept drifting to the what-ifs. What if something was wrong? What if she couldn't be the donor? What if all this was for nothing?

Dr Brothers adjusted her glasses and glanced down at the papers in front of her. "We've got quite a bit to go through. How have you been feeling since the last time we spoke?"

"Nervous," Lorna admitted. "I just… I don't want to mess this up."

Dr Brothers nodded. "That's perfectly normal. This is a big decision, and it's natural to have reservations. Let's start by going over your test results."

Angela flipped through Lorna's file, nodding as she reviewed the results. "I've got all your test results here. You've been through quite a few, haven't you?"

Lorna forced a small smile. "Yes, it's been... a lot."

"I know it can be overwhelming," Angela said, her tone reassuring. "But you've done really well so far. Let's go through everything."

Lorna listened as Dr Brothers methodically went through the results. The blood and urine tests were normal, the DTPA/GFR tests showed good kidney function, and the oral glucose test was within acceptable ranges. The echocardiogram and electrocardiogram didn't raise any red flags either. Each piece of good news was a small relief, but Lorna's anxiety lingered.

"Your recent cervical screening was all clear," Angela continued, flipping to the next page in the file. "That's great news."

Lorna nodded, but her mind was fixated on one specific concern. "Dr Brothers," she began hesitantly, "I noticed during some of the tests, my blood pressure seemed high. I'm worried... what if I fail the blood pressure test? What if it means I can't donate?"

Angela looked up from the file, her expression softening. "I did see your blood pressure was elevated during a few of the tests. That's why we're going to have you wear a 24-hour blood pressure monitor, just to make sure we're thorough."

Lorna's stomach knotted. "But what if... what if I fail that test? Will everything I've done so far have been for nothing?"

Sue, her transplant coordinator who'd been sitting quietly in the corner, spoke up. "Lorna, it's normal for blood pressure to spike when you're under stress, and discussing a procedure like this can definitely cause that. We want to make sure we're getting accurate readings, so the 24-hour monitor will give us a better picture of what your blood pressure is really like in your everyday life."

Lorna's mind raced. "But if the monitor shows my

blood pressure is high... does that mean I can't donate?"

"We don't want to jump to conclusions just yet," Angela said, her voice calm and measured. "If your blood pressure is consistently high, we'll look into managing it, but it doesn't automatically disqualify you from donating. It's just something we need to keep an eye on. And remember, we're being thorough to make sure it's safe for you."

Lorna took a deep breath, trying to absorb the information. *It's just precautionary*, she told herself, but the fear of failing this last hurdle was very real.

"The good news," Angela continued, "is that all your other screenings, your bowel cancer test, and mammogram, have come back clear. However, because you're over 50, we want to be extra cautious and rule out any potential heart issues. That's why we're going to schedule a stress test at a cardiologist's office. It's an exercise test where you'll walk on a treadmill while your heart is monitored."

Lorna's heart sank further. "And... what happens if I don't pass that test?"

Angela leaned forward. "Lorna, we're not here to put you through unnecessary tests. We're here to make sure if you do decide to donate, you're doing it safely. If the stress test reveals something concerning, we'll discuss our options. But try not to worry about that right now."

Try not to worry, Lorna thought, the words echoing in her mind. How could she not worry? Every test felt like a step closer to a decision she wasn't sure she could make.

"Your next step," Sue interjected, her voice steady and reassuring, "is your appointment next Wednesday with your Transplant Urologist. They'll explain everything about the actual day of the transplant, what to expect, which kidney will be removed, and how the procedure will be done. That appointment is scheduled for later in the afternoon, here at Sydney Hospital. And since you'll already be here, I've contacted Cardiology, and they've managed to secure you an appointment that morning for your stress test."

Lorna nodded slowly, trying to absorb the information. The transplant, the tests, the endless waiting, it was all starting to feel overwhelming.

"And in regards to the 24-hour blood pressure monitor," Sue continued, "we've arranged that with your local pathology. They have a monitor available, and you're scheduled to wear it from Friday morning to Saturday morning next week."

Lorna nodded again, her mind racing with what felt like a thousand different thoughts. "So, I can have that test done locally?"

Sue gave her an encouraging smile. "Yes, you won't need to travel for that one. It'll be more convenient for you."

Lorna appreciated Sue's attempt to ease her burden, she looked at Sue, her voice quiet. "I just… I don't want to let anyone down. What if… what if I'm not strong enough for this?"

Sue reached out, gently placing a hand on Lorna's arm. "Lorna, you've already shown so much strength by coming this far. It's normal to feel overwhelmed, but you don't have to do this alone. We're all here to support you."

Lorna tried to hold on to Sue's words, but the doubts continued to swirl in her mind. "Thank you, Sue," Lorna said softly, hoping her gratitude would mask the anxiety she couldn't quite shake. "I'll take it one step at a time."

"That's all you can do," Sue replied, giving her arm a reassuring squeeze. "And remember, you're not alone in this."

Angela closed the file and gave Lorna a reassuring smile. "You're doing great, Lorna. I know this is a lot to process, but remember we're here to support you, whatever you decide."

Lorna forced another smile, but inside, she was anything but calm. The thought of wearing the monitor, of potentially failing the tests, made her feel sick with anxiety. *What if I go through all of this and find out I can't donate? Or worse, what if I get to the end and realise, I just can't do it? What will Jakob and Henry think of me then?*

She thanked Dr Brothers and Sue, her mind a whirlwind of doubts and fears. After the appointment, as she and Sue left the office, Lorna couldn't shake the feeling of uncertainty that clung to her. The sun was setting, casting long shadows across the pavement as they walked to the car. Sue gave her a reassuring smile as they parted ways, but Lorna's mind was already racing ahead to the blood pressure monitor, to the stress test, to all the possibilities that could go wrong.

As she drove home, Lorna replayed the conversation in her head, the words of encouragement from Dr Brothers and Sue mingling with her own fears. She'd come so far, would it all be worth it? Had she set herself up for failure? And if she did fail, would Jakob and Henry understand? Would they forgive her? She'd promised Jakob and Henry she would do this, that she would try to save their mother's life. But the closer she got to the final decision, the more uncertain she became. She tried to push the thoughts away, focusing instead on the steps ahead. The blood pressure monitor, the stress test, it was all part of the process, part of making sure she was ready. But deep down, the worry remained constant.

When Lorna finally pulled into her driveway, she sat in the car for a moment, gathering her thoughts. She'd promised herself she would do everything she could to help her sister, to be there for her nephews. But now, as the reality of the situation settled in, she couldn't help but wonder if she was in over her head. Taking a deep breath, Lorna stepped out of the car and walked inside, trying to shake off the lingering doubts. Tomorrow was another day, another chance to face her fears. She would take it one step at a time, just as Dr Brothers had said. For now, that was all she could do.

Forty

2010
Escalation

Lorna watched through the kitchen window as Jakob and Henry raced their remote-control cars across the backyard, their laughter echoing into the house. It was the perfect distraction, the perfect opportunity to finally bring up the topic that had been gnawing at her for weeks. She took a deep breath, trying to steady herself. This conversation had to happen, and it had to happen now. She turned to Cara, who was casually flipping through a magazine at the kitchen table. "Cara," Lorna began cautiously, "have you spoken with Dad about his house?"

Cara didn't look up. "What about it?"

"He needs to sell it. He's in the nursing home, paying more money than he should because he hasn't paid the bond and without the sale of his house, he hasn't got the money to cover the bond. He needs to sell it, Cara."

"Well, he can't. I won't let him."

Lorna felt a familiar frustration rise, she'd known this would be difficult, Cara's stubbornness was like a wall, but she kept her tone calm. "Come on, Cara, I'm asking you… please, just let Dad sell the house. This has gone on for far too long. He repaid you all the board you paid him. We even agreed you could get more money; we signed the agreement you had drawn up. What more do you want? Can't you see what it's doing to him? For God's sake, I didn't get all the board I paid returned to me when I moved out. That was a living expense, and the same goes for you. Dad was more than generous helping you out so you could get a house, just like Byron and I did."

Cara closed the magazine with a sharp snap and finally looked at Lorna. "Not my problem. The house is worth more now."

Lorna's heart sank. She'd expected resistance, but not this level of callousness. "But it's not your house, Cara. You have your own home."

"Dad agreed to put me on the title," Cara replied, her voice calm. "And with my name on the title... it is my house."

Lorna stared at her sister, disbelief mingling with anger. "That was his mistake," Lorna replied. "He trusted you, but you know it's only in writing. You never paid a cent for that house. You're screwing him over, ripping him off."

Cara's eyes narrowed. "Like I said, my name is on the title. It's nothing to do with you. It's between me and Dad. Mind your own business."

"This is my business!" Lorna's voice trembled with frustration. "He's my father, and you're my sister. There has to be a way to work this out. This arguing isn't good for anyone. I'll talk with Dad, if you want? I'll be the go-between. Don't you want to work things out?"

Cara shook her head, her posture stiffening with defiance. Lorna could see the stubbornness in her sister's eyes, the same defiance she'd seen a hundred times before, only now she seemed more hostile and much colder.

"Come on!" Lorna's voice cracked with desperation. "You helped him, just like I helped you. That's what family does. Don't you remember when you were having custody issues with Jakob?"

"What's your point?" Cara's voice turned icy.

Lorna's heart pounded in her chest as she tried to rein

in her emotions. "I'm just saying that's what family should do, they help each other. Like I helped you when you had custody issues with Jakob. Remember how you couldn't afford a solicitor, so I loaned you the money? I went without so you could keep full custody of Jakob. I let you pay me back when you could. I never asked for anything in return."

"And what's your point?" Cara snapped. "You want me to pay you interest? Is that what this is about? Go ahead, dig up your records. Tell me all the details. I'll pay you your bloody interest."

Lorna shook her head. "I don't want your money, Cara. I don't want any interest. I just want you to understand. I helped you because you're my sister, and you needed help. Just like you helped Dad when he needed it. But now... let him have it, Cara. Let him sell his house. This stress is killing him, it's making him sick. Don't you care? What about your agreement?"

"Oh, that's right. You're the bitch who keeps all the records, aren't you?" Cara snarled, her voice rising. "Well, Lorna, you can go and get fucked. This is none of your business. It's between Dad and me, so why don't you just fuck off?"

Lorna was stunned into silence, she couldn't believe what she was hearing, the venom in Cara's words... Cara could be difficult but this was something else entirely.

How can she be like this? How can Cara be so heartless, so greedy? Why can't she see the damage she's doing to dad?

Lorna had seen it before, Cara's manipulation, her ability to twist situations to her advantage. Uncle Bernard had ended up buying Cara a new car, Cara didn't know Lorna was aware of this detail, but Uncle Bernard had let it slip in one of their phone calls. Prior to the car it had been the new pool sails after Lorna, in her concern, had inadvertently convinced him Cara needed help.

Lorna remembered how Cara had twisted the truth to make herself appear the struggling single mother in need, at one stage telling Uncle Bernard that Lorna was "loaded with money." Lorna had confronted her sister about it, trying to explain she worked hard, saved where she could, and followed their mother's advice: The harder you work, the luckier you become. But Cara didn't care about any of that.

The whole situation left Lorna feeling sick to her stomach, how Cara projected an image of a struggling single mother to garner sympathy, yet in truth it had been less than a year ago when Cara had proudly announced her promotion, practically glowing as she boasted about her new six-figure salary. Lorna had been happy for her at the time, genuinely pleased her sister was doing well. Lorna remembered the conversation vividly. Cara had asked her about her own income, and when Lorna told her it was significantly less than what Cara earned, her sister had thrown her head back and laughed. "I wouldn't get out of bed for the money you're making," Cara said, her voice condescending.

The words had stung. Lorna had calmly explained it wasn't just about the money for her, she valued a balance between work and home life. Lorna wanted to enjoy the simple things, things that didn't require a hefty pay packet or a luxurious lifestyle. She cherished picnics with friends, having people over for barbecues, sitting in the sun with a great book, or watching a movie. These moments brought her true happiness. But Cara seemed determined to live in a world where worth was measured in dollars and cents.

"Did you hear me?" Cara snapped.

Lorna jumped and stared towards her sister, ready for

her next tirade.

Cara leaned towards Lorna, pointing her finger. "Let me tell you nice and slow so you understand, so you get it through your thick head." Cara paused, her eyes narrowing. "I'm not interested in what you have to say, Lorna. I'll do what I want, and no one will stop me. If you get in my way, I'll knock you to the fucken ground."

Lorna blinked, stunned by the threat. There was no reasoning. She couldn't believe what she was hearing. Her own sister, the person she'd once trusted and loved so deeply, was now acting like a stranger, cold, calculating, and heartless. The boys were still outside, but Lorna knew she had to stop. They didn't need to hear this, didn't need to see their mother like this. Lorna forced a smile, dropping the subject and walked outside to join Jakob and Henry.

The rest of the evening was unbearably tense. Lorna felt like an unwelcome guest in her sister's home, sensing Cara's simmering anger. They ate dinner in near silence, the only conversation coming from the boys, who were excited to watch a movie after the meal. Lorna tried to focus on the movie, but her mind was elsewhere, replaying the conversation with Cara over and over.

When the movie ended, Lorna excused herself early, claiming tiredness. She retreated to the guest room, relieved to be alone, away from Cara. She lay awake for hours, replaying the conversation in her head, wondering how things had come to this. Lorna's heart sank as she realised her sister would stop at nothing to get what she wanted.

The next morning, Lorna was up early, eager to leave. She'd prearranged her departure, telling Cara she had things to do before work on Monday. After a quick story time with the boys, who'd already picked out their book, and a light breakfast of toast, Lorna said her goodbyes and left.

As she drove home, Lorna fumed, her hands gripping the steering wheel tightly. The anger she felt for Cara was overwhelming, but so too was the sadness. How had her sister become so twisted, so selfish? Or maybe Cara had always been like this, and Lorna had just refused to see it. The memories of an old conversation surfaced, it was a conversation they'd had years ago, during one of their rare moments of closeness.

They'd been celebrating their birthday together, a few drinks in, when Cara had said something that had stuck with Lorna ever since. "People are like prawns," Cara had said, her voice casual as she sipped her drink.

Lorna had laughed, thinking it was a slip of the tongue. "Don't you mean pawns?"

But Cara's expression turned serious as she looked at Lorna over the rim of her glass. "No. Prawns. They're the cockroaches of the sea. Tasty in small doses, but they have a shelf life. When they get old or start to stink, you discard them. People are no different. You use what you can, and when they're no longer useful, you move on."

At the time, Lorna had been disturbed by the comment but hadn't realised just how deeply it reflected Cara's worldview. Now, it made perfect sense. Cara saw people as disposable, tools to be used and discarded as she saw fit.

For Cara, lying was as natural as breathing. She wove her deceptions effortlessly, convincing others of her sincerity while hiding her true motives. Most people never saw her for who she really was, instead, they were seduced by her charm, her apparent trustworthiness, her ability to make them feel special, to draw them in with her warmth and engaging ways. First, there was a lie to gain acceptance. Then, flattery to stroke egos and gain followers. Sympathy to gather supporters, and finally, stories spun to grant her hero status. Ultimately, underneath that façade was a cunning woman and what Cara wanted, Cara generally got.

As Lorna drove, the memories and realisations tumbled through her mind. Cara was like an artist, crafting her lies into a perfect patchwork quilt, colourful pieces of imagination, delusion, and deceit stitched together to form the perfect picture. And once the picture was complete, it was almost impossible to tell where the truth ended and the lies began. *Did Cara even know the truth anymore?* Lorna wondered. Or had she lost herself in the stories she told?

When Lorna arrived home, she tried to call Cara, desperate for one last chance to reason with her. The phone rang twice before Cara picked up.

"Don't call me again," Cara warned. "If you do, I'll call the police and have you charged with harassment."

Before Lorna could respond, Cara hung up, leaving her staring at the phone in disbelief.

Lorna sat in stunned silence, she felt an overwhelming sense of loss, not just for the relationship she once had with Cara, but for the family they'd once been. Her sister, her own flesh and blood, the person she'd once been so close to was now a stranger, she'd turned into someone she barely recognised.

Cara was out of control. Where would it all end?

Forty-One

Saturday, 29th June, 2024
Surprise

Lorna strolled around the edge of the dam; her breath visible in the chilly morning air. The countryside was quiet, peaceful, the kind of stillness she'd hoped for before the world woke up. It wasn't even 6 a.m. Lorna loved this time, the moment before everything stirred to life, the trees, the birds, the frost-covered ground, which crunched softly under her boots. The edge of the dam had iced over, and the air was sharp, nipping at her cheeks and nose. She rubbed her hands together and cupped them to her mouth, trying to warm them.

Her thoughts, however, were anything but peaceful. They wandered to Cara. How was she holding up? Lorna couldn't help but wonder. Was she feeling the weight of the assessment, the stress of waiting to see if she was suitable for the transplant? Was she scared? Stressed? Cara hadn't reached out. Not a word, not since her phone call when she'd discovered Jakob had made contact.

Then she thought of Jakob and Henry. It had been two months since she'd last seen her nephews, but those two months felt like a lifetime. Before that, it had been over a decade since their last meeting… so much time lost, so many missed opportunities.

During those years, she'd grown used to their absence. Of course, she missed them, but she'd learned to focus on other things, pushing aside the emptiness they left behind. Now they were back in her life, the longing to be part of their world had returned, more intense than before. Their absence filling her with a sadness she hadn't allowed herself to feel in a long time.

They'd grown from boys into young men, and it pained her to realise Cara had robbed them all of the loving bond they'd once shared.

The silence stung more than Lorna liked to admit.

A sigh escaped her, a slow exhale of the tension that had built up over the past few weeks. Did Cara even wonder how she was doing? Lorna doubted it. She shook her head, turning her gaze to the thin layer of frost that covered the landscape. The forecast had predicted snow next week, and she hoped it would hold off until after her trip to Sydney, for appointments she couldn't miss.

Today, though, she had the day to herself. A day to do something normal, to forget about hospitals and assessments, even if just for a little while. She would head into town, buy some fresh fruit and vegetables, pick up the newspaper, and maybe treat herself to a cappuccino. Simple things. Distractions. A quiet day, a day to read, to breathe.

Inside, she grabbed her keys, slipped them into her coat pocket, and headed off. The small joys of a simple routine calmed her, grounding her in something familiar. She needed that right now.

In town, the fruit shop was just as it always was: neat rows of vibrant produce, the scent of fresh apples and oranges filling the air. As she picked through a pile of avocados, she heard a familiar voice behind her.

UNDER THE COVER OF CLOSENESS

"Lorna? Is that you?"

She turned to see an old friend; someone she hadn't seen in months. They exchanged warm smiles and fell into easy conversation, catching up on the little things, life, the weather, plans for the week. Lorna smiled and nodded. But then came the inevitable question.

"So, what's been happening with you?"

Lorna hesitated. She thought about mentioning the tests, the potential surgery, but she held back. How could she explain something so personal? The tests, the possibility of donating a kidney... people would only ask why. They always did. Why would she even consider doing such a thing? And it wasn't like she had all the answers, she wasn't even sure she'd fully convinced herself.

"I'm just keeping busy," she finally said. "You know how it is."

Her friend nodded, thankfully moving on to another topic, but Lorna's mind lingered. The truth was, she still had doubts.

They parted ways at the checkout, and Lorna loaded her bags into the car, her thoughts heavy once again.

Could she really go through with it? She still wasn't sure. But the clock was ticking. The final decision would have to be made soon. For now, though, she would try to enjoy her quiet day, take comfort in the simple pleasures, and push the questions to the back of her mind. At least for a little while.

As she drove into her driveway, her heart skipped a beat. Parked there was an old red Ford, unfamiliar and battered, with faded paintwork and a front passenger side that looked like it had lost a battle with a kangaroo. She remained in her car, cautiously scanning her surroundings. *Where's the owner? Why is this car in my driveway?*

Gathering courage, she stepped out and approached her

front door, nerves tingling as she unlocked it and slipped inside. She placed her bags just inside the entrance, then turned to survey her home. Silence. Instinctively, she locked the door behind her and slowly made her way around the outside of the house, her eyes darting towards the old shed she used for storage. Still, there was no sign of anyone.

Lorna's gaze returned to the mysterious car. The closer she got; the more questions whirled in her mind. Who'd brought it here, and why?

Returning inside, she moved through the house, her thoughts spinning in a thousand directions. She busied herself, taking her bags to the kitchen where she unpacked her groceries, she kept glancing out the window, her pulse racing each time she thought she saw movement out of the corner of her eye.

A sudden noise. A knock at the front door made her jump. Her heart pounded as she hesitated, trying to gather herself.

"Who's there?" she called.

"It's me. I wanted to see you."

Lorna's breath caught in her throat. She recognised the voice. Flinging the door open, she was greeted by a familiar face, one she hadn't seen in what felt like a lifetime.

"Oh my gosh, Henry... you scared me. I saw a strange car in the driveway but I never would've guessed it was yours."

Henry smiled. "It's not mine. I borrowed it. I think we need to talk. Can I come in?"

"Yes, of course, of course, come in." Lorna stepped aside, her mind racing with a thousand possibilities. "I just got home, let me put the kettle on. Would you like a cup of tea?"

"Sure," he replied.

UNDER THE COVER OF CLOSENESS

As she made her way back to the kitchen, Lorna couldn't help but wonder what had brought Henry here, unannounced and looking so solemn. Had something happened? Was everything okay? Her mind raced as she prepared the tea.

When she entered the lounge room, Henry was sitting on the edge of the lounge, his posture tense. He looked up at her, his eyes searching her face as if trying to find the right words.

"I'm sorry for showing up like this," he began, his voice hesitant. "I probably should've called first."

"No, no, it's okay," Lorna reassured him, handing him a cup of tea. "Is everything alright?"

Henry took a deep breath. "Yes... and no," he finally said. "I've just been thinking a lot since we last talked. I was so young back then, before..."

Lorna leaned in closer, her voice soft. "A lot has happened, Henry. Unfortunately, we can't change the past, as much as we might want to. Once time has passed, it's gone. But we can shape the present, and the future... that's something we can influence."

Henry looked at her, tears welling in his eyes. "I remembered something... after our last conversation."

Lorna studied her nephew, her heart aching at the change in him. Henry's hands were so much bigger and stronger in comparison to those she remembered, the little delicate ones she'd hold as they crossed the street. His voice was deeper now, the innocence she remembered replaced by a maturity. The sweet, squeaky excitement of his childhood was gone, replaced by a seriousness. She wished she could wrap him in her arms, take away his pain, and reassure him the future still held brightness and hope.

"We were happy," Henry said, interrupting her thoughts.

Lorna felt her throat tighten, emotion threatening to overwhelm her. "Yes, we were happy," she nodded.

"You used to tell us stories," Henry continued, his eyes distant as if he was looking back into another time. "We were the characters in those adventures."

Lorna chuckled softly, memories flooding back. "Yes, you were. You and Jakob would always decide how the adventures would start, and I'd weave the stories around your ideas. We were very happy, Henry... extremely happy."

Suddenly, Henry jumped to his feet, startling Lorna. "Wait here. I have something for you... I'll be right back."

Lorna watched, confused, as Henry hurried out of the room. She sat there, trying to make sense of what was happening. They'd lost so much time, years that could never be recovered. Maybe, just maybe, they could find their way back to each other.

A noise at the front door signalled Henry's return. He entered the room with a mysterious smile on his face. "Close your eyes," he said, a hint of excitement in his voice. "You have to close your eyes and hold out your hands."

Lorna hesitated, feeling a mix of curiosity and nervousness, but she complied. "Okay... my eyes are closed."

"Keep them closed," Henry insisted as he placed something in her hands.

Lorna's fingers brushed against the object, sensing the soft, smooth texture beneath her touch. *It feels like plastic*, she thought, as her hands traced the contours. The largest portion was round, almost like a small ball, but two jagged protrusions stood out at the top. Below the rounded part, she found a firmer section, with small extensions jutting out to each side. Further down, her fingers encountered two smaller pieces with flat, wider surfaces, possibly legs.

UNDER THE COVER OF CLOSENESS

What on earth has legs and spiky horn-like things on its head? She moved her hands over the object, trying to make sense of its shape. It was about the size of her palm, with a flexible part that seemed like it could be the back, and at the end of the bend, she felt another jagged form. Henry's laughter filled the room, light and carefree in a way that Lorna hadn't heard in years. "You should know what this is," he teased, clearly enjoying her confusion.

Lorna's mind raced, but she couldn't quite figure it out. "I have no idea," she admitted.

"Okay," Henry said, still chuckling, "open your eyes."

Lorna slowly opened her eyes and looked down at the object in her hands. The moment recognition hit her, she gasped, tears springing to her eyes. It was a figurine of Red, the character from Fraggle Rock, a nickname the boys had affectionately given her years ago.

"Oh, Henry," she whispered, her voice breaking as tears streamed down her face. "You remembered."

Henry nodded, his own eyes glistening with emotion. "How could I forget? You were always Red... and I was Wembley. Jakob was Gobo. Those were some of the best times of my life."

Lorna clutched the figurine to her chest, overwhelmed by the flood of memories and the realisation Henry had held on to those moments just as tightly as she had. Despite all the years that had passed, the connection between them was still there, still strong.

She reached out and pulled Henry into a hug, the kind of hug that spoke of love, loss, and the possibility of healing. "We were happy," she repeated. "And we can be happy again. We have the future ahead of us, Henry. We can make new memories."

As Lorna and Henry sat together, the small figurine of Red Fraggle between them, Henry shifted and reached behind his back. "I've got something else," he said with a teasing smile, "something I thought we could enjoy together."

Lorna blinked, overwhelmed by his gesture, still not fully believing her nephew was really here, sharing this moment with her. His presence felt surreal after so much time apart. His thoughtfulness in bringing the figurine, the memories they shared, it was almost too much to take in.

"Really?" she asked, her voice soft with disbelief.

"Close your eyes," Henry instructed. "And hold out your hand."

With a smile, Lorna obeyed. She heard the rustle of plastic and felt something light placed in her palm. When she opened her eyes, she burst into laughter, tears welling up again. "Oh, Henry! Where did you find this?"

"It took some searching," he admitted. "But I thought... I haven't seen it in years, and I figured you might remember."

"Oh, I remember it all right," Lorna said. "I'd love to watch it with you, if you've got time?"

Henry glanced at the DVD case in her hand. "Now? Do you have popcorn?" He chuckled.

Lorna stood up quickly. "Actually, I think I do! You sit tight, and I'll go make some."

She dashed into the kitchen; her heart lighter than it had been in months. It wasn't just the nostalgia of their shared past; it was the simple joy of having Henry there with her, like nothing had changed between them.

Moments later, she returned with a large bowl of popcorn. Henry had the DVD already loaded, the TV screen glowing with the familiar intro to *Fraggle Rock*.

As Lorna sat beside her nephew, the scent of buttery popcorn filled the room. She couldn't help but smile as Henry picked up the remote and pressed play. "Do you remember the opening theme song?" he asked.

UNDER THE COVER OF CLOSENESS

"I certainly do," Lorna replied.

The familiar tune burst from the speakers, and the two began singing along, just like they had when Henry was a little boy. Tears welled in Lorna's eyes as she sang. The song, so full of joy and hope, transported her back to simpler times. She felt overwhelmed by the tenderness of the moment, by Henry's thoughtfulness. She'd missed this, missed him.

When the movie ended, Henry leaned forward, a bit of hesitation in his voice. "I should probably head out soon. I've got a long drive ahead of me and I have to return my friend's car. I don't want Jakob or Mum to find out I've been here."

Lorna nodded. "You've driven so far. I can't tell you how much I appreciate you driving all this way. Are you sure you wouldn't want to stay?"

Henry's expression softened. "I'd love to, but I have to get back. I just wanted to make sure you were okay. I wanted you to know I haven't forgotten you, Aunt Lorna."

Lorna's throat tightened. She didn't realise how much she needed to hear that. "I've missed you, Henry. I'm so glad you came by."

Before he could respond, she added, "I'm heading back to Sydney next Wednesday. I've got a cardiologist appointment in the morning, a stress test to make sure my heart is strong enough for the donation. Then I've got an appointment with my urologist... and if that's not enough, I have to go to an educational seminar at the hospital afterwards."

Henry's face turned serious. "A seminar?"

Lorna nodded. "Yes, it's about the transplant process. Sue, my transplant coordinator, said they'll have doctors, specialists, even people who've gone through it sharing their stories. I'm nervous, to be honest. My friends Jamie and Jill can't come with me, they can't get the day off work."

Henry's brow furrowed. "I'll go with you. If you want."

"You'd do that?"

"Of course," Henry said. "But there's one condition."

"A condition?"

Henry shifted; his expression more serious now. "You've got to promise not to tell Jakob or Mum."

"Why? Why can't Jakob know?"

"If Jakob finds out, he might let it slip," Henry said, leaning back in his chair. "And if my mum hears I went to a transplant seminar with you, she's going to get angry."

Lorna's heart ached. She couldn't understand why her sister, her own twin, would feel such resentment and expect her children to share in it.

"I don't want to cause any issues," she said.

"I don't want to cause any issues, either," Henry replied, his voice softer now. "But I also don't want you going to the seminar alone. Especially since..." He hesitated, glancing down at his hands. "Since you're doing all this for Mum, and to be honest, sometimes I think she's been a bit ungrateful. Rude, even."

Lorna wasn't sure what to say. Henry rarely spoke this openly about his mother. She reached out, placing a hand gently on his arm. "Henry..."

He shook his head, cutting her off. "I know I live under her roof, and I have to follow her rules, but sometimes... it feels like we're just different, you know? Different principles. Different values."

Lorna understood all too well the complicated family dynamics that simmered just below the surface, but hearing Henry express his frustrations so clearly made her realise how much weight he was carrying, too.

"I promise I won't tell Jakob or your mother."

Henry gave her a relieved smile. "Good. Then it's settled. We'll go together, and you won't have to worry about anything else."

UNDER THE COVER OF CLOSENESS

Lorna gave him the details of the seminar, and after a lingering goodbye, Henry left to return his friend's car. As Lorna closed the door behind him, she felt a renewed sense of hope.

Forty-Two

2010
A Public Rant

Lorna sat in her car, staring at the familiar highway that stretched endlessly between her rural home and Sydney. Living in the country had its advantages, quiet mornings, open spaces, and a break from family drama, but today, the distance felt more like a burden than a blessing. She sighed, remembering the countless trips she'd made back and forth, the drive used to be manageable, but ever since her father's health had started to decline, the kilometres had piled on, and so had the emotional weight.

Today, she was headed back to Sydney to visit friends and family, but the last few past months had drained her. She'd spent countless hours with her brother Byron, clearing out their father's house in preparation for a garage sale. The property was going to be sold, as her father, Gerald, needed the money to pay for his nursing home bond.

As she drove, she thought of her father, now settled in the nursing home, he'd made the move because he didn't want to burden his children, feeling more secure with the nursing staff to assist him. It broke Lorna's heart, but she understood. What she couldn't understand was Cara's refusal to help their father.

Gerald had talked about selling the house, his frustration

clear. "I don't want to fight her, Lorna," he'd said during one of their last conversations. "But Cara still refuses to help. She won't even talk to me about it, just demands half of the sale price. She says the house has gone up in value, so she's entitled to more. And she doesn't care that I gave her over $30,000 when she moved out in 1996, she doesn't care we all agreed and settled things with a signed agreement." His voice broke slightly. "That was money from her board and living expenses, in essence she lived with me for free. She's a…"

"Dad," Lorna had said cutting him off. "Try not to upset yourself, it only makes you sick. You never know, she could still change her mind." Lorna had tried to console him, but deep down, she shared his frustration. Cara's selfishness seemed to know no bounds. How could she demand more when Gerald's health was failing and all he wanted was peace?

Byron and Lorna had already spent hours clearing out rooms, sorting through old belongings, deciding what was worth selling and what would be tossed. Every corner of the house was a memory, and every memory seemed to carry the weight of the family's dysfunction. Their father, though frail, insisted on being part of it. He moved slowly, pointing out things he wanted to keep or let go. Lorna could see the exhaustion in his eyes, but he was determined to help.

"Are you sure you're okay, Dad?" she had asked.

Gerald had waved her off with a shaky hand. "I'll be fine. It's just... hard seeing it all go."

Lorna nodded, understanding all too well. This was more than just preparation for a garage sale, it was the dismantling of his family home, piece by piece. And yet, Cara was nowhere to be found.

Their father had told Cara about the garage sale, he'd mentioned she still had an old wardrobe in the house and some clothes, but Cara hadn't been interested in any of it, she'd said she didn't care, it was probably just junk.

Now, standing in her father's house, Lorna thought about Cara's distance. It was infuriating. Cara's refusal to even show up, her dismissal of their father's efforts, it all grated on Lorna's nerves. She'd always been the one to defend her sister growing up, always standing by her side, but as an adult, Lorna had witnessed how manipulative and selfish Cara had become. Yet no one seemed to believe her. People still lumped them together, as if they were the same. *Why can't they see the truth?*

"Is everything okay?" Byron's voice snapped her out of her thoughts.

"Yeah," Lorna said. "Just thinking about how much work we've got ahead of us."

By the end of the weekend Lorna and Byron had spent hours cleaning the house, sorting through decades of belongings. Lorna had decided to take a couple of weeks off work to help finish the task, especially since Cara had made no effort to assist. Cara's silence was loud, and Lorna had no desire to break it. Instead, she'd bought a sleeping bag and would sleep at her father's house on the lounge so she could continue to work late into the night. The garage sale was advertised for the following weekend and within the following week a large for sale sign was placed on the front lawn.

The day of the garage sale arrived, and as had been expected, people showed up early. Byron manned the garage while Lorna kept an eye on things inside the house. Their father, too frail to do much, sat on the lounge, watching as his possessions were sold off bit by bit.

As the morning wore on, a few familiar faces stopped

by. A woman Lorna vaguely recognised approached her, introducing herself as Melissa, one of Cara's coworkers. "I saw the sign out front," she said, glancing around with mild interest. "Didn't know the house was up for sale. I've been watching the values of houses around here; the market's hot right now, you should get a good price."

"I'm not sure, it's Dad's home," Lorna replied, not wanting to get into any details.

Melissa nodded, not really interested in the details and wandered off.

Lorna continued talking to those who wandered through the house, completing sales and rearranging items left to be sold.

Just after lunch her phone rang, Lorna saw Cara's name flash on the screen. Realisation dawned on her, Melissa probably told Cara she was at the garage sale. She hadn't told Cara, but she didn't need permission to help her father clear out his own home.

Lorna walked outside, away from listening ears, and hesitantly answered.

"Who the hell do you think you are?" Cara's voice exploded through the speaker. "Did you think I wouldn't find out?"

Lorna took a deep breath. "Find out what?"

''I know where you are and what you've been saying."

"I know where I am too, Cara, I'm here helping Dad and I haven't been saying anything."

"You're a fuckin' bitch, Lorna! Going there behind my back. I told you, if you're not with me, you're against me!"

Lorna's hand tightened around the phone. "I'm here to help Dad. That's all, I haven't done anything behind your back."

"You're in my house!" Cara shrieked. "I know what you've been saying about me. You're butting into my business, talking about how much I'm getting from my house!"

Lorna's patience snapped. "It's Dad's house, Cara. And I haven't said a word about it. How much dad gets for his house has nothing to do with me. You're being ridiculous."

"Shut your mouth, or I'll shut it for you," Cara snarled. "You have no right to be there."

"I have every right to be here and you need to pull your head in. I don't care what you say, Cara, I'm here helping Dad which is more than I can say about you." Lorna had had enough. "It's Dad's house" she repeated, "and I didn't say anything about it. You need to get your facts right."

But Cara didn't let up, as her tirade intensified her anger changed to hatred. Her insults grew louder, more vicious, and Lorna could hardly bear to listen anymore. Enough was enough. After enduring a lifetime of abuse, Lorna realised it was time to stand up for herself. She didn't deserve her sister's relentless attacks, and she wasn't going to let Cara control the situation any longer.

No more allowing Cara to manipulate her with threats and demands. Lorna had decided: from now on, she would challenge her sister's opinions, call out her flaws, and stand firm when she disagreed. It was time to take back her power.

She pulled the phone away from her ear, the sound of her sister's screeching voice still audible. Her hands shook as she pressed the speaker button, letting everyone hear what was being said.

Byron, their father, and the few relatives who had gathered for the sale stopped and stared, listening in stunned silence as Cara's tirade continued.

"You fucking bitch!" Cara shrieked. "Get out of my house!"

Lorna stood tall, no longer willing to hide her sister's toxic behaviour. She was done being compared to Cara, done being treated as if they were one and the same. It was time for everyone to see who Cara really was.

UNDER THE COVER OF CLOSENESS

As Cara continued her assault, oblivious to the audience on the other end, Lorna waited for the right moment. When she'd finally heard enough, she brought the phone to her face. "That's enough," she said, her voice steady. "Goodbye, Cara." With a calm tap, she ended the call.

The show was over.

The silence that followed was heavy, but Lorna stood firm, feeling a mixture of relief and sadness. The show was over, and everyone had witnessed the real Cara. Her father shook his head, and Byron looked stunned. The relatives whispered to each other in disbelief. But Lorna? She felt something shift, a renewed sense of clarity, a weight lifted from her shoulders. She was no longer just Cara's twin… she was Lorna, standing on her own.

Forty-Three

Wednesday, 3rd July, 2024
Victory To Beethoven

Lorna sat in the waiting room at Sydney Hospital, glancing at the clock every few minutes. Her appointment with the cardiologist, Dr Beach, was first on the agenda today. The thought made her smile as she glanced at the name on her appointment card.

The nurse called her name, breaking her from her thoughts. Lorna followed her into the exam room, where she was met by Dr Beach himself. A tall man with a friendly smile. "Good morning, Ms Martin. I'm Dr Beach," he said with a handshake.

Lorna couldn't help but chuckle.

Dr Beach raised an eyebrow. "Something funny?"

"Sorry," Lorna smiled, shaking her head. "Just a bit of wishful thinking. Beaches, relaxing… you know."

"Ah, I get that a lot," he replied, with a grin. "Unfortunately, the only relaxing you'll be doing today is after we push your heart to its limit."

Lorna nodded, a wave of unease passing over her.

Dr Beach went over the basics of what the stress test would entail, though Lorna had already prepared by reading up the night before. She'd worn comfortable clothes, skipped her morning coffee, and made sure not to eat anything. As she listened to him explain the treadmill portion of the test, she couldn't help but think about how surreal it all felt. The test itself wasn't particularly scary, she walked everywhere at home, but it was one more step on the road to seeing if she was suitable for kidney donation. That was where her real nerves lay.

"Alright, ready for the treadmill? We're going to get started," Dr Beach said, snapping her back to the present. "Just let me know if anything feels off during the test."

Lorna nodded. "Okay, yep, I'm as ready as I'll ever be."

As the treadmill began to hum and pick up speed, Lorna found her mind drifting. It wasn't just today's appointment that weighed on her; it was everything. Her parents, Cara, and now this transplant process. Could she really do this? The machine beeped and the incline increased, pulling her back to focus.

She worked hard to keep up, her breath steady as her legs moved faster. Dr Beach and a nurse monitored her vitals closely, their eyes darting between her and the machines. Lorna's heart rate climbed, but she felt steady. For now, everything seemed fine.

I can do this. One step at a time.

The test didn't last long, though it felt like an eternity as her body worked harder and harder. Eventually, Dr Beach slowed the machine to a stop and gave her a nod of approval.

"Great job," he said, unhooking the leads from her chest. "Your heart handled that well. We'll monitor you for a few more minutes before you can head out."

Lorna nodded, grateful for the break. As her heart rate gradually returned to normal, she took a deep breath, trying to steady her thoughts. "One hurdle down."

After grabbing a quick lunch at a nearby park, Lorna found herself back at the hospital for a meeting with the transplant urologist to discuss her upcoming surgery.

Ushered into a small, brightly lit office, she was greeted with a warm smile. "Lorna, welcome. I'm Doctor Tony Batley, pleased to meet you. Let's talk about the big day," the doctor said.

They dove into the details of the kidney removal, the surgery, and what she should expect. As Dr Batley explained the procedure, Lorna found herself listening intently, though her mind caught on something small but amusing.

"I have to ask," Lorna said, grinning. "I noticed the incision pattern you mentioned is three dots and a dash. Do you know that's 'victory' in Morse code?"

The urologist raised an eyebrow, and smiled. "Yes, it's quite fitting, don't you think."

Lorna laughed. "I like the idea. It feels symbolic in some way, victory. Over this whole process. It even reminds me of Beethoven's Symphony No. 5. The opening notes: dot-dot-dot-dash. I'll be walking around with a piece of history on me."

Dr Batley chuckled. "Well, I'm glad you're looking at it that way." As the conversation shifted back to medical matters, Lorna took a deep breath. This whole process was terrifying, but moments like these, finding humour, seeing meaning helped her push forward. Dr Batley handed her some pre-admission paperwork, but not before expressing a concern. "One thing we'll need to keep an eye on is your blood pressure. It's a bit higher than we'd like."

Lorna sighed, nodding. "Yeah, I've got a 24-hour monitor coming up. I've got the monitor starting Friday, all the way through Saturday morning."

"Try not to worry. We'll see how it goes," Dr Batley said, encouragingly. "For now, keep doing what you've been doing. Your kidney is in great shape."

His comment brought a small comfort to Lorna as she left the office. *At least my kidney is holding up*, she thought. *One less thing to worry about.*

UNDER THE COVER OF CLOSENESS

Later that afternoon, Lorna met her nephew, Henry, at the hospital for an educational seminar on kidney donation. His presence meant so much, being by her side was a comfort. As they walked towards the seminar room, Henry tapped her shoulder. "You'll be fine."

Lorna gave a half smile. "Thanks, and thank you for being here, I really appreciate it."

"100%. I wouldn't have it any other way. I told Jakob and Mum I'm at a friend's house studying," Henry whispered as they took their seats.

Lorna frowned, she didn't like the fact he felt he needed to lie, but understood the issue it could cause if her sister found where he was, with her.

The seminar was eye-opening. Experts in the field spoke about the medical side of things, but it was the personal stories that really resonated with her. At one point, a mother and daughter shared their transplant experience, bringing tears to Lorna's eyes. Henry, ever the caring nephew, handed her a tissue and squeezed her hand reassuringly. By the end of the seminar, Lorna felt a mixture of exhaustion and renewed determination. The four hours had flown by, and the shared experiences of others gave her a sense of peace she hadn't expected.

As they left the hospital and sat down for dinner, Lorna felt a little lighter. "Sue, my transplant coordinator was right. That seminar... I really needed to hear those stories," she said, glancing at Henry. "It's one thing to hear about the medical part, but those families... they're living proof everything will be okay."

Henry smiled, nodding in agreement. "And you'll be okay too, Aunt Lorna. You've got this."

Lorna smiled back, feeling the weight on her shoulders

lessen, if only a little. *I can do this*, she thought once again.

One step at a time.

Forty-Four

2011 / 2012
Devastation And Accusations

Lorna sat on the edge of her father's bed in the dimly lit nursing home room, the faint scent of antiseptic mingling with the garlic prawns they'd shared for lunch. Her father loved garlic prawns, a small indulgence that brought him a brief period of happiness. Lorna made sure to bring in something special whenever she visited, hoping to create small moments of comfort amid the weight of everything else.

The warmth of the meal had passed, Gerald sat across from her in his worn armchair, his hands trembling as they rested on his lap. His face was drawn, a shadow of the man who once commanded their family with pride. Now, all that was left was the hurt.

"I can't believe it," he whispered, his voice cracked as he spoke. "Your sister... she sickens me. Her greed is worse than I ever imagined." He glanced towards the window; his eyes vacant with disbelief. "I want nothing to do with her. Nothing."

Lorna shifted uncomfortably, wringing her hands together. She'd heard this before, the same searing disappointment, the same broken record of betrayal. She couldn't defend Cara, not after what had happened. But still, it hurt to hear their father speak like this. "Dad, I could try talking to her again," Lorna offered gently, knowing the futility of her words even as she said them. "Maybe now the house is sold, she'll... reconsider. Maybe she'll give you what's rightfully yours."

But even Lorna didn't believe that. Cara wasn't going to change.

The sale of the house had been devastating, its price staggering in the booming market, a small fortune could have secured Gerald's final years. But half of it was gone. Gone to Cara, who hadn't paid a cent into the home but had swooped in like a vulture to claim her share. Hundreds of thousands of dollars, money that should have eased Gerald's burden, was now in Cara's hands, and no amount of reasoning had convinced her to relinquish any of it.

Months had passed since the sale, and Lorna continued to visit her father in the nursing home. But Cara? She was nowhere to be found. Lorna could see it, the devastation in Gerald's eyes, the simmering rage that threatened to consume what little peace he had left.

"You have to try and let it go, Dad. You can't change what's happened. The doctor explained how the stress is only making things worse, holding onto this anger is making you more tense, and that's adding to your physical pain. Please, try to let it go. I don't want this to make you any sicker."

"I can't help it! I can't let it go." Gerald shook his head violently, his voice rising with emotion. "Look what she's done! She doesn't care about me. She took what was rightfully mine, half the sale price, hundreds of thousands. And she paid nothing for that house!"

"I know Dad. We all know. This isn't just about Cara anymore; this is about what it's doing to your health."

"I was going to say your sister is like a hyena," Gerald growled, his voice low and rough, "but that would be too kind. She's more like pond scum, an oxygen thief, a danger to anyone in her path."

Lorna pressed her lips together, torn between her own anger and her deep sorrow. "She's still your daughter. She's still…"

"Not to me," Gerald snapped, his fists clenching. "I want you to promise me something, Lorna. I want you to promise me."

"What, Dad? What do you want me to promise?"

"When I die," Gerald's voice faltered, "I don't want her told. I don't want her at my funeral. She doesn't deserve to mourn me, not after what she's done."

"Dad, I can't promise that. I just… I can't."

"Why not?" His voice grew sharper. "She doesn't care about me."

Lorna looked down, unable to meet his gaze. "She's still your daughter. And my sister. I have to live with my choices, and I can't sit here and lie to you. I can't promise I won't tell her when the time comes. What about Jakob and Henry, they love you and you love them. What would they think to one day find out their grandfather died and no one told them?"

Gerald's face twisted in anguish. "Your brother, Byron, promised me. He'll respect my wishes."

"That's Byron's choice," Lorna said firmly. "I have to live with mine. I don't know what will happen when the time comes, but I won't make a promise I can't keep. Right now, all I can do is be honest."

Gerald stood abruptly, his chair scraping against the floor. "I need some air," he muttered, shuffling towards the door, leaving Lorna alone with her thoughts.

As the months dragged on, Gerald's bitterness only deepened. He raised the topic of Cara again and again, desperate for validation, for someone to understand his betrayal. Lorna was always there, patient but firm, refusing to make promises she couldn't keep. She felt trapped between loyalty to her father and her obligation to her own heart.

Meanwhile, Cara had vanished from their lives. Any attempt to reach out to her had been met with silence or hostility. When Lorna tried to follow up a planned weekend away with Cara and the boys, the trip was suddenly cancelled. Phone calls went unanswered, texts were curt. Cara always claimed she was busy, but Lorna knew the truth. How could Cara face their father and look him in the eyes after what she'd done? The thought made Lorna's stomach turn.

One evening, while relaxing at home and flipping through a magazine, Lorna's phone buzzed with a call from a friend who lived near Cara. The conversation quickly took a turn that left Lorna reeling. Her friend shared some unsettling news: Cara had been driving Jakob and Henry over an hour away to swimming lessons in an affluent suburb. The boys were already confident swimmers, so there was no practical reason for such extravagance. But it wasn't about the lessons. It was Cara's relentless need to associate with wealth and status.

The conversation took a darker turn when her friend, laughing, casually mentioned how Cara had attended the funeral of a wealthy stranger, someone she didn't even know. "She said she signed the attendance book," the friend chuckled, "hoping she might inherit some of his money."

Lorna's stomach turned. How far had her sister fallen? How far would Cara go for money? Swimming lessons in elite suburbs, showing up at a stranger's funeral for a chance at cash... What else would Cara do in her pursuit of wealth?

UNDER THE COVER OF CLOSENESS

An additional blow came weeks later in the form of an unexpected text message from Cara. "You're a fucking termite. You condone abusive partners," Cara wrote. "You let people hit my boys, and you did nothing about it."

Lorna's heart raced at the sickening accusation, which had absolutely no basis in reality. "What are you talking about? I would never let anyone hurt Jakob or Henry," she replied.

But Cara didn't listen, her response was immediate, ignoring Lorna's comments, the accusations flying like arrows. Lorna knew Cara's tactic, deflection, projection, anything to avoid accountability. Lorna didn't bother bringing up the affairs Cara had, the relationships that had crumbled under her lies. That wasn't the issue now. The issue was how far apart they had drifted, how Cara used her children like pawns in a game Lorna was powerless to stop.

Lorna sat there for a long time, staring at her phone. Would she ever see her nephews again? Would this fractured family ever heal?

The era had changed, and so had the people in it. Once as solid as rock, the bonds that held them together were now crumbling beyond repair.

Forty-Five

Friday, 5th July, 2024
The Pressure

Lorna sat in the quiet waiting room of her local pathology clinic, fidgeting with the magazine on her lap. She was there to be fitted with a 24-hour blood pressure monitor, but her mind wasn't on the test. It was stuck on the past, looping through the tangled mess of her relationship with her twin sister, Cara. *Why am I even doing this?*

She glanced towards the door, contemplating whether she should just get up and leave. *Why not?* Cara had walked out of her life without a word, without an explanation. Blood didn't mean much when loyalty and respect were absent. But what did that make Lorna? What was her word worth if she didn't go through with the testing? She'd promised her nephews she would undergo this process. What kind of person would she be if she didn't keep her commitment?

Her phone buzzed in her bag, snapping her out of the haze. It was Jill. Lorna hesitated for a moment, then answered, grateful for the distraction.

"Hey, Jill," she said, leaning back in her chair.

"Lorna, how are you doing? I know today's the big day with that blood pressure monitor. Are you alright?" Jill asked.

Lorna glanced around the quiet waiting room, lowering her voice. "I'm here now. Just waiting for them to call me in. Honestly, I'm not sure how I feel about it."

"What do you mean? Is it the test, or...?"

Lorna sighed, running her fingers through her hair. "It's not the test. It's everything that comes with it. I keep thinking, why am I putting myself through this for someone who's caused so much damage?" She lowered her voice even more, glancing towards the nurses' station. "Maybe they've only been in touch with me because Cara needs something. This whole thing with her boys... I want to believe Henry when he says he wants to rebuild what we lost, but I don't know, Jill. I just don't know."

"Do you seriously think they're only reaching out because of Cara needing a kidney?"

Lorna swallowed hard. "Part of me feels like I'm just another piece in her game. I mean, Jakob told me they can't meet me anymore because Cara's afraid it'll look like they're trying to coerce me into helping her. But was that the real reason? Or was it all just to soften me up, to make me feel obligated to go through with the kidney testing?"

"That's not fair, putting you through this? If it's manipulative... you don't deserve that."

"I know, but... what if Henry's being honest? He seems different, Jill. He says he wants to reconnect, but I don't even know if I can trust my own judgment anymore. Cara's been playing these mind games for so long." Lorna's voice cracked. "I don't want to cut the boys off. I don't want to walk away. But I also don't want to be used."

Jill's voice softened. "It's okay to feel conflicted. You've been pulled in so many directions, but you don't owe Cara anything. You're here because you want to be and you made a promise to your nephews, not to her. Don't forget that."

Lorna stared at the door, wondering if she should just get up and leave. "I don't know what I'm doing anymore. I promised them I'd go through with the testing, but what if

I'm just letting myself get sucked back in? Cara's not going to change, and part of me wonders if the boys have learned her ways too. What if everything Henry said is just part of the plan?"

Before Jill could respond, a nurse stepped into the waiting room, glancing at her clipboard. "Lorna Martin?"

Lorna's heart sank. She wasn't ready to be done with the conversation, but there was no avoiding the inevitable. "I've got to go, Jill. They're calling me in."

"Alright, but listen…don't doubt yourself. You've always been strong. Call me after, okay?"

"I will. Thanks, Jill."

Lorna ended the call and slipped her phone back into her bag, her mind still buzzing with doubt. *How did I get here?* she wondered. A loud sigh escaped her lips, as the nurse led her into a small room, explaining the blood pressure monitoring process. Lorna listened, her mind drifting. The technicalities felt distant, overshadowed by her internal turmoil.

"How is the test done?" she asked, trying to focus on something other than her worries.

"We'll place the cuff snugly on your upper arm. It'll inflate, tighten, and then deflate slowly, allowing us to measure your blood pressure. We monitor it over 24 hours to see how it fluctuates throughout the day and night. This helps your doctor understand when and why your blood pressure rises or falls."

Lorna nodded, feeling the pressure of the situation.

As the nurse finished explaining the procedure, Lorna's thoughts began racing again. She'd have to wear the monitor which was very much the size of a hand-held radio strapped over her shoulder for the next 24 hours, with readings taken every 20 to 30 minutes. She was supposed to follow her normal routine, but avoid bathing, swimming and heavy exercise and keep her arm still during each measurement, and make sure the monitor stayed securely attached. But all she could think about were the implications of her choices, her nephews, her sister, the tests, the promises.

Returning to the clinic the next morning, Lorna felt a mix of anxiety and relief as the nurse removed the monitor. The past 24 hours had been a haze of emotions, doubts swirling in her mind, but now, as the nurse removed the cuff, a strange mix of relief and uncertainty washed over her.

"You did well," the nurse said with a smile, gently disconnecting the monitor. "All set."

Lorna forced a smile, nodding, though her thoughts were elsewhere. *At least that's done. I kept my word*, she thought, but the nagging doubt about her nephews, Cara, and the future continued.

As she walked out of the clinic, her phone buzzed. It was Jamie. Lorna smiled. Jamie had always had this uncanny sense of knowing exactly when to check in. The night before, after Jill had mentioned Lorna's conversation at the clinic, Jamie had called. She didn't press, didn't push for details, she just offered her company. "Let's have a girls' night in. Takeaway, movies, no pressure," Jamie had said.

Lorna had jumped at the chance. She needed a distraction, and Jamie's presence always had a way of grounding her.

Later that evening, Lorna arrived at Jamie's house, the comforting smell of Chinese takeout filling the air. Jamie greeted her with a wide grin and two sets of chopsticks already in hand.

"You look like you could use this," Jamie said, waving containers of spring rolls, fried rice and Mongolian lamb at

Lorna.

Lorna let out a tired laugh, slipping off her shoes and sinking into the familiar warmth of Jamie's living room. "You have no idea."

As they settled onto the couch, Jamie leaned back, her eyes studying Lorna. "So, how are you really? I know the monitor thing's done, but what's going on in that head of yours?"

Lorna sighed, poking at her food with the chopsticks. "I don't know, Jamie. I did what I promised. I went through with the test for the boys. But I can't shake this feeling I'm just being pulled back into Cara's mess again. What if this was all just part of her plan?"

Jamie raised an eyebrow. "And what if it wasn't? What if Henry really does want to rebuild something with you? Look, I'm not saying Cara hasn't messed with your head, she's done a number on nearly everyone, but the boys... they're not her. Maybe they really do want to have you in their lives."

Lorna stared at her friend and patted little Daisy who had sat next to her on the floor. "I don't know. I mean, Henry seems genuine, but Jakob said Cara's worried about people thinking they're coercing me. Coercing me? Really? That just sounds like something Cara would come up with."

Jamie nodded and placed her food on the table. "It does. But listen, Lorna, you're not responsible for Cara's actions or the way she manipulates things. You were always there for those boys before Cara disappeared, and if Henry's reaching out, that's on him. You're allowed to protect yourself, but you're also allowed to let them in if that's what you want."

Lorna leaned her head back against the couch. "It's just hard, you know? I promised myself I wouldn't get sucked back into this, but here I am, doing the testing, questioning everything again."

UNDER THE COVER OF CLOSENESS

Jamie smiled, leaning over to nudge Lorna's arm. "You're doing the best you can. And that's enough. You've been a good aunt, a good sister, even when Cara didn't deserve it. But you don't owe her anything, Lorna. You've got to do what's right for you, not just for them."

They sat in silence for a while, the movie playing quietly in the background. Jamie was always like this, never pushing too hard, but always knowing exactly when to remind Lorna of her own strength.

As they finished their food, they shifted the conversation to lighter topics, holiday plans, future ambitions, random inside jokes that had them laughing so hard their sides hurt.

"You know," Jamie said through giggles, "if you ever get tired of Cara's drama, we can just move to some tropical island and start a new life. No manipulative siblings allowed."

Lorna snorted, wiping a tear from her eye. "That sounds like heaven. You and me, living the dream."

"Deal," Jamie grinned. "No more stress, no more family drama. Just sun, sand, and cocktails."

The laughter felt good, for the first time in days, Lorna allowed herself to just be in the moment, appreciating her friend's unwavering support.

As the night wore on, and Jamie fell asleep mid-movie, Lorna sat quietly, gazing at the screen but lost in her thoughts. She was lucky, lucky to have people like Jamie and Jill in her life. They were her anchor, her reminder that no matter how chaotic things got with Cara, she had solid ground to stand on. But still, the doubt lingered, quietly gnawing at the edges of her mind. Could she really trust Henry? Would things with Jakob ever be the same? She didn't have the answers, but at least, for tonight, she didn't have to. Tonight, she was simply Lorna, laughing with her best friend, eating takeaway food, and enjoying the moment.

When the results came in, Lorna's blood pressure was perfect. Relief washed over her, but a deeper unease remained. The past was a mess, and the future remained unclear. Yet, she'd kept her promise. In a world where relationships were unravelling, loyalties were questionable and trust seemed distant, Lorna found solace in knowing she'd stayed true to her word.

Tomorrow was another day.

Forty-Six

2013
The Passing

Lorna was awoken in the early hours by the persistent ringing of her phone. Her heart raced as she saw Byron's name on the screen. *Something's wrong!*

"Lorna," Byron's voice trembled. "The nursing home called. You need to come now."

Throwing on the first clothes she found and grabbing her keys, Lorna raced to her father's side. She'd only visited her father the previous afternoon. He hadn't been well, but the doctor had reassured her with some rest, he might improve in the coming days. He'd been unwell before and pulled through, hadn't he? Yet as she rushed to his side, dread filled her. A nagging feeling in the pit of her stomach. Was it really happening this fast?

When Lorna finally arrived, the scene before her confirmed her worst fears. Her father lay frail and still, his complexion pale and his breathing shallow and laboured. She could hardly recognise the man who'd once been so strong.

"Dad," she whispered, taking his hand in hers, willing him to hold on, to fight just a little longer. But within minutes of her arrival, his chest rose and fell one last time. And then, he was gone. Lorna's world crumbled, a dull ache filling her chest as her legs gave way, dropping her into the chair. She sat, hands trembling, staring. Her father, the man who'd always been there, was no longer. Tears streamed down her face as she held onto his hand, unable to let go. Byron stood nearby, stunned into silence, his face pale with shock. The room felt too small, too suffocating for the weight of their grief.

After what felt like an eternity, Lorna finally spoke. "We need to tell people... they need to know what's happened."

"I promised him I wouldn't tell Cara," Byron murmured, his voice thick with emotion. "He didn't want her to know."

Lorna closed her eyes, remembering the countless conversations she'd had with their father about this very moment. "Byron, I told him I couldn't keep that promise. I didn't agree with it. She's his daughter too, no matter what's happened between them."

"But..." Byron began, but Lorna cut him off.

"I have to do what I feel is right," she said firmly. "I have to live with my actions and decisions."

Byron's eyes flashed with anger. "No, Lorna. You can't tell her. I promised Dad I wouldn't."

"She has a right to know. And I told Dad I couldn't make that promise," Lorna replied, her voice firm. "You can keep your promise, you don't have to tell her, but I have to live with my decisions, Byron. And I have to do what I believe is right."

Byron shook his head, but he didn't argue further. Lorna could see the conflict in his eyes, the desire to respect their father's wishes.

She took a deep breath and dialled Cara's number. The phone rang several times before Cara answered, her voice groggy and irritated. "What do you want, Lorna?"

Lorna's throat tightened. "Cara... it's Dad. He passed away."

There was silence on the other end, followed by a sharp intake of breath. "What? I... I didn't even know he was sick."

"I know," Lorna said softly, her heart aching for the sister who'd been so distant. Of course she wouldn't know, she hadn't appeared to care for several years. "It was sudden. I'm sorry, Cara."

The conversation was brief. Cara didn't ask for details, and Lorna couldn't offer much. The words felt hollow, empty. How could she explain the loss, the finality of it all, in just a few sentences? She couldn't. And Cara, in her shock, didn't push for more.

Lorna then called their mother, who, despite being separated from their father for nearly twenty-five years, had remained in contact with him, visiting him regularly at the nursing home. Their mother was understandably upset, her voice breaking as she thanked Lorna for letting her know.

The next calls were to Uncle Bernard and Aunt Victoria, their father's siblings. Both were heartbroken, but understood that Lorna had many more calls to make. They promised they'd talk later.

The day dragged on in a haze of mourning, reflection, and countless phone calls. Each one felt like reopening a wound, forcing Lorna to confront the reality of her father's death over and over again. Byron suggested they speak with the funeral home and begin making arrangements. Lorna agreed, though she sensed her brother was still upset about her decision to inform Cara.

As they discussed the overwhelming details of the funeral, Lorna felt a heavy burden of responsibility settle on her shoulders. She would create a photo slideshow, and prepare the eulogy. She reached out to Cara several times, asking if she wanted to contribute, but each time, Cara declined. Until the last moment.

"I want to have a song played," Cara demanded.

Lorna, exhausted and emotionally spent, sighed. "It's too late, Cara. Everything's already arranged."

Cara didn't argue, but Lorna could sense the tension between them, a tension that only grew as Byron's resentment simmered beneath the surface.

"He didn't want her to know," Byron muttered again, his anger barely concealed. "You went against his wishes."

"I couldn't keep that from her," Lorna replied, her voice soft but firm. "I had to be honest with Dad and with myself. I knew he didn't agree, but I had to live with my conscience. You can organise everything else, I'm happy to agree with all your decisions."

As the day of the funeral arrived, Lorna prepared herself for what would undoubtedly be one of the most difficult days of her life. She prayed Cara would attend without causing a scene. As she sat in the front row of the chapel, she couldn't help but feel the weight of everything that had happened. Cara sat next to her, with Jakob and Henry by her side, and Uncle Bernard beside them. Lorna glanced at her sister, wondering if they could ever find a way to move forward.

Delivering the eulogy Lorna stood and spoke of her father with love and reverence, recounting memories that painted him as the kind, strong man she'd always known. As she spoke, she felt her emotions rise, but she held them in check, determined to honour her father's memory.

Returning to her seat, Lorna was taken aback when Cara leaned in and whispered, "What happened to Dad's safe? Where's Dad's money?"

Lorna stared at her sister in disbelief. "Cara," she hissed, "this is neither the time nor the place."

Cara's words echoed in Lorna's mind, the audacity of

the question. The service ended, and Lorna felt the urgent need to distance herself from Cara's probing questions. Today was meant to be about celebrating their father's life, not about inheritance or greed.

After the service, a celebration of life gathering was held. It was a bittersweet occasion, with photos and stories bringing both tears and laughter. Lorna found herself outside in the garden, needing a moment to herself. The cool air was a welcome relief, and she closed her eyes, trying to steady her emotions, opening them after a short while she stared at the blue sky, wondering what her father had thought of her actions. Would he have been annoyed with her contacting Cara? Or would he have known Lorna was a person of her word and understood the reason for her actions?

As she stood alone, lost in her thoughts, she saw little Henry peek out from behind the glass door. He disappeared for a moment, then returned and pushed the door open. He dashed out to her. He jumped up, wrapping his arms around her in a tight hug.

Lorna held him close, feeling his warmth and innocence. "I miss you, Aunty Lorna," Henry whispered, his voice trembling.

Lorna kissed his cheek, her heart aching. "I miss you too, Henry."

Tears welled up in Henry's eyes as he looked at her. "Why doesn't Mummy like you anymore?"

Lorna's chest tightened with the weight of his question. "I'm not sure, but I'm sure we'll work it out."

"I hope so, Aunty Lorna. I don't like it when she's mad and cries. We get into trouble."

Lorna stroked his hair, trying to offer comfort. "You make sure you're a good boy, won't you? I know you can be good. You're a good listener and a great little helper, my little Wembley."

Henry laughed, a sound that brought a brief moment of light to the darkness. "Haha! My Red Fraggle. I will, little Wembley's always good," he said.

Lorna chuckled softly, remembering the special moments they'd shared watching Fraggle Rock. Jakob had been nicknamed Gobo Fraggle for his love of Gobo's purple hair, while Henry had been dubbed Wembley Fraggle. They'd all laughed and declared Lorna's new name to be Red Fraggle because of her love for the colour red and her habit of wearing her hair in pigtails. Those memories felt like a lifetime ago.

"I am, Aunty Lorna. I promise I'll be a good boy."

"And I promise we'll work things out. So don't you worry."

Lorna set Henry down, and he looked over his shoulder at the door as if making sure no one was watching. He hugged her again, then ran back inside, turning around to call out, "Love you, Aunty Red." He blew her a kiss before disappearing back into the house.

Lorna stood there, tears streaming down her face with the realisation of how much she missed those simpler times. How could she work things out with Cara when their relationship seemed so broken, so damaged beyond repair?

With the funeral behind them, Byron phoned Lorna. "I'm going to Dad's solicitor to find out about the Will. You should come with me."

Lorna agreed, but nothing could have prepared her for the shock that awaited her. As the solicitor disclosed the details of their father's Will, Lorna felt the ground shift. Cara had been excluded. She couldn't believe it. How could their father have done this without telling her?

What will Cara think?

UNDER THE COVER OF CLOSENESS

Lorna asked to see the Will, not because she doubted the solicitor, but because she needed to understand when and why her father had made such a drastic change. The Will was dated 2011, after the sale of his house. But what stunned Lorna even more was the Statutory Declaration her father had created in 2012 to support Cara's exclusion. As Lorna read the four-page document, her heart broke. Her father had felt bullied, manipulated, and betrayed by Cara, it detailed events leading up to the sale of the house, money transactions, broken agreements and the actions Cara had taken that left him with no choice but to change his Will.

"Why didn't he tell me?" Lorna whispered; her voice barely audible. Her mind raced back to 2008, when her father had stayed with her and expressed a need to see a solicitor. They'd updated his power of attorney and enduring guardianship, ensuring all siblings were equal. He'd insisted there was no need to update his Will, as it was valid, and all his children were treated equally.

Now she was left with the realisation that her father had concealed the truth, she'd been kept in the dark about something that would drive even a greater rift between them.

Her father's words echoed in her mind as she read the final page. "It is my sincere wish that my daughter Cara realises the impact of her actions, but until then, I cannot, in good conscience, include her in my Will."

The truth was there, in black and white, but it offered no comfort. Lorna knew her sister's reaction would be explosive. And as she looked at Byron, she could see he too understood the gravity of what they'd just learned.

As they left the solicitor's office, Lorna felt a sense of dread settle over her.

Cara's reaction was swift, it came within days.

Lorna sat at her kitchen table, her phone buzzed

again, her fingers trembling as she received yet another notification from the social media platform where Cara had decided to air their family's dirty laundry. Lorna hesitated, then opened the app, bracing herself for what she might find. Her sister's latest post was there, laced with venom, dripping with anger.

"How could you?" Lorna whispered to herself, scrolling through the words. Cara's posts had started subtly, almost innocently, a vague comment here, a cryptic remark there. But it hadn't taken long for her anger to escalate, each post more vicious than the last. And as Cara's rage grew, so did her audience.

Lorna's heart ached as she read the comments, strangers and acquaintances alike joining in, egging Cara on. "You're so strong!" one person wrote. "Don't let them get away with it," another encouraged, "You're a dam crack up, cutting family off can be one of the most refreshing things to do." Lorna felt sick, how easily they were swept into Cara's narrative, completely unaware of the real story. The lies. The manipulation. They were cheering for a reality that didn't exist, fuelling Cara's hatred with every like, every comment, oblivious to the damage they were causing.

Jamie's words echoed in her mind, "Ignore it, Lorna. Don't give her the satisfaction. She's just looking for a reaction."

Jill had agreed, insisting it was best to stay silent. "She's just trying to provoke you," Jill had said, "but you're stronger than that. Don't stoop to her level."

Lorna was used to the abuse, to Cara's outbursts, her denials, the cycle of anger and blame. But this time Cara's attacks weren't limited to Lorna alone. She went after their parents, their brother, anyone who dared to be associated with the truth.

Why does she do this? she wondered. *Does it make her feel powerful to tear others down? Does she feel important*

UNDER THE COVER OF CLOSENESS

when she can rile up a crowd to cheer her on?

With every screenshot, Lorna noted the names of those who engaged without a care for the repercussions. As the weeks passed, Lorna's folder of screenshots grew thicker, a tangible reminder of the battle she was fighting in silence. Her father's death, the reading of the Will, Cara's exclusion, everything had spiralled into a public spectacle. But Lorna stayed silent, hoping the storm would pass, hoping that one day Cara would come to her senses. She couldn't tell their mother or Byron. There was no point in dragging them into this, no reason for them to know the sickening depths to which Cara had sunk.

Then, one day, as suddenly as they had begun, the posts disappeared. Lorna was stunned. She checked and rechecked, scrolling through Cara's profile in disbelief. Every last post, every hateful word, gone. Erased as if they'd never existed. Lorna couldn't believe it. *What's Cara up to?* Why had she suddenly decided to delete everything? Had she finally realised the damage she was doing? Or was this just another move in the game she was playing?

Lorna hoped and prayed Cara had seen the error of her ways. Maybe, just maybe, her sister had come to her senses. Maybe, in time, they would be forgotten.

But the relief was short-lived. The phone rang, Byron's name flashing on the screen.

"Lorna," his voice was heavy with concern. "You need to see this."

The email he forwarded left her speechless. It appeared Cara had deleted the posts at the same time their father's solicitor received a letter. Cara intended to contest the Will. Lorna had braced herself for some form of protest, but what stunned her was the letterhead. It wasn't from Cara's usual solicitor, the one who had handled her custody battle. No, this was from their Uncle Bernard's legal firm.

"Uncle Bernard? Why would he help her?" Lorna whispered to herself, her mind racing. Cara had already received half of their father's estate when the house was sold. Did Uncle Bernard believe her? Did he think their father would exclude Cara without good reason?

The next day, Byron called again. He had met with their father's solicitor, who had reviewed all the files. The solicitor had sent a copy of the Statutory Declaration to Cara's new solicitor, along with a letter stating intent to investigate the sale of the house.

Lorna felt her chest tighten. Her breath caught in her throat. How would Cara react to this? Something was off, terribly off. The more Lorna thought about it, the more unsettled she became. Something didn't feel right. She couldn't shake the feeling there was more to it, Cara was up to something.

As Lorna sat in the quiet of her kitchen, she closed her eyes, she knew one thing for certain: this was far from over. The silent war Cara had started was just beginning. What was Cara planning? And how far would her sister go to get what she wanted?

Forty-Seven

Friday, 9th July, 2024
The Evaluation

Lorna sat in the waiting room; her hands clasped tightly in her lap. Today was the day, the psychological evaluation. Every potential kidney donor had to go through this step, a final hurdle to determine whether they were emotionally and mentally prepared for what lay ahead. But for Lorna, this felt like more than just a routine assessment. Would her fractured relationship with Cara cast doubt on her ability to go through with it?

She'd considered every possible outcome, preparing herself for the emotional weight of donating her kidney. But now, as she waited, a new question gnawed at her. *Could they deny me because of the complicated relationship with Cara?*

Cara and Lorna had shared a bond once. Twins. Identical twins. Closer than most people could understand. They'd practically read each other's thoughts, felt each other's pain. But that was a lifetime ago, Lorna thought, her mind drifting back to when Cara had disappeared, taking her two young sons with her and leaving no explanation. It had shattered her. Would the psychologist see this fracture as a sign she wasn't fit to donate?

"Lorna?" The soft voice broke through her thoughts.

She looked up to see a woman standing by the door, with a kind but professional smile. "I'm Dr Lewis. Please, come in," the psychologist said as she gestured towards the open office door.

Lorna stood, trying to calm the nerves fluttering in her stomach. *Just be honest,* she reminded herself as she followed Dr Lewis into a small corner office. Sunlight streamed through the blinds, casting warm light over the cosy chairs and small coffee table between them. The space felt more like a comfortable living room than a clinic room. Lorna took a seat, suddenly feeling exposed.

"Thank you for coming in today, Lorna," Dr Lewis said, her voice steady and reassuring. "Before we begin, I just want to assure you this evaluation is not about 'passing' or 'failing' in the traditional sense. It's about making sure you're making this decision of your own free will, that you understand the emotional implications, and that you're in a good place mentally and emotionally prepared to cope with the process. It's a significant decision, and we want to make sure all donors are fully informed and feel no pressure."

Lorna nodded, though her stomach still churned as she anticipated where the conversation might lead. "I understand. I've been thinking about this a lot."

Dr Lewis smiled. "I'm sure you have. Let's start by talking about what brought you here. Why did you decide to undergo the testing to see if you could donate a kidney?"

Lorna hesitated for a moment then exhaled slowly. "Jakob, my twin sister Cara's eldest son, tracked me down. I hadn't seen him in over ten years, and suddenly he showed up at my doorstep, telling me Cara, needed a kidney transplant." She paused, her fingers twisting the hem of her sleeve. "It wasn't an easy decision, but after thinking it through, I promised him and his brother Henry I'd at least complete the tests to see if I was a match and well... here I am."

UNDER THE COVER OF CLOSENESS

"That's a big decision, and I imagine it wasn't an easy one. How do you feel about your decision now?"

"I'm nervous," Lorna admitted, the words tumbling out faster than she'd expected. "I'm nervous about the surgery, of course. But more than that, I'm nervous about... us. My relationship with Cara is complicated."

Dr Lewis nodded, as if she'd expected this. "It's perfectly natural to feel nervous. It's understandable to feel conflicted, especially with family dynamics. Sibling relationships can be complicated, even under the best circumstances. Can you tell me more about your relationship with Cara?"

Lorna shifted in her seat, unsure how to sum up years of tangled emotions in just a few sentences. "Cara and I were incredibly close growing up. Identical twins. It was like we shared the same mind; we could practically feel each other's thoughts. When she was pregnant with Jakob, I felt her morning sickness. I even knew the exact moment she gave birth. But over time, something shifted. Cara changed. She started lying more, manipulating people, our family. It was like she lost her empathy. She became selfish, and demanding, as if the world owed her something. Every problem in her life was someone else's fault. If you disagreed with her, it wasn't just a disagreement, it was viewed as an attack. Everything had to revolve around her, and if you didn't conform to her way of thinking, you became the enemy. She'd lash out, verbally, sometimes cruelly, insults, threats, whatever she could use to cut you down. She broke our father's heart when she took half of the proceeds from the sale of his house, even though she hadn't contributed a cent. Then, after he passed away, she vanished. No explanation, no goodbye. She took her boys and disappeared like our bond meant nothing to her. It was as if she cut ties without a second thought."

Lorna's voice caught, but she pressed on. "It devastated me. But over time, I moved on. I found peace. I think. I focused on the positives in my life. But it doesn't mean I've forgotten what she did."

Dr Lewis listened carefully, her expression never wavering from compassion. "That sounds incredibly painful, Lorna. Many families experience disharmony. In fact, I'd be more surprised if you didn't mention any conflict at all. If someone tells me they have a perfect family, I tend to wonder how they define 'perfect.'"

Lorna managed a small smile. "I suppose that's true."

"It sounds like you're carrying a lot of conflicting emotions," Dr Lewis said gently. "What you've described, your sister ghosting you, that's a deeply hurtful act. It shows a level of immaturity and can be emotionally damaging to those left behind. Some mental health professionals even describe it as a passive-aggressive form of cruelty. It's understandable that you feel hurt by Cara's actions. Yet here you are, considering something as significant as donating a kidney to her. That speaks volumes about the love and care you still have for her, despite everything."

Lorna let out a shaky breath. "I may not like what she's done. I don't agree with how she's treated people, especially me. But I do love her. She's my sister, no matter what's happened between us. I wouldn't want anything bad to happen to her."

Dr Lewis leaned back, her brow creasing as she gently removed her glasses, folding them with care. She paused for a moment, clearing her throat before speaking, her eyes focused on Lorna, conveying genuine interest in what she had to say. "That's understandable and it's perfectly natural to feel conflicted. It's common for people in your position to have mixed emotions, love, frustration, even anger. It sounds like you've spent a lot of time reflecting on the anger you still carry and the love you continue to have for her. And it's important to remember those emotions aren't mutually exclusive, you can feel both at the same time. You don't have to choose between them. That balance between love and frustration is complex, but it's also a natural part of being human. What's important is you're not letting those emotions dictate your decision. You're taking the time to process and reflect on them, which shows emotional maturity. This assessment is about ensuring you're doing this for the right reasons, not out of guilt or pressure."

Lorna nodded, feeling a strange sense of relief. "Absolutely, I've thought a lot about it. I'm not being coerced. I know the risks, and I've respected the process."

"That's important," Dr Lewis said. "Because being a living donor is a personal decision. And part of this evaluation is ensuring no one feels coerced into it, either directly or indirectly. You need to be doing this for you, because you want to."

"I am," Lorna said quickly. "I've had a lot of time to think it through, and I've had a lot of support along the way. I know this is not just about Cara, it's about me too, about doing something that feels right."

Dr Lewis smiled. "It sounds like you've approached this with a lot of thought and care. And that's exactly what we want to see. You're aware of the risks, both physical and emotional, and you've accepted them. And you have a support system in place, which is crucial."

"I do," Lorna said, feeling a bit lighter. "I've got a great support network. Friends, family, people I can rely on."

"Good. That will make a huge difference in your recovery, should you decide to go through with the surgery."

After a few more questions and a discussion about the potential emotional challenges of the donation, Dr Lewis closed her notebook. "Well, Lorna, I'll be completing my report. You've been incredibly open, and thoughtful today, I appreciate that. But please remember, this is your decision. You can change your mind at any time, even if you decide at the last moment, it's not right for you."

Lorna smiled, feeling a surge of relief. "Thank you. I'll keep that in mind."

Dr Lewis stood, extending her hand. "Thank you, Lorna and I wish you all the very best."

As Lorna left the office, the tension in her chest eased. She'd been honest and vulnerable, and still, she'd come out the other side and passed the evaluation. The psychological hurdle, at least for her, was behind her. Yet, as she walked towards the exit, her thoughts drifted back to Cara.

Will Cara pass her psych test?

Lorna wasn't so sure. Cara's mind worked in mysterious ways. She was unpredictable. But that wasn't Lorna's concern, that was Cara's problem. Lorna had done her part; her mind was clear.

Whatever came next was out of her hands.

Forty-Eight

2014
Gone

Lorna met Byron at the solicitor's office, her mind swirling with disbelief. News of Cara changing her mind left her flabbergasted. *Why would Cara do a complete turn?* There had to be something far greater at play. Cara didn't do anything unless there was something to gain. Lorna closed her eyes, trying to think as her sister would. "Think," she whispered to herself.

The response from Cara's solicitor had been short and to the point. "In the interest of family harmony, our client no longer wishes to pursue the matter."

Lorna's eyes flew open. "Oh my God, I'm a fool…I'm such a fool," she said. "Look at it, look at it!" Lorna flapped the piece of paper in her hand.

"What? What is it?" Byron asked, leaning in.

"She's not interested in the remains of Dad's estate; she never has been." Lorna laughed and shook her head. "Oh my God! We've been played. We've played right into her greedy little paws."

"I don't know what you mean. You saw the letter from her solicitor; she wanted to know why she hadn't been included before she stated her intentions."

"Yes, that's right. That was the first part of her plan. Her first move. It set the scene. And she received the reply she'd been expecting. Dad's solicitor replied, bringing up the sale of the house and how Cara had already pocketed half of the proceeds. You said the solicitor also sent a copy of the agreement Cara had created and we'd all signed and the Stat Dec Dad had written. Dad's solicitor indicated his intention to investigate the legality of it through the courts." Lorna shook her head and laughed, flapping the paper again.

Byron nodded. "And now she's dropping her claim."

"Yes, but you're missing the point... she's no longer contesting the Will, in the interest of family harmony." Lorna paused and laughed again. "Family harmony... Cara isn't interested in family harmony, she's only interested in people believing she's interested in family harmony... well, not even people. She's only interested in one person's thoughts...Uncle Bernard."

"You've lost me," Byron said, shaking his head.

"This has given Cara everything she's been after. She was never after this little pot of gold; she was after the vault. It's here, the letterhead, her legal representative isn't her solicitor, it's Uncle Bernard's solicitor. I've seen it all before: first, it's the meals, the pool sails, then the car which cost a fortune."

"What are you talking about? This is the first time I'm hearing about pool sails and a car."

"You had your life. I thought I could stop her lying, but she's got it now. He'd be handing it out and she'd be lapping it up," Lorna said, frustration creeping in.

"Who...who's he? Dad's not letting her get another cent; he despised her."

"No, not Dad...Uncle Bernard...She's got it now."

"Got what?"

"Sympathy!" Lorna shook her head again and chuckled. "His sympathy... this is her crème de la crème, her ultimate performance. She got us hook, line, and sinker. She was never interested in Dad's estate. She needed to portray herself as the victim, the poor struggling single mum who's been shunned by her family. Written off by her own father. She built on Uncle Bernard and Dad's tension; she used their differences. This has been in play for years, bad-mouthing us all for being so inconsiderate as to not even attend Aunt Sally's funeral, when all along it was Cara who told us we would be going against Uncle Bernard's wishes if we showed. And who was there, the only compassionate family member...Cara, of course. Dad always said Uncle Bernard was a sucker for a sob story. The pool sails were her first test, and I foolishly played along like a puppet, talking to Uncle Bernard, highlighting my concerns for Cara's safety should she attempt to replace them herself. It wasn't long after I realised, then came the car. You probably don't know Uncle Bernard paid for the nice set of wheels she drives."

Byron shook his head. "That greedy, manipulative, lying bitch."

Lorna raised her eyebrows and nodded. "Yes, she is." Looking towards her brother she could see the anger in his eyes. "And she knows I know. I see it in my dreams just as I knew what she was up to when we were younger. If I try really hard, I can still tap into her thoughts. That's what she hates about me, that's what she can't stand. She knows I know, and there's nothing she can do but lie."

"Oh my God! Are you serious?"

"Yep. And I'm not going to let her get away with it. I'm going to confront her. I'm going to tell her what I really think."

Lorna left Byron to speak with the solicitor and headed for Cara's. She was determined to let her sister know exactly what she thought, she would know that not only was Lorna a wake up to her schemes, she was prepared to do everything possible to expose her for who she really was. And she had the element of surprise on her side, Cara was unaware Lorna had come to Sydney.

She arrived in Cara's Street within the hour, her heart racing, she didn't want to get into a huge argument, she just wanted to confront her sister. As she turned the corner she gasped. She couldn't believe her eyes. *What the heck! No way!*

Lorna parked her car in the driveway and dashed to the front door, pushing the door bell repeatedly. No answer. She stood back looking at the front of the house. Disbelief. "This can't be... this can't be happening."

Dashing over to the front window she tried to peer inside, but the blinds were closed. Nothing. Lorna ran to the side of the house. The gate was locked. She jumped trying to see over. Nothing. She dashed to the other side of the house, climbed the retaining wall and dropped behind the fence. Shock. Cara's bedroom was empty. Jakob's bedroom empty. Little Henry's things gone. Everything was gone. Nausea swirled. Lorna dashed to the lawn and vomited. Glancing over her shoulder she could see the top of the For Sale sign. How can this be? Why would she move? Grabbing her phone, she called the number she'd call so many times. No answer. Lorna collapsed.

Where's Cara? Where's Jakob and Henry who I adore? What the heck is going on? Why the hell would Cara sell her house and not say anything?

None of the neighbours knew where Cara had gone. Uncle Bernard also denied any knowledge, saying he kept in contact but didn't want to get involved.

UNDER THE COVER OF CLOSENESS
Emptiness

"Cara entered my dreams last night; I could see her smile and feel our connection. Did I jump into the world behind her eyelids?" Lorna whispered to softly to herself as she sat up in bed, sweat running from her brow.

Reaching for a glass of water, she struggled to comprehend how Cara could be so cruel as to disappear without explanation, without reason, without a single word. She thought she knew her better than anyone in the world. But did she know her at all?

Devastation

Those first moments were almost suffocating. How could someone switch off like a light switch? Light, dark, and not just dark where you can still see the remnants of things... black. Lorna thought about the black hole abyss her Aunt Victoria believed people went to when they died. Nothingness. She closed her eyes in an attempt to feel the connection that had existed since the beginning of time. Still. Silent. Emptiness. Cara was gone. The inner glow of twinship extinguished.

The sense of abandonment felt like a cruel joke. She replayed the moments in her mind, trying to pinpoint when things had gone so wrong, but there was no clear answer. Cara's decision to leave without a word felt like the ultimate betrayal. It was as if her sister had looked at their relationship, at the bond they had shared since birth, and deemed it worthless.

The betrayal hit her in waves, each one more intense than

the last. She felt disrespected, used, and utterly discouraged. Lorna's relationship with Cara had been tumultuous, marked by years of Cara's manipulation and rage, but there had always been a part of her that hoped things would get better. That hope had been shattered. She felt like a fool for believing in the possibility of reconciliation, for thinking their bond as twins meant something.

"I feel like an idiot." Lorna murmured to herself. *Why didn't I anticipate this? How could I have been so blind? What did I do to deserve this?*

Cara's ghosting was one of the cruellest forms of emotional torture, it gave no answer on how to react. Lorna began creating scenarios in her mind. *Should I worry? Is Cara injured and lying in a hospital bed? Should I be upset?*

Anger grew as she reflected on the situation. How could Cara move away, taking Jakob and Henry without telling her? How could she sever the bond they had shared since birth? Lorna was furious with herself for not seeing the signs sooner. Cara had removed social media posts and announced to the world that Lorna was dead to her. What would Cara tell the boys? How would she explain Lorna's absence to Jakob and little Henry? Henry had already told her that he missed her when they'd been at her father's funeral. What would he think now, now they'd moved without a chance to say goodbye? Would Jakob and Henry think she didn't love them anymore?

Tears welled in Lorna's eyes. Anger grew. Resentment. She'd always tried to be there for her nephews, to be a source of stability in their lives. Now, that stability had been ripped away. "This is emotional cruelty," she whispered, her voice trembling with anger. The realisation that Cara had manipulated their uncle to gain control over his finances was infuriating, but there was nothing she could do.

Lorna knew she had to move forward. Cara's actions said more about her inability to maintain healthy, mature relationships than they did about Lorna's worthiness of love. Lorna needed to keep her dignity intact and let go of the hope that Cara would return or provide the answers she so desperately sought. She had to focus on the things that made her happy and remember she was a person who treated others with respect and honesty.

Lorna took a deep breath, wiping the tears from her face she acknowledged the existence of her anger, it was normal for anger to exist as long as she felt loss.
"I will not let Cara's actions define me," she promised herself. In releasing a loud sigh, she let go of her sister's control. "I will cherish the memories of Jakob and Henry; I hope one day they might find their way back to me. In the meantime, I will rebuild my life, I will nurture relationships with those who value and respect me.

With renewed determination, Lorna got up from her bed. It was time to shower, dress and face the world outside. "You are worthy of genuine happiness and love. Today is another day."

Truths Over the Seas

Lorna's phone rang in the stillness of the early morning, jerking her from a deep sleep. Her hand fumbled in the dark, knocking over a book on her bedside table before finding the phone. Squinting at the bright screen, she didn't recognise the number. It was international, London.
"Hello?" Her voice was groggy, disoriented.
"Hello, is that Lorna Martin?" The voice on the other

end had a highly distinguished English accent, precise and formal, which made Lorna sit up in bed.

"Yes," she replied, rubbing her eyes. A sinking feeling settled in her stomach.

"My name is Anne Swadling, I'm calling from Kingston Hospital in London. I…"

Lorna cut the woman off. "Is everything alright? Are you calling about my Aunt Victoria?"

"Yes, Dear, everything is alright… well…" Anne, replied gently, but there was a hesitation in her voice, "your aunt wanted me to contact you. She's in hospital."

"In the hospital? What's wrong?" Lorna straightened, wide awake now, her heart racing.

"I'll hand the telephone over to your aunt. She'll explain."

There was a shuffling sound, muffled voices in the background, and then the line went quiet for a moment. Lorna swallowed hard, bracing herself. People didn't just end up in hospital for nothing. She'd only spoken to Aunt Victoria a few days ago. How could things have changed so suddenly?

"Hello, Lorna," came the soft, frail voice of her Aunt Victoria. It was a voice that had always sounded strong, full of life. But now, it seemed almost fragile and trembling.

"Aunt Victoria!" Lorna gasped. "Are you alright? What happened?"

"I wasn't feeling well. I thought it was my eyes, but then my speech went funny. And I had trouble keeping my balance, walking straight. I thought I might be having a stroke, so I called the ambulance and well…." Her voice cracked a little, but she kept a brave tone. "Here I am."

"Did they test you? Are you okay? Was it a stroke?"

"No, no stroke." There was a long pause before her aunt continued, her voice even softer. "They found something else. I have brain cancer, Lorna. Fancy that. At my age."

UNDER THE COVER OF CLOSENESS

"Brain cancer?" Lorna whispered, her breath catching. The room seemed to close in around her. She didn't know much about brain cancer, but it was enough to terrify her. "What... what do they say? What can they do?"

"They're not going to do anything, Dear," Victoria said softly, her voice calm, almost accepting. "They've given me possibly three months. I've accepted that. I've lived a lucky life."

Lorna's world crumbled around her. The thought of losing Aunt Victoria so soon after her father was too much. Her throat tightened as she fought back tears. *Not another loss*, she thought. *Not so soon.* The grief from losing her father had barely healed, and now this?

"I'm coming to be with you," Lorna said, the words spilling out before she had time to think.

"You don't have to do that, Lorna."

"I know I don't. But I will." The resolve in her voice was unshakeable. She wasn't going to let her aunt face this alone.

There was a pause on the other end, and Lorna could almost hear the smile in her aunt's voice when she spoke again. "Thank you. And will you do something for me?"

"Of course. Anything."

"Can you tell Bernard?"

"Of course, I'll let the family know."

"Thank you, Lorna. I know I can count on you. My brother is hard of hearing these days, bless him."

The line fell silent again before Aunt Victoria added, "I'd better go now. They've been kind enough to let me call from the hospital."

"Okay, Aunt Victoria, you take care of yourself. I'll be in touch to let you know what I'm doing," Lorna said, her voice thick with emotion. "Can I speak to the nurse?"

After a brief moment, Lorna was connected to the nurse, who confirmed everything her aunt had said. The prognosis was grim. There would be no treatment. Victoria had refused any invasive measures and only wanted to be kept comfortable for whatever time she had left. Lorna asked the nurse to reassure her aunt that she would inform the family and make arrangements to be there soon.

When the call ended, Lorna sat in the darkness, the phone still clutched in her hand. It felt unreal. Aunt Victoria, with her warm laugh and steady wisdom, was dying. And there was nothing anyone could do. How could everything change so suddenly? One minute her aunt was vibrant, full of life, and now she had only months left.

Lorna strolled to the kitchen and made a cup of tea, trying to settle. Watching the clock, she waited for a more respectful hour to break the news to Uncle Bernard.

She dialled his number with shaky hands. He answered after a few rings.

"Uncle Bernard, it's Lorna."

"Oh, Lorna, my dear. Is everything alright?"

"No, Uncle. I'm afraid I have some difficult news." She hesitated, then pushed forward. "It's Aunt Victoria. She's in the hospital... She has brain cancer."

The line went quiet, and for a moment, Lorna feared he hadn't heard her. Then came a muffled sob, breaking her heart all over again.

"She... she doesn't have long, a few months at most." Lorna's voice cracked as she spoke. "I'm going to London. I'll make arrangement to be with her."

"Oh, Lorna... That would mean the world to me; to know she had family by her side. Thank you, thank you so much," he said between sobs. "I wish I could go, but... well, you know me, my age is an enemy now. Flying across the world... it might as well be the moon."

"I understand, it's a long way, and you're not alone in this. I'll be there for her, for you."

They spoke for a while longer, the conversation drifting from Victoria's diagnosis to memories of her unbreakable spirit. Uncle Bernard shared stories of their once regular phone calls, how they'd dwindled then finally stopped, not because of the desire to connect, but because his hearing was fading, making it difficult to understand her. Lorna listened, her heart aching with the knowledge that age had stolen so much from both of them.

As the conversation began to wind down, Lorna hesitated before bringing up her sister. "Uncle Bernard, could you let Cara know about Aunt Victoria?"

She knew he kept in touch with Cara, even though Lorna and her sister hadn't spoken in months.

Uncle Bernard sighed. "I'll let her know, Lorna. I'm aware of the tension between you two, but I'd like to stay out of it. I want to maintain my relationship with both of you without being placed in the middle."

Lorna respected his position, though it stung. She wished she understood what had caused the distance between her and Cara, but the silence had stretched on without explanation. "I don't know what the issue is," she admitted softly, more to herself than to him. "I just hope, in time, Cara will tell me."

Would Cara even care? Her sister had distanced herself from the family, even their mother, and hadn't been in touch for ages. Yet, despite the estrangement, Lorna felt a sense of duty.

There was more on Lorna's mind, something she'd wanted to discuss with her uncle but now didn't feel like the right time. Recently, she'd been unable to reach him for several days, and it had caused her sleepless nights worrying from afar. When she finally got through, she'd learned there had been an incident, something minor but enough to make him uncontactable for a while. What had hurt the most was finding out Cara knew about it and hadn't bothered to inform Lorna, leaving her in the dark, worrying for days. It was another layer of frustration she planned to address later, but now wasn't the time. London and Aunt Victoria were her priority.

When Lorna arrived in London, she found Victoria much weaker than she'd expected, her aunt now frail and for the most part confined to a wheelchair, had moved into a nursing home, her appetite had diminished, and she required assistance for even the simplest tasks. The brain tumour had ravaged Victoria's body, but her spirit remained as sharp as ever. Victoria's nursing staff were lovely, kind and so compassionate, even Patrick had a particular charm, despite his teeth resembling a line of vertical turds. Patrick's rancid breath made Lorna's stomach churn but he was always available when needed and much to aunt Victoria's delight he followed her request in closing her door when leaving.

Together, they embarked on a journey to fulfil Victoria's bucket list dreams, savouring each meal as if it were their last. The first meal they enjoyed was lemon drizzle cake with a cappuccino, from there it was full steam ahead. Red wine with a full English breakfast, white wine with smoked salmon, beer with shepherd's pie. These meals became a celebration of life, every bite savoured not just for its flavour, but for the warmth and love it represented.

Despite her deteriorating condition, Victoria insisted on making the most of time. From picnics in The Pheasantry

UNDER THE COVER OF CLOSENESS

Plantation where Lorna would push Victoria around in her wheel chair for hours taking in locations Victoria had sat intently painting its beauty, to quiet moments reminiscing over old photos.

Victoria, a keen observer of human nature, shared her observations about the elderly residents around them. She deliberated about how age seemed to amplify selfish tendencies and create an 'I want attitude' a stark contrast to her own acceptance of impending death.

"I'm just going to die, disappear into a black abyss and be no more." Victoria's voice broke through Lorna's thoughts. "Isn't it ironic, Lorna, all these years worrying about ending up like my mother, only to find myself here. I laughed, you know, when they told me about the tumour. People didn't understand. But it was the absurdity of it all, the realisation that after all those years fearing the inevitable... the worry was all wasted energy, energy I could have used elsewhere. You see my brain tumour diagnosis released me from years of fearing a fate worse than death, a slow decline into the abyss of Alzheimer's." Victoria chuckled and shook her head, her voice trembled with emotion. "Why waste so much time on worry? Promise me you'll never waste your time on worry. Enjoy life, Lorna. Learn from my mistake. Promise me that, will you promise me?"

Lorna took her aunts hand and nodded with a smile. "I promise you, aunt Victoria, I promise never to waste time on worry."

In quiet moments between their outings, Victoria confided in Lorna about family matters. She spoke of her disappointment in Cara, who had stirred trouble within the family. Then one day she revealed the shattered feelings of Lorna's father.

"Lorna, dear, I want you to have a letter from your father, he wrote it some years ago, about the time he went into the nursing home. The letter is no use to me now, I've never disclosed its existence before, but I think it's time you knew how your father felt," Victoria said, her voice barely a whisper. Lorna straightened and looked towards her aunt whose delicately veined hand was holding a folded piece of paper. Lorna's stomach churned with a mixture of anxiety and curiosity. She reached forward with trembling hands and slowly unfolded the paper. The twiggy handwriting was unmistakably her father's. Lorna began to read, the words searing themselves into her mind.

My dearest Victoria,

I write this with a heavy heart and a sense of betrayal I can scarcely comprehend. Cara's actions have left me shattered, not just financially but emotionally. How could my own daughter deceive me so? I was a fool to trust her assurances that she would only take her fair share of the estate. I believed her when she promised and even signed that declaration so many years ago.

But when it came time to sell the house, her name on the title gave her the right to claim half of the proceeds. Half, Victoria. Despite it being my money that paid for the house, my hard-earned savings, she took it without a shred of remorse. While she lived under my roof, she paid a fair share for board and lodging. However, when she bought her own home, I repaid her every cent of those living expenses. Cara acknowledged this and yet still, it wasn't enough. Her offer of assistance I had once praised only disguised her predatoriness.

This act of greed has left me no choice. I had to change my Will, to ensure my other children receive a share in what little remains after my nursing home expenses. It breaks my heart, but Cara has left me with no other option.

I hope you understand why I had to do this. Please, keep this to yourself. I feel embarrassed by the betrayal,

from being so gullible and I don't want to burden the others with this knowledge unless absolutely necessary.
  With deepest sorrow,
  Your brother,
  Gerald

Lorna wiped away tears, lost for words, she knew her father had been upset, but reading his devastation was heart wrenching.

"Family dynamics are always complex, but one should never steal, especially from family. Your sister has proven herself to be a liar and a thief, unworthy of inheriting anything from me."

"Aunt Victoria, I understand your concerns," Lorna began gently, "but Cara, she's still family. People make mistakes."

Victoria nodded. "Yes, they do. But mistakes have consequences. And I don't see why I should leave anything to a liar and a thief. What she did to my brother."

"What about Jakob and Henry," Lorna interrupted. "Her boys. Children are innocent. I'm sure Cara would use some of the money to assist with their education and future."

Victoria straightened in her chair and inhaled deeply releasing a loud sigh. "Then if I do include her, I hope she'll see beyond her own selfish desires, I suppose I could include her for the sake of Jakob and Henry. Yes, children are innocent, Lorna," Victoria murmured, her gaze distant. "Perhaps my inheritance could still do some good."

Their conversation shifted to Bernard, Victoria's eldest brother and Lorna's uncle. Concern etched lines on Victoria's face as she spoke of Cara's growing influence over him. Lorna listened, silently absorbing her aunt's wisdom about the true nature of family bonds and the dangers of selfishness. Only time would tell what would happen with uncle Bernard.

As their time together drew to a close, Victoria handed Lorna several artworks, cherished pieces from her collection. "Take these," she said softly, "share them with the family. Keep those you like, let them remind you of our time together."

Lorna clenched her jaw, pushing her tongue firmly against her teeth she held back tears, overwhelmed by the generosity and finality of the gesture. She leaned in to hug her aunt, whispering words of love and gratitude before turning and making her way to the door.

"Don't forget to shut the door," Victoria said, with tears in her eyes. "And remember, love is a word meant for special moments."

As Lorna bid farewell to her aunt and the nursing home that had become a temporary haven, she carried with her not just the artworks and her father's letter, but the profound lessons Victoria had imparted. In those fleeting weeks, Lorna had learned that life's most enduring truths often emerge when facing mortality.

Forty-Nine

Monday, 16th September, 2024
Final Tests

The day had started like so many others, with Lorna attending another medical appointment. Only today was different. Today, she'd completed her final test at Sydney Hospital. Her final blood test for tissue typing was over, but instead of relief, she felt a deep well of anxiety rising within. She was at a crossroads, torn between two drastically different paths, both of which would change her life, and Cara's, forever.

As she drove home, she rolled down the window, letting the cool wind whip through her hair, but the fresh air couldn't ease her anxiety.

Am I really ready to give Cara a kidney?

The road stretched ahead like her two conflicting thoughts. On one hand, donating would be a selfless act of sisterhood. Cara, her twin, needed her. Saving Cara could restore the connection they once had, bringing back not just a sister, but also a family. Jakob and Henry, Cara's boys, could finally have a healthy mother. Lorna could be the one to give them that, to fill the void Cara's illness had left. She'd missed her nephews, missed watching them grow, missed being the aunt they could turn to.

But then there was the other side. The side that told her to stop, to protect herself. Cara hadn't spoken to her in years, hadn't even offered a single gesture of reconciliation. Their once-close bond had been shattered, replaced by silence, distance, and a decade of unresolved hurt. Why was it only now, when she needed something, that Lorna had heard from them? *Am I simply a resource to Cara? An identical twin with a matching kidney?*

Lorna blinked away the thought, but it lingered in the rear-view mirror, staring back at her like a ghost of doubt. What if Cara never changed? What if her nephews were only trying to manipulate her? Would they even care about her if she wasn't offering them hope? The questions circled in her mind. Was it worth risking her health, her life, for someone who had treated her like a convenient solution, not a sister? The thoughts persisted; doubt gnawed.

Lorna arrived home late, but thankful to see her friends waiting. Jamie and Jill had agreed to meet up, after a few minutes of small talk they made their way inside Lorna's house and sat at the kitchen table. Lorna trusted her two friends more than anyone else, she spoke of her uncertainty moving forward, about her fears and the feeling of pressure to make the right decision.

Jamie broke the silence. "I can't imagine how tough this is for you. I wouldn't want to be in your shoes. But I'll tell you this, you have to stay true to yourself. Know who you are. Your decision will be the right one if it aligns with your core values. Who is the real Lorna? What would she do?"

Lorna looked at Jamie trying to absorb her words. *Who am I?* she thought, *the sister who gives life or the sister who protects her own?*

"But what if I don't know anymore? I thought I knew what I wanted. To help Cara, to do something that would bring us closer. But now, I'm not so sure," she replied.

Jill leaned forward and gave her a sympathetic smile. "It's okay to be scared. But don't let fear be the reason you make a decision. Take fear out of the equation and ask yourself: without it, what do you want?"

Lorna closed her eyes, imagining a life without fear. Without the constant pressure of expectations, of old wounds that hadn't yet healed. She envisioned each path ahead of her, the left one, leading towards the donation and the uncertain future it held, and the right one, leading back to her own life, unburdened but forever haunted by the 'what-ifs.'

"You've got time, Lorna," Jamie said softly. "Don't rush into this. Trust yourself. You've always made good decisions in life, and this will be no different. You've said it yourself; you have the right to make this decision on your terms. No one can force you, not Cara, not her boys, not anyone. If you're having doubts, you need to honour that. The transplant team is there to support you, and they'll understand if you choose not to go through with it. You have every right to step away. No one should judge you. It's your body, your choice."

Lorna nodded, knowing Jamie was right. The transplant team had told her the same thing, she could walk away at any time, for any reason, and no one would need to know why.

"What about the boys?" Lorna asked, her voice trembling. "Do they really want me in their lives, or are they just playing along for their mother's sake? I don't even know them anymore, not really."

Jamie gave her a small, understanding smile. "Maybe you don't, but I don't think anyone can fake that kind of hope, Lorna. They're probably just as confused as you are. But you can't make this decision based on what they think or what they might want. This has to be about you."

Jill added, "If you're afraid of saying no, you can ask for help. The transplant team can handle it for you if it comes to that. You don't have to be the one to tell Cara directly. You don't owe anyone anything, Lorna, not even an explanation."

The room grew quiet. Lorna bit her lip, looking down at her hands. "I'm still not sure," she admitted. "But it feels better, talking about it. I'm starting to see that maybe... maybe this isn't just about saving Cara's life. It's about making sure I don't lose mine in the process."

When the conversation ended, and her friends had gone home, Lorna retreated to her bedroom. She stood in front of the mirror, studying her reflection. Her reflection stared back at her, but all she could think of was Cara, her twin, her mirror image. Were they still identical after all these years? They shared the same face, the same DNA, but they were worlds apart. Cara was a stranger to her now. A stranger she once knew as well as herself, but who'd become something else entirely. Lorna had changed too. A decade of distance had left its mark, on their faces, their bodies, their lives.

Lorna traced the lines and creases on her forehead with her fingertips. They told stories, of laughter and pain, of a life lived, of love given, lost and found again in different ways. Of moments spent trying to understand why Cara had left, and why she'd come back now, only to ask for the ultimate sacrifice. But this wasn't the past anymore. They weren't the same children who used to finish each other's sentences, who once shared a bond that seemed unbreakable. They were no longer the girls who shared secrets and dreams. These marks on her face were hers. They weren't Cara's.

"Cara isn't my mirror anymore," Lorna whispered to her reflection. "I have to stop pretending we can recreate that."

She sighed, brushing a hand across her cheek. Donating her kidney wouldn't guarantee a renewed relationship. All it guaranteed was she would have one less kidney. And what about her? Was this truly what she wanted? Or had she become so wrapped up in trying to fix things for others that she'd lost sight of herself? She couldn't answer those questions now. All she knew was she had to be true to herself, to stop dwelling on what-ifs. There were no guarantees in this life, but she had to trust that whatever choice she made, it would be the right one for her.

She closed her eyes, finally allowing herself to let go of the fear, the doubts, the guilt. She had to make this decision for herself, not for Cara, not for Jakob or Henry, and not for anyone else.

"The decision is mine," she whispered into the darkness. "I can change my mind at any stage. This is my journey."

Fifty

2015
Sharing Love

Lorna stepped off the plane, utterly exhausted, both physically and emotionally. The trip to England had taken a toll on her, but she felt an immense sense of peace for having spent time with Aunt Victoria. The memories she created with her aunt were priceless, moments she would cherish for the rest of her life. Aunt Victoria had once said, "One day, I'll be forgotten, and it will be as if I never existed." Lorna had gently reassured her, promising, "As long as I'm alive, you'll always be remembered. You'll always be in my heart."

Back in Australia, Lorna carefully unpacked the artwork her Aunt Victoria had gifted her before she left. Victoria had been a talented and accomplished artist, and Lorna wanted to honour her in a special way. She spent hours creating calendars for the family, using some of her aunt's most beautiful pieces. Each calendar was wrapped with care, along with a slideshow she had made, featuring photos of the artwork set to Victoria's favourite classical music. As Lorna handed them out, she felt a deep sense of pride, celebrating the incredible talent her aunt possessed.

When she visited Uncle Bernard, she left a selection of the artwork with him, along with the calendars, making sure he had enough to pass on to Cara. "These are from Aunt Victoria," Lorna said, "I wanted to bring back something meaningful for everyone."

"These are wonderful, Lorna," Uncle Bernard said, though there was a trace of hesitation. "Thank you. I'll make sure Cara gets hers. You know how much I appreciate these things, but I just want to remind you, I don't want to be caught up in any tension between you and your sister. I enjoy our chats, and Cara helps me a lot since she's close by. I don't want to end up in a nursing home, and I need to rely on her."

Lorna nodded. "I understand, I just wanted to bring something back for everyone, something from Aunt Victoria."

The days passed, and Lorna found herself filled with joy when she heard Aunt Victoria had received her calendar in the nursing home. The staff had called, telling Lorna how thrilled her aunt was, proudly showing it off to everyone. Lorna had also sent a copy of the slideshow set to the music her aunt loved so much. Hearing about the smile on Aunt Victoria's face had made it all worth it, but it also brought tears to her eyes. She could hear the deterioration in her aunt's voice, the toll the illness was taking. Time was running out.

Weeks passed, and still, there was no word from Cara. Not a single thanks. Lorna tried to tell herself it didn't matter, but the absence of acknowledgment hurt. She hadn't needed to return with gifts or make the calendars and slideshow. The least Cara could've done was say thank you.

Three weeks later, the dreaded call came. Aunt Victoria had passed away. Surprisingly, Uncle Bernard seemed to take the news of his sister's passing better than Lorna had expected. He was calm, reflective. Lorna promised to let the rest of the family know while Uncle Bernard said he'd inform Cara.

Days passed, and Lorna made a point to check in on her uncle, ensuring he was managing the loss well. When she called next, she wasn't prepared for the bombshell.

"You know, Lorna, Cara's been very upset," Uncle Bernard said, his tone more serious than usual. "She told me she didn't inherit anything from Victoria. Poor girl, she's devastated, first your father, and now Victoria. Everything went to you and Byron. I don't know why they've both been so cruel to her. She's done so much for me. She's here all the time, you know, calling in, shopping for me, even hired a new gardener. I'm starting to wonder how I managed without her."

Rage surged through Lorna. "That's not true, Uncle Bernard. Aunt Victoria divided her estate equally. Cara wasn't excluded. I have the documents. I can send them to you."

Uncle Bernard hesitated. "Well, I don't know, Lorna..."

Lorna forced herself to stay composed. *Of course, Cara is weaving herself into his life,* she thought, *she's making him dependent on her, filling his mind with lies.*

"I think there's been a misunderstanding, maybe you heard her wrong," Lorna said carefully. "I'll send you a copy of the Will. That way, you can see for yourself."

Her uncle hesitated again. "If you think that's necessary..."

"I do," Lorna insisted, already determined to prove the truth. "I'll send it this week."

After hanging up, Lorna sat for a moment, seething. How could he believe Cara's lies so easily? Aunt Victoria had been clear with her intentions, and Uncle Bernard had even been told about them. Yet now, he was swallowing Cara's manipulations without a second thought.

The next morning, Lorna mailed a copy of the Will, along with a violet crumble chocolate bar she remembered her uncle loved. She sent it via registered mail, ensuring it would be delivered without delay.

A few days later, she received confirmation of delivery. She called her uncle immediately. "Did you get the letter and the little gift I sent?"

"I did, and I loved the chocolate," Uncle Bernard said. "Thank you, Lorna. It's been so long since I've had one."

Lorna smiled at the sound of his laughter. "I'm glad you liked it. But did you look at the Will? You'll see Cara wasn't left out. Aunt Victoria divided her estate equally."

A long silence followed. "I saw it," her uncle finally responded, his tone curt and cold. The warmth from their earlier exchange vanished. He cleared his throat and began coughing.

Lorna's heart sank. Was he upset? Had Cara lied again? She listened intently, wondering if her uncle's coughing was a distraction from his discomfort. He continued coughing and spluttering, then dropped the phone. Lorna pressed the receiver hard against her ear, her heart racing as she strained to hear any sign of distress.

Moments later, Uncle Bernard returned. "Sorry about that," he muttered. "My allergies are acting up again."

"Are you sure you're alright?"

"Yes, yes," he said hurriedly. "Just hay fever. I think I'll take an antihistamine and lie down. We'll talk next month. Thanks again." With that, he hung up.

Lorna sat with the phone still in her hand, her mind racing. What did he think? What did he really think? He'd been so adamant that Cara had been left out, and now he had proof that wasn't true. Had he believed her lies for so long that the truth was too much to handle? Lorna hadn't wanted to upset her uncle, she just wanted to believe he would see the truth, that he'd finally recognise Cara's manipulations. But maybe he never would. Maybe he didn't want to.

Why did Cara insist on lying?

It had been happening for too long. Cara weaving her stories, manipulating the family, making everyone doubt what they knew to be true. Lorna had stayed silent for too long, and that silence had only given Cara more power.

But no more.

Lorna was done protecting the lie. If it upset people, so be it. At least now the truth was out there, undeniable, in black and white.

As the days slipped by, it was time for Lorna's monthly phone call with Uncle Bernard. She hoped by now he'd come to terms with the fact Cara had been included in Aunt Victoria's Will. When the call connected, Lorna was relieved, their conversation was light and familiar, as it often was.

"How's the weather on your side of the mountains?" Uncle Bernard asked.

"A lot drier than the forecast has said it's been there. Although we've been getting some wild storms. How are you surviving over there?" Lorna replied.

"It's been miserable, really, I think we'll all turn into ducks soon with all this rain, " he chuckled. "But that's nothing new for this time of year. I've been keeping busy, though. Been looking into some new shares. These markets, Lorna, they're a nightmare. And don't get me started on American politics, the world has gone mad."

Lorna laughed, enjoying the normality of their chat.

UNDER THE COVER OF CLOSENESS

They'd always found common ground on topics like politics and the world's strange turn of events. But as her uncle rambled on about his shares, Lorna's mind was elsewhere. She had something she needed to bring up.

After a moment, she found an opening. "Uncle Bernard," she began, "I've been thinking. You know, last time I couldn't get a hold of you for nearly a week. It really worried me. I didn't know if something had happened to you. Is there anyone nearby I could contact if you don't answer your phone? A neighbour or maybe someone else?"

Her voice trailed off, knowing she was stepping into territory he might brush off. She could sense him hesitating on the other end of the line.

"Oh, Lorna," he said with a chuckle. "I knew where I was. I wasn't lost! There's really no need to worry so much."

Lorna smiled at his attempt to lighten the mood, but her concern lingered. "I know, but what if something did happen? Cara knew you were fine last time, but she didn't let me know. I spent days wondering. It's hard being so far away and not having any way to check on you."

There was a pause. Then Uncle Bernard's voice softened. "I see your point, Lorna. But if something serious happened, I'm sure Cara would let you know. You know, she checks in on me regularly. She'll do the right thing."

Lorna nodded even though he couldn't see her. She wasn't so sure. Cara had already proven her willingness to withhold information when it suited her. But what could she do? She had to trust Uncle Bernard's judgment, even if her gut told her otherwise.

"Would you speak to her? Just to make sure she knows how important it is for me to be kept in the loop if something happens to you."

Her uncle sighed. "I will, Lorna. I will. If it'll make you

feel better, I'll speak with her, but I'm certain she would do the right thing."

"Thanks, Uncle Bernard. It's just hard sometimes, being so far away. I just want to make sure you're alright."

She hung up a few moments later, filled with a lingering doubt. As much as she wanted to trust Uncle Bernard's assurances, could Cara really be relied on when it mattered most?

Lorna wasn't so sure, but for now, she had to accept her uncle's word.

Fifty-One

Monday, 30th September, 2024
The Home Stretch

So far Lorna had passed all her work-up tests, and now, standing on the precipice of her final appointment, it should have felt like a victory but instead she felt a mixture of relief and dread. *One last hurdle before surgery,* she thought. One last trip to Sydney for the pre admission appointment at Sydney Hospital. What if this last test put an end to everything? Uncertainty worried as she made her way to the hospital.

Surgery was scheduled in just two days, and with each step closer to the operation, Lorna's doubts grew. She tried to shake them off, but they followed her within the shadows, they appeared in her quiet moments. When she arrived at her appointment, Sue, her transplant coordinator, was already waiting.

"Lorna," Sue greeted her warmly. "How are you feeling?"

Lorna offered a weak smile. "Nervous, to be honest. I still have doubts... even if the last test results come back all clear, I'm not sure I can go through with this."

Sue nodded. "It's completely normal to feel that way. Remember, this decision is still in your hands, Lorna. Even after all the tests, you have the right to change your mind. You could pull out right in the anaesthetic bay if you wanted to."

Lorna knew Sue was trying to be supportive, but it didn't ease her mind. Would backing out make her a coward? Was she really ready for this?

As she sat in the waiting room, her heart pounding, a familiar voice pulled her from her thoughts.

"Aunt Lorna?"

She looked up to see Henry standing there, a small smile on his face.

"Henry... what are you doing here?" she asked, surprised.

"I wanted to be here for you," he replied. "I wanted you to know I care. I'm so grateful for what you're doing for Mum and I've really enjoyed spending time with you. Surely, you didn't think I'd let you go through the last bits alone?"

Lorna felt a lump in her throat. She nodded; reached over and squeezed his hand. "Thank you, Henry. That means a lot to me."

The pre admission appointment was over and done in no time. Henry hugged his aunt on her return to the waiting room and suggested they go for coffee, and Lorna agreed, needing the distraction.

As they sipped their coffee, Henry leaned in, his voice dropping to a whisper. "I'd still like to keep our meetings between us," he said cautiously, "just so it doesn't cause any waves."

Lorna understood his concern. "Of course," she agreed, though it saddened her that their connection had to be kept hidden.

Henry sighed as he stirred his coffee and his expression grew serious, Lorna could sense there was more on his mind.

"I've missed you, Aunt Lorna," he said, his voice tinged

with sadness. "I've missed the rest of the family too. I can't wait until all of this is over. Maybe then... I can reconnect with everyone I lost after we moved."

Lorna's heart ached at his words. "We all missed you, too, Henry. Losing you was hard. Losing everyone... it felt like losing a part of myself. Everyone would love to catch up with you."

Henry smiled then looked down at his coffee, his eyes clouded with memories. "Losing Poppy... was the worst. And then we moved, and I lost you, Aunt Lorna and Nanny, we couldn't see Nanny anymore and I loved going to her house... then Aunt Victoria in England died, I didn't know her but mum was upset so that made me upset... by the time we lost Uncle Bernard, I was scared of who else I'd lose. It felt like everyone I cared about just... disappeared."

Lorna took a deep breath, then swallowed hard, memories of those losses flooding back. She decided it was time to ask the question that had been burning in her mind. "Henry, what happened with Uncle Bernard?"

Henry hesitated; the pain evident on his face. "I'm sorry, Aunt Lorna. He didn't just die."

Lorna's heart skipped a beat. "What do you mean? What happened?"

"He had a fall, a bad fall. He broke his hip and was in terrible pain," Henry said quietly, his voice thick with sorrow.

"He broke his hip? When?"

"A long time ago," he replied, looking away. "Not long after we moved. Mum moved him."

Lorna's confusion deepened. "What do you mean?"

Henry struggled to find the words. "I don't remember everything, but I know he was in the hospital for a long time. After that, he couldn't go back to his house. Mum said it would be too far for her to travel all the time, so she convinced him to buy a new place near us. That way, she told him, she wouldn't have to put him in a nursing home, and he could pay for a private nurse to assist him."

Lorna's mind raced, trying to piece together the fragments of information. "But what about his house?"

Henry's face darkened. "It's Mum's now... and his new one, too. She looked after him, and she said he had to look after her." Henry paused as if thinking what to say next. Lorna stared, shocked by what she was hearing.

"Mum said he was loaded," Henry added. "She said it was only fair since she did the right thing by him, he did the right thing by her... so she spoke with him and Uncle Bernard had his solicitor draw everything up. Mum said she had to make sure there were no loops or holes."

"Loop holes?" Lorna questioned.

"Yep. That's it. She said she couldn't have any loop holes."

Lorna's heart sank as the implications of Henry's words hit her. "But what happened? Was he in pain? Did he suffer? When did he die?"

Henry looked pained, but he answered quietly. "Not long after he moved into his new place. He... he wasn't the same. He looked sad. I'd ask if he was okay, and he'd always say he was, but... but his eyes were different. It looked like he was just lost in his thoughts. He'd stare out the window, I wondered if he just liked looking at the clouds in silence. He didn't talk as much either, not like he used to." Henry swallowed hard, his voice breaking. "Mum said he probably couldn't get over the fall, sometimes old people just don't recover. She said he needed strong painkillers, and... and his heart just gave out."

A wave of nausea washed over Lorna as the pieces began to fall into place. Uncle Bernard's fall had been the opportunity Cara needed to isolate him, to control his life. Henry didn't seem to know the full extent of what had happened, but he'd said enough. Cara had used their uncle's vulnerability to secure her own gain. Lorna felt sickened to her core, the confirmation of her sister's greed more than she could bear.

She forced herself to stay composed for Henry's sake. "I would have been there if I'd known, Henry. I would have. But no one told me. Your mum... your mum moved him, disconnected his phone. He had all my contact details at his old house, but they were in his old home phone which was left behind."

"He never went back to his old house, Mum said he couldn't as he was too unwell, she said it would have been too upsetting, that a new place and a fresh start would make him feel better, there was no use in living in the past."

"But what about his computer? He was always on his computer."

"Mum bought him a new laptop, she set it up from him. She said it was easier for him to use on the lounge or in bed while he recovered."

Lorna closed her eyes now understanding why her emails were no longer answered, her sister had taken full control. Tears welled in her eyes. "I couldn't reach him. I tried everything. I exhausted all my options. My point of contact was at his old house. There was nothing I could do."

Henry looked at her, the pain of years of misunderstanding evident in his eyes. "I thought... I thought you didn't care."

Lorna shook her head, her voice trembling. "I cared, Henry. I always cared. I wish I could have been there for him. I wish I could have been there for you. It was the distance; I didn't live around the corner. I couldn't just pop over. Before he disappeared, I spoke with Uncle Bernard regularly. I sent him gifts; we'd exchange emails and jokes. Uncle Bernard was a deep thinker, a practical person, we'd talk about cooking ingredients and shopping lists, we'd talk about current affairs, about movies and literature and the stock market. We had so many conversations about everything. Uncle Bernard knew of the strained relationship between your mother and I, he said he didn't want to involve himself as he appreciated and valued both relationships, I respected that. He'd tell me how much he looked forward to our conversations, how he was unable to visit me in the country but how he'd googled where I lived and worked so he felt he had a greater involvement in my life. He was afraid of going into a nursing home. He told me so many times. And I supported him when he wanted to stay in his house... his family home. There were also times in our conversations when he'd appear to slip up and tell me small details about you and your brother. I'm not sure if it was on purpose, but I loved hearing about you, no matter how small the detail. But as your mother got more involved ... everything changed. I couldn't stop it, I lived too far away."

Lorna hesitated, unsure if she should continue, but why not, there was nothing wrong in telling the truth, her sister had silenced her for far too long. "It was the little things at first...the change in gardener, the switching of utility companies, how your mother would insist on paying for his shopping with her debit card and he'd reimburse her in cash. Then there was that vet bill... it went into the thousands. Your mother said it was easier for her to pay with her credit card to earn points, and Uncle Bernard would reimburse her. He was always vocal about how she was just trying to make his life less stressful. But... I always wondered, at what cost?"

Henry listened quietly, absorbing her words. Lorna could see the conflict in his eyes, the loyalty to his mother, the growing awareness of what had really happened.

"And there was nothing I could do," she continued, her voice tinged with frustration. "I sat on the sidelines, hoping your mother would do what was right. But she didn't. She took control, slowly but surely, and by the time I realised what was happening... it was too late. Uncle Bernard was gone, he'd disappeared without a word just like you, and I was heart broken once more. I was devastated beyond belief.

Henry looked down, his voice barely a whisper. "I'm sorry, Aunt Lorna."

Lorna placed a hand on his, trying to offer comfort. "It's not your fault, Henry. None of this is your fault."

The truth of her sisters' actions was worse than she'd imagined. Lorna sat holding Henry's hand, a wave of nausea washing over her. Cara had taken advantage of their uncle, used his vulnerability to secure her own gain. It was just as she'd suspected, and now the confirmation was like a knife twisting in her heart. The realisation she'd been powerless to stop it, that she'd lost her uncle not just to death but to her sister's greed, was more than she could bear.

Why should she offer her sister the chance at a better quality of life when Cara had shown such blatant disregard for everyone else?

Fifty-Two

2016
No More

Hearing about Uncle Bernard from Henry brought Lorna back to that last moment of contact. After she returned from England, life had gone on as usual, work, home, friends, catching up with family, and her monthly phone calls with Uncle Bernard. Days, weeks, and months passed without drama. Conversations with him had been routine, just another part of life. She never imagined one of those calls would be their last.

Did she take those moments for granted? Did she not see the finality that could come without warning?

It had been over three years since her father Gerald passed, and two since Aunt Victoria was gone. Now Uncle Bernard wasn't answering his phone. That was unlike him. He'd always been reliable, reassuring her that Cara would keep her informed if anything happened. But all she got was silence, his phone rang out.

Lorna had called for three days straight with no response, and on the fourth day, the line played a recording.

"The number you have called is not connected. Please check the number before calling again."

Lorna stared at her phone. Her mind spinning. *This can't be right. What do I do?* She dialled again more carefully, double-checking each number, but the message repeated, over and over. Nausea churned in her stomach as panic started to creep in.

Something was wrong. Slumping onto the lounge, tears welled up as she cradled her head in her hands. Why hadn't Cara called her? What had happened? Was Bernard dead?

In desperation, she tried to think of someone who could help, but she didn't have the numbers of any neighbours.

Lorna decided to call her uncle's phone company, hoping they might provide some clue. The first operator she spoke to was no help, citing privacy laws. Frustration simmered, she paced her lounge room, determined not to give up. She tried again, this time explaining her circumstances more clearly, how she lived hours away, and her aging uncle hadn't answered for days.

The operator hesitated before offering a lead. "I can't tell you specifics, but I can give you the last three digits of a mobile number with authority connected to the account, this is related to the disconnection."

Lorna's heart raced. *Finally, a clue.* But when the numbers were read out, her excitement vanished. She slumped into the lounge, whispering bitterly, "Fucking Cara."

She immediately dialled her sister's number. Cara answered with cold detachment.

"Hello, Cara, it's Lorna. I'm trying to get in touch with Uncle Bernard."

"And?"

"Do you know where he is?"

"Yes."

Lorna's grip on the phone tightened. "Then can you tell me, please?"

"I'm not sure I'm at liberty to say. I'm not sure if Uncle Bernard would want me divulging his private information."

"What are you talking about? He's my uncle, Cara! This isn't a game. Is he okay? Please."

Cara's tone was sickeningly calm. "I'm respecting Bernard's wishes. He didn't ask me to inform you, so I'm protecting his privacy."

Lorna fought to stay composed. "Please, Cara, I'm asking you respectfully."

Cara laughed. "Respectfully. I'm simply the conduit, I'm respecting my uncle, he hasn't asked me to tell you and I wouldn't want to invade his privacy."

"He's my uncle too."

"Calm down, Lorna, you're starting to become emotional. I will pass on your message, although I can't guarantee if he wants to talk to you. I'm looking after him just fine, I'm his Enduring Power of Attorney and his Enduring Guardian, you my dear sister don't have to worry yourself. Please don't call me again, I answered this call out of politeness, now I'm asking you respectfully... don't call again. I will not answer."

The phone clicked. Silence.

Lorna stared at her phone in disbelief. Rage coursed through her, and she fired off a text: "Further to our conversation, I'm concerned I can't contact Bernard. If I don't hear from him soon, I'll contact the police."

Cara's response was quick. "He had a fall, and he's been in the hospital. He's responding to rehabilitation. If you need more, let me know. Best regards, Cara."

Lorna felt her blood boil as she typed back. "Which hospital? When did he fall? What injuries does he have? I'd like to talk to him to ease my concerns. Thank you so much, I look forward to hearing from you."

She stared at the screen, waiting, her fingers gripping the phone.

A few minutes later Cara responded: "He's out of the

hospital now and in private accommodation near rehab. No phone. No NBN. If you have a message, I will be seeing him tomorrow and I'll pass it on."

Lorna's heart pounded. Cara was avoiding giving any real answers. No phone? No NBN? It didn't make sense. How could Cara know their uncle had fallen, watched him spend weeks in the hospital, and still be this evasive? The anger inside her grew, her patience gone. Did Cara enjoy leaving her in the dark, worrying about the worst?

"I'd like to speak with Uncle Bernard to ease my concerns. He's my uncle, and I'm worried about him. Where is he? I don't think that's too much to ask."

This time, the reply was slower, but just as dismissive.

"When I'm with Bernard tomorrow, I'll call your number, and if he chooses to, he can speak with you. Clearly, you're using me as a conduit to communicate with him, and I'll do my best to enable that. But it's up to him to give you his details, not me. I trust you understand my position."

Lorna gritted her teeth, her hands trembling with a mix of rage and helplessness. How could Cara be so cold?

She quickly shot off another message. "What time do you expect to see him?"

Her eyes stayed glued to the phone, waiting for the typing bubble that never came.

Lorna's phone buzzed the next day, and when she saw Cara's number flash on the screen, her heart raced. She answered it quickly, a knot of anxiety tightening in her chest.

"I have Uncle Bernard with me," Cara said flatly. "He's tired, but you can talk to him for a moment."

Lorna heard voices in the background, faint and indistinct, as if Cara had put the phone on speaker. Her pulse quickened, and she leaned forward, holding her breath.

"Hello, Uncle Bernard."

"Hello, Lorna," came Bernard's voice, weak and distant. It was him. "Don't worry, dear, your sister is looking after me."

Tears filled Lorna's eyes, spilling down her cheeks as she pressed the phone closer to her ear. *He's really there*, she thought, her relief mixing with the ache of not knowing what had happened.

"I couldn't reach you," Lorna stammered, her voice cracking. "I tried calling for our regular chat, but... you didn't answer."

"I'm okay, Dear," Bernard replied, though his words were slow, as if each took effort. "I had a fall... but your sister is taking care of me."

Lorna's stomach tightened. "But I didn't know. She didn't tell me."

There were muffled voices again, distant and unclear, as if someone was whispering just out of reach. Lorna strained to listen, her anxiety rising as the conversation felt like it was slipping away.

"Uncle Bernard? Are you there?" she called, straining to hear anything that made sense.

More muffled voices, then Cara's firm tone returned, sharp and final. "He's exhausted. But now you've spoken to him. You need to let him recover. Goodbye, Lorna."

The line went dead before Lorna could say another word. She stared at the screen, her fingers trembling. The conversation had been so brief, leaving her with more questions than answers. But at least she'd spoken to him. That alone brought some comfort.

She prayed she'd hear more soon, that Cara wouldn't continue keeping her in the dark. All she could do was wait, hoping her uncle had heard her concern and that he'd be okay.

Weeks passed with no updates. Lorna decided to contact

UNDER THE COVER OF CLOSENESS

Cara again, this time through a carefully worded message: "I've tried reaching Uncle Bernard several times. Where is he? Is he okay? It's been a month since we spoke. I would like to know what's happening? I'm deeply concerned and would appreciate any update."

Cara's response was swift and cutting: "You severed your relationship with me when you meddled in Dad's Will and pressured him to change it. Your relationship with our uncle is independent to me. He is free to access his devices and communicate. As you have chosen not to have a relationship with me, I find it deeply offensive that you would either text or telephone me as a conduit to Bernard. Bernard has your email, your telephone and your address. Perhaps you should reflect on why he has chosen not to communicate with you. He is fine, maybe he doesn't want to talk to you. Live with it. My life has been so much better without you. Don't contact me again."

Lorna felt the sting of the accusation, knowing it was a lie. She had no part in their father's Will. Cara had a twisted view of the past and Lorna had proof, if only her sister would bother to listen and look, but there would be no reasoning.

She sent one last reply. "Given your perception of events I understand why you might feel this way. I know the truth and maybe one day you will too. Take care. Hi to the boys. Love Lorna."

As the weeks dragged on, Lorna drove to Bernard's house, only to find the mailbox overflowing and neighbours clueless. No one had seen him for months.

In a final attempt, Lorna went to the local police, hoping for help. But after a welfare check, they informed her that Cara, as his legal guardian, had the final say. There was nothing they could do. Uncle Bernard was safe, they assured her.

Safe. Yet, he was lost to her.

Lorna couldn't help but wonder, was Uncle Bernard too afraid to reach out, fearing Cara might cut off the help he needed? Was he choosing silence to preserve his care? He was aging, after all, perhaps sacrificing contact with his niece for his own survival.

The uncle she knew was gone.

Fifty-Three

Tuesday, 1st October, 2024
Choices Of the Heart

Lorna lay on the hospital bed, staring at the clock on the wall. Fear and uncertainty causing her heart to race, the nurse had reassured her, she could change her mind about donating her kidney to Cara at any time, even now. Recent memories and swirling emotions had been gnawing, causing her to question her decision, her mind drifting back to the events that had led her to this moment.

"Why am I doing this?" she whispered to herself, "Why am I risking my own health for someone who has shown me nothing but cold heartedness and betrayal?" Her thoughts interrupted by the feeling of another presence.

Lorna turned her head, her breath catching as Cara stood in the doorway. Her presence filled the small room, along with a familiar tension. Neither spoke. Lorna could see Cara was clearly stewing on something, her arms crossed, her expressions hard, eyes staring. She stepped into the room and walked to the foot of the bed. Lorna braced herself for the onslaught.

When Cara finally spoke, her voice was quieter than usual, likely to avoid drawing attention from the hospital staff, yet her words carried seething anger.

"All I ever hear from Jakob and Henry is 'Aunt Lorna this, Aunt Lorna that,' and I'm sick of it," Cara began,

"Dear little Lorna always on a pedestal. Always wanting to be on top. Just like when we were kids and you insisting on having the top bunk. You just had to be above me, didn't you?"

Lorna straightened. "What are you talking about?" she couldn't believe what she was hearing, the absurdity of her, Cara's comment was near laughable. "I don't know who made the decision for me to have the top bunk," she replied, her voice remained calm. "I can't recall if I'd asked for it, or if you wanted the bottom. It's just how it was."

Memories of their childhood room flashed in Lorna's mind. She would have relocated to the bottom bunk in a heartbeat had she known it caused such grief. In truth, she didn't particularly like the top bunk. Up there, she had to sleep facing the wall to avoid the glare of passing headlights reflecting off the dresser mirror. On the bottom bunk, Cara had the comfort of darkness, safely tucked beneath overhanging blankets, her only hazard the occasional dropping boogies she'd picked and wiped on the underside of Lorna's mattress.

"This is ridiculous." Lorna shook her head trying not to laugh.

Cara snapped, and pointed towards her sister "Don't call me ridiculous."

"I never called you ridiculous, I said this is ridiculous, as in this situation. All we do is go around in circles. But let me tell you something, Cara, I'm not on your merry go round, I jumped off years ago. You need to stop, now!"

Lorna closed her eyes and released a loud sigh. Frustration. How could something so trivial stir such deep-seated bitterness after all these years?

Cara's mouth opened to protest "I- "

"Stop! I said stop!" Lorna felt her patience snap, her frustration boiling over. "I can't believe this. You're bringing up the top bunk from over fifty years ago? Where are your priorities, Cara... here, in the present, or stuck in the past? You need to move on."

Cara's eyes flashed with anger. "And you need to learn your place. Giving me this kidney changes nothing. And don't you forget they are my boys, not yours. you chose not to have kids, so don't think you can come in here and take mine. You want company, get a dog and leave my boys alone."

Lorna struggled to contain her rage. "Let's get a couple of things straight," she said, her voice firm and unwavering. "They are not your boys, as you put it. You don't own them. You gave birth to them, you raised them, and yes, you even took them away from the rest of the family. But they are young men now, capable of making their own decisions. Like everyone else, they will live by the consequences of their actions. YOU don't control them."

Cara's face twisted with indignation, but Lorna pressed on, her voice gaining strength. "A mother doesn't control the decisions of a mature, free-thinking individual. A good mother lets her children live their own lives, offering encouragement and support, praising them along the way. I don't need to have children to understand this. People don't OWN people, Cara. You don't own Jakob, you don't own Henry, and you certainly don't get to come in here trying to boss me around because YOU, Cara, you don't own me either. I might be your twin sister, but I'm a free-thinking individual. Now, if you don't mind, I need to be alone to think."

With that, Lorna, turned away from Cara. Rolling onto her side, her focus returned to the clock on the wall.

Silence.

Retreating footsteps.

The argument with her sister had left Lorna emotionally

drained and close to tears, while the certainty she once felt about donating a kidney to her twin sister now seemed splintered.

"Why am I doing this?" she whispered to herself, "Why am I risking my own health for someone who has shown me nothing but cold heartedness and betrayal?"

A soft knock on the door interrupted her thoughts. She turned her head, expecting a nurse, but instead, Jakob and Henry stepped into the room, their faces etched with concern.

Jakob, approached first, the maturity he displayed through his tall frame and serious expression was beyond his years. Henry followed close behind, his eyes red-rimmed, clear evidence of recent tears. "Mum told us about the argument," Jakob said, stepping closer to her bed. "Are you okay, Aunt Lorna?"

Lorna forced a smile, her heart ached from his concern. "I'm fine," she replied softly. "Just…I'm just trying to process everything."

"We were worried you might change your mind about the kidney donation," Henry blurted, his voice tinged with desperation. "We came to make sure you're still going through with it."

Seeing her nephews in distress added another layer of complexity to her emotions. "I haven't made any final decisions yet," she admitted. "I thought I had… I need time to think."

Jakob glared at his brother then leaned forward. "Being a twin is a magical thing," he said gently. "You should be thankful for that magic and share what you've been blessed with. Maybe this was the reason you were born a twin… to help, to be able to save a life."

Lorna felt a lump form in her throat. The bond of twinship, for all its complexities and heartaches, was indeed something special. The notion of their shared existence had always held a mesmerising allure. But how could she ignore the anger and resentment? She knew she had a part to play, still Cara's abusive tirades had left deep scars, and her final departure all those years ago had felt like both a relief and a devastating blow.

Henry, burst into tears. "When we moved away, I thought I'd done something wrong," he sobbed, "I thought you didn't love me anymore, Aunt Lorna. It hurt so much."

Lorna reached out and held Henry's hand as she fought back tears.

"Oh, Henry, you didn't do anything wrong. I've always loved you, both of you. It's just… complicated."

He nodded, tears streaming down his face. "I know, I know it's complicated, but please go through with the kidney donation. Even if you and Mum never talk, even if she never says thank you... we need you to do this. I need you to do this."

Jakob placed a comforting hand on his brother's shoulder and nodded in agreement. "We know it's a lot to ask," he said quietly. "But saving her… You'll be giving her a second chance and we'll be forever grateful."

Lorna looked at the two young men standing before her, their faces a mixture of hope and fear, she knew they were desperate. But the decision wasn't just about Cara anymore, she wasn't doing this for Cara's gratitude, or even for reconciliation. The decision wasn't even about family and two boys caught in the crossfire. Yes, Jakob and Henry were two innocent victims, and their love and concern for both her and Cara shined through in their eyes. But more importantly, the decision to donate a kidney was about Lorna, what did she want? She understood the gravity of their request, but at that moment, she needed space. "I need time. To think," she said softly. "I'm sorry. I wasn't prepared for this. It's just... too much. I understand what you're saying, but your mum... I just need a moment. I'm sorry, but this decision is mine. I have to do what feels right for me."

Jakob's eyes flickered with pain, and Henry's face twisted with a mix of hope and fear. The pressure was suffocating, but Lorna reminded herself: This is my journey. This is about me. She couldn't lose sight of that. It had to be her choice, her path. She placed her hands against her forehead, trying to block out the world around her.

"I just need to close my eyes for a moment," she whispered.

In the darkness behind her eyelids, she shut everything out, their pleading faces, the weight of the decision, the noise. Her thoughts turned inward, into quietness.

Breathe, she told herself, *just focus on your breath.*

Slowly, she felt her mind settle. *What do you truly want? Forget about the external noise. Forget about the past. Be true to yourself, Lorna. Be true to your values.*

Her breaths grew deeper, steadier. *Who am I?* she asked silently. *What kind of person am I?*

Am I a giver? Someone who lets go without expectation? Could this be an altruistic gift, an act of kindness to someone I once knew?

She breathed in with purpose. *This is my journey. My decision. My life.*

Her mind, usually swirling with emotion and doubt, stilled.

Stop.
Quiet.
Focus.
Forget.

She could feel the tension slowly releasing. She inhaled deeply, then released the breath in a slow, controlled exhale, remembering how she had been taught when she had learnt meditation.

Remove the emotion, she told herself.
Inhale.
Exhale.

Lorna felt her body relax. She repeated her internal mantra, finding strength with each breath.

Who am I? Why should I?
Inhale - *I am strong.*
Exhale - *I will endure.*
Inhale - *I am resilient.*
Exhale - *I will recover.*
Inhale - *I am brave.*
Exhale - *I can confront.*
Inhale - *I am giving.*
Exhale - *She needs it.*

Tears slipped from the corner of her closed eyes, sliding down her cheek. Her breathing slowed, becoming more deliberate, more at ease. With each inhale, she drew in clarity; with each exhale, she released doubt. Her mind found a new, unexpected clarity, a stillness she hadn't known she could reach.

When Lorna finally opened her eyes, the room seemed brighter, though the atmosphere remained tense. Jakob and Henry stood silently, their eyes locked onto hers, waiting.

"Okay," Lorna said at last, her voice steady, her decision made. She met their gazes. "I'll do it. I'll donate the kidney." There was no turning back now. But this time, Lorna knew it was her choice, her decision to give, to heal, to be true to herself.

The relief on Jakob's and Henry's faces was immediate, as they leaned in to hug her, Lorna felt a renewed sense of purpose. As they pulled back, their smiles were tinged with a mixture of hope and relief. Lorna knew this act of giving, while it might not heal all wounds, would be a step towards freeing herself from the shadows of the past.

"Thank you, Aunt Lorna," Jakob said, his voice thick with emotion. "You're giving us all a chance to be a family again."

Henry nodded, his eyes still glistening with tears. "Thank you. We'll never forget this."

As the boys left the room, Lorna leaned back against her pillows. The decision was made. She would give her sister the gift of life, not out of obligation or for the hope of reconciliation, but out of love. Lorna closed her eyes and whispered a silent prayer. She prayed for strength, for courage and for forgiveness. If there was even the slightest chance that her sacrifice could save her sister's life, then it was a risk she was willing to take. Taking a deep breath a sense of calm washed over her. She was ready to embrace the magic of her twinship.

Fifty-Four

Wednesday, 2nd October, 2024
The Awakening

On the morning of the surgery, Lorna could feel the nervous tension in the air, in the quiet she could hear the blood pulse in her veins as she tried to steady her breathing.

"Good morning, Lorna. How are you feeling today?" one nurse asked.

"Nervous," Lorna admitted, forcing a small smile. It was the truth. Her stomach twisted into tight knots, and her heart raced with a mixture of fear and anticipation.

The nurse's eyes softened as she nodded. "That's perfectly normal. We're going to ask you a few questions, and you might hear them more than once. It's just to make sure everything goes smoothly."

Lorna's fingers fidgeted against her chin and she bit her lip as her mind raced. The questions came, each one a small checkpoint on the way to the unknown. Name, date of birth, allergies, medical history. She answered them automatically.

As they wheeled her into the anaesthetic bay, the anaesthetist introduced himself. "Lorna, I'm Dr Frost. I'll be taking care of you today."

Lorna tried to smile but felt it falter. "Thank you," she managed to say.

"We're going to insert a small cannula into one of your veins," he explained, holding up the needle. "You should feel just a little sting."

Lorna winced as it pricked her skin, then looked away, focusing on the sterile white ceiling, the room was bright, filled with the soft beeps and hums of medical equipment. Her thoughts drifted to Cara and the weight of what she was about to do.

More devices and lines were attached to her, each one a tether to the world she was about to leave behind for a few hours. The coldness of the operating table seeped through the thin fabric of her gown as she was wheeled into the theatre.

"Just relax, Lorna," the anaesthetist said, his voice soothing. "We're going to give you something to help you sleep now."

Lorna nodded, taking a deep breath. As the anaesthetic agent was administered, she felt her body growing heavier, her mind starting to drift. Her last conscious thought was a fleeting one, a whispered hope that everything would be okay. The last thing she remembered was the soft hum of machines and the gentle murmur of voices fading away.

Then, nothing.

The next thing she knew, she was waking up in the recovery unit, disoriented and groggy. Her body felt heavy, disconnected, but there was a strange sense of relief too. *It's over*. The surgery was done. She allowed herself to slip back into sleep, comforted by the knowledge she'd made it through.

When Lorna woke in her hospital bed, a dull pain radiating from where the doctors had removed her kidney.

UNDER THE COVER OF CLOSENESS

For a moment, she lay still, letting the reality of the situation sink in. Tears fell from her eyes. The surgery was over. She'd done something remarkable. She'd saved her sister's life. Despite Cara's insistence on wanting nothing to do with her. Despite the years of silence and abandonment, Lorna had stepped up. She'd undergone the tests, faced her fears, and given a piece of herself. The finality of it all hit hard, the realisation settled in.

A nurse entered the room. "Hello, Lorna. How are you feeling?"

Lorna winced as she shifted in the bed. "I've been better. There's this dull ache and a bit of sharp pain when I move."

"That's to be expected. The pain could be due to the gas we pump inside during the operation. It helps us see better, but it can cause some discomfort afterwards."

"Gas?" Lorna asked, wincing slightly as she shifted in the bed.

"Yes, it's perfectly normal. The gas will dissipate over time, and moving around can help speed up the process. Your operation went by the textbook. The surgeon was extremely pleased with how everything turned out."

"That's good to hear. What happens next?" Lorna asked.

"We'll be back later to get you up and walking. Moving around will help with your recovery. It might be uncomfortable at first, but it's important."

"Okay," Lorna said. The thought of moving around made her nervous, but she'd been told by other donors that it was important. The living donors she'd met along her journey had been amazingly supportive, they'd offered so much advice and words of encouragement. Lorna would be forever grateful to them.

The nurse finished her checks and gave Lorna a gentle pat on the arm. "You're doing great. Just take it one step at a time."

As the nurse left, Lorna's mind drifted and tears welled in her eyes. She'd done it. She'd really done it. She'd saved her sister, even if Cara might never acknowledge it. Despite everything, Lorna had found the strength to give a part of herself to someone who had turned her back on her. She sighed, and wiped the tears from her eyes thinking about the future. This was the end of a long, painful chapter. Soon, she would return home, back to normality. It was time to move forward with her life, to find joy and happiness despite the unchanged, frustrating circumstances around her. She could only hope Jakob and Henry would continue to stay in touch. As for Cara, she had little to no hope for reconciliation.

Questions swirled.
Panic.

She hadn't asked... had Cara undergone her surgery? If so, was it successful? Was she in pain? Could she feel Lorna's presence in some inexplicable way? Lorna chuckled at the irony of the situation. Cara had insisted she wanted nothing to do with Lorna, yet now she carried a part of her inside her body.

A new nurse entered the room. "Lorna, I'm just checking in. How's the pain now? Do you need anything for it?" Her eyes brightened as she gestured towards the bedside table. "Oh, and by the way, did you see those beautiful flowers? Your lovely nephews, Jakob and Henry dropped them off. They waited for you to wake, but unfortunately, they had to go. They wanted me to tell you they loved you, appreciated all you've done and they promised they would see you as soon as possible."

Lorna turned her head, her eyes widening as she took in the sight of the large bouquet, vibrant colours dazzled, red, yellow and purple and white, the roses in particular stood out, their intoxicating scent filled the room.

"Oh my! They're beautiful!" she gasped; her voice filled with emotion.

"Yes, they are," the nurse replied with a smile. "You must be one loved Aunt."

Lorna took a deep breath, feeling a wave of gratitude, she was touched by the thought of her two loving nephews. The flowers a reminder of the strong bond they shared.

The nurse gently interrupted her thoughts. "So, how's the pain? Do you need anything?"

Lorna shook her head gently. "It's bearable, thank you. I'm just trying to process everything."

"That's understandable, the surgeon will be around later to see how you're doing. In the meantime, just rest as much as you can."

"Before you go… Do you… do you know…did Cara have her surgery? Is she okay?"

The nurse checked her notes. "Yes, Cara had her surgery shortly after yours. She's in recovery now, and from what I've heard, everything went well."

Lorna exhaled a sigh of relief. "That's good to hear."

The nurse smiled. "I'll be back later."

Lorna nodded and relaxed into her pillows closing her eyes.

"Cara entered my dreams last night. I could see her smile and feel our connection. Then I jumped into the world behind her eyelids. I held her hand and kissed her cheek. Then I whispered in her ear… Goodbye, my sweet, Cara," she said quietly to herself as she rolled over in bed.

A mix of emotions washed over her, sorrow, relief, a strange sense of peace. She'd done what she could. It was time to let go and live her own life. The pain in her side was a reminder of her sacrifice, but it was also a symbol of her strength. She'd faced her fears and emerged on the other side. Now, it was time to heal, both physically and emotionally.

Tomorrow was another day.

Fifty-Five

Friday, 4th October, 2024
Rocks And Hope

Lorna left the hospital, her mind swirling with reflections on her relationship with Cara. The notion of their shared existence had always held a mesmerising allure for her. The idea that Cara and she were once one entity, seamlessly halved into two distinct individuals, felt like a wondrous feat of nature. Cara had been Lorna's rock, and Lorna had been hers, but Lorna finally realised rocks came in different shapes and sizes. They could also crack, crumble, and fall apart, unable to be put back together. Under pressure, even rocks turned to dust and were carried away by the wind.

Lorna pondered if their lives resembled rocks. Their original form, being one, divided into two distinct parts, weathered over time. Lives sculpted and relationships broken down, their bond eroded. What once was, was no more. Carried away in the breeze.

She looked up at the sky, the clouds drifting lazily overhead. Each one a fragment of a once larger whole, moving on a path controlled by unseen forces. She wondered if their relationship was destined to be like those clouds, forever changing, forever moving, drifting further apart.

Standing on the hospital steps, Lorna took a deep

breath. The air was crisp, carrying the scent of possibility and the promise of new beginnings. She realised while their past was etched in stone, their future was still being written. She could choose to carry the dust of their broken bond with her, or she could let it be swept away by the breeze.

With a final glance back at the hospital, Lorna felt a sense of peace wash over her. She had done what was right and she knew the journey ahead wouldn't be easy, but she was ready to face it. Just like the rocks, she would endure, adapt, and find her way.

Travelling home she found herself silently acknowledging the countless individuals who'd walked this path before her. Those brave souls who'd chosen to donate, who'd given a part of themselves to save another, and those who'd received such profound gifts.

She thought of the people still waiting, their lives hanging in the balance, longing for the call that would bring them hope, a second chance at life. She silently acknowledged those who had passed and whose final act had been a gift to strangers and she had a new found appreciation for donor families, families who in their darkest moments, had found the strength to say yes to donation. Without them, the miracle of organ donation would be impossible. They were the unsung heroes.

Lorna sent a silent prayer of thanks to the universe. Thanks for the process that made organ and tissue donation possible, for the doctors, the surgeons and nurses, for the coordinators who navigated the logistics, and for the advocates who tirelessly promoted the cause.

She hoped more people would take just a minute of their time to register at Donate Life and then have the crucial conversation with their families to ensure their wishes were known and supported. It was such a small act with such a monumental impact.

Finally, she envisioned a world where everyone understood the importance of organ donation. A world where no one had to wait in desperation for a chance at life. She hoped her story, their story, would inspire others to make that commitment and help make a difference.

Lorna smiled.

Tomorrow is another day and where there is life, there is always hope.

Printed in Great Britain
by Amazon